T0267093

STAR-CROSSED

STAR-CROSSED

JERRY FRISSEN - ROBERTO ZAGHI

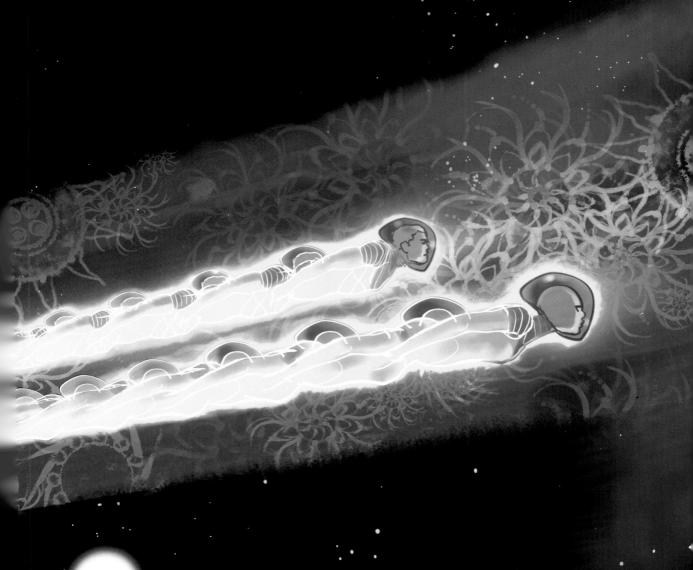

HUMANOIDS

JERRY FRISSEN
Writer

ROBERTO ZAGHI
Artist

Ive Svorcina
Colorist

Montana Kane
Translator

Jake Thomas & Tom Williams
English Language Edition Editors

Camille Thélot-Vernoux
Original Edition Editor

Caroline Melamed
Designer

Jerry Frissen
Senior Art Director

Fabrice Giger
Publisher

For Marisa, Marica, and Margot.

Many thanks to Jerry, Camille, and Humanoids for this fascinating story that made me draw and dream at the same time. Thanks to Germano, Marco, and Grégory for their invaluable help and to Ive for his magnificent color work.

—Roberto Zaghi

Rights and Licensing - licensing@humanoids.com
Press and Social Media - pr@humanoids.com
Sales - sales@humanoids.com

Esther Kim - Marketing Director
Holly Aitchison - Sales Director
Amanda Lucido - Operations Director

Library of Congress Control Number: 2023942719

First published in France in 2023 under the title "Attraction" by Les Humanoïdes Associés (Paris, France).

This book is a publication of Humanoids, Inc. 8033 Sunset Blvd. #628, Los Angeles, CA 90046.

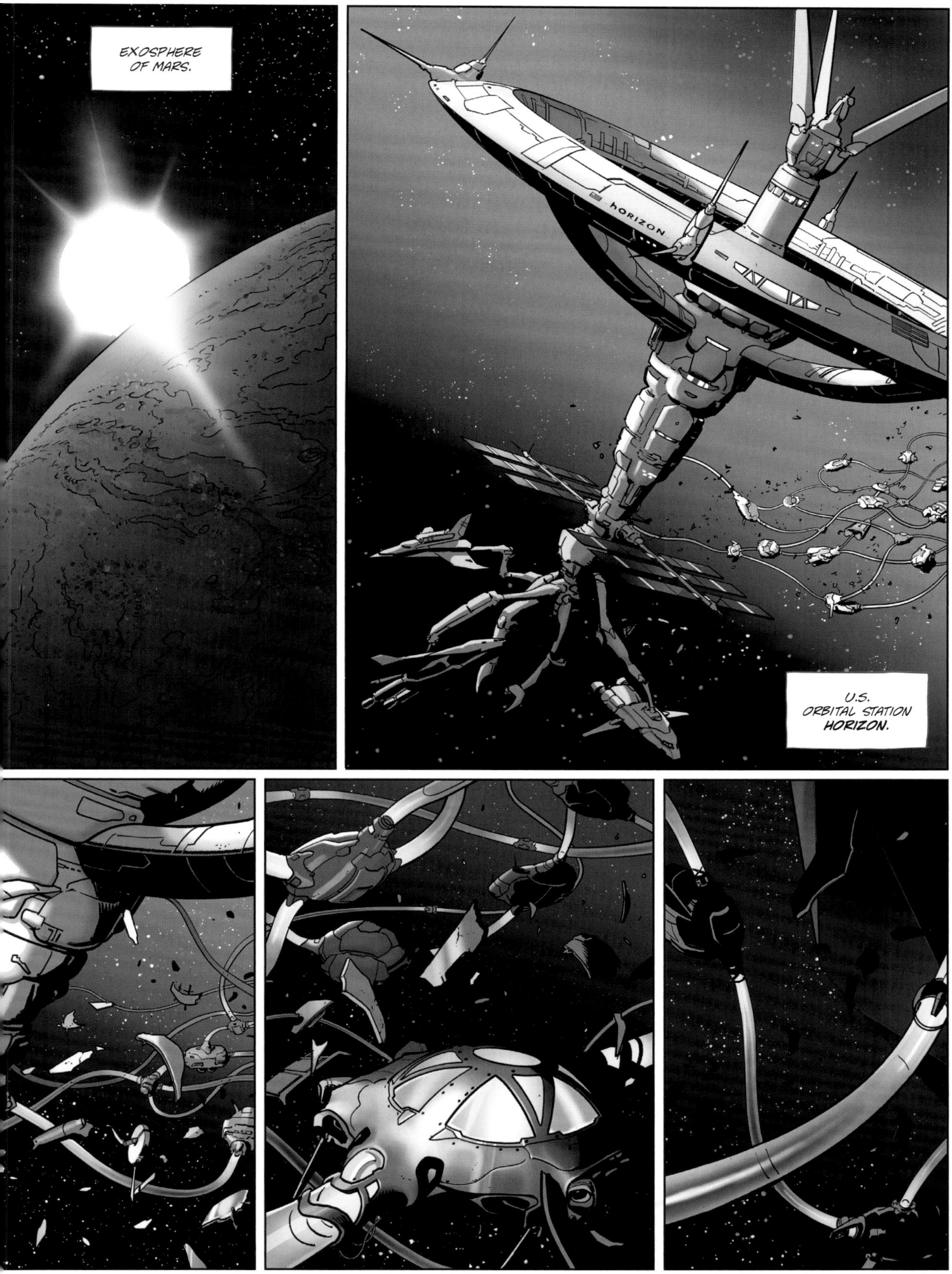
EXOSPHERE OF MARS.
HORIZON
U.S. ORBITAL STATION **HORIZON.**

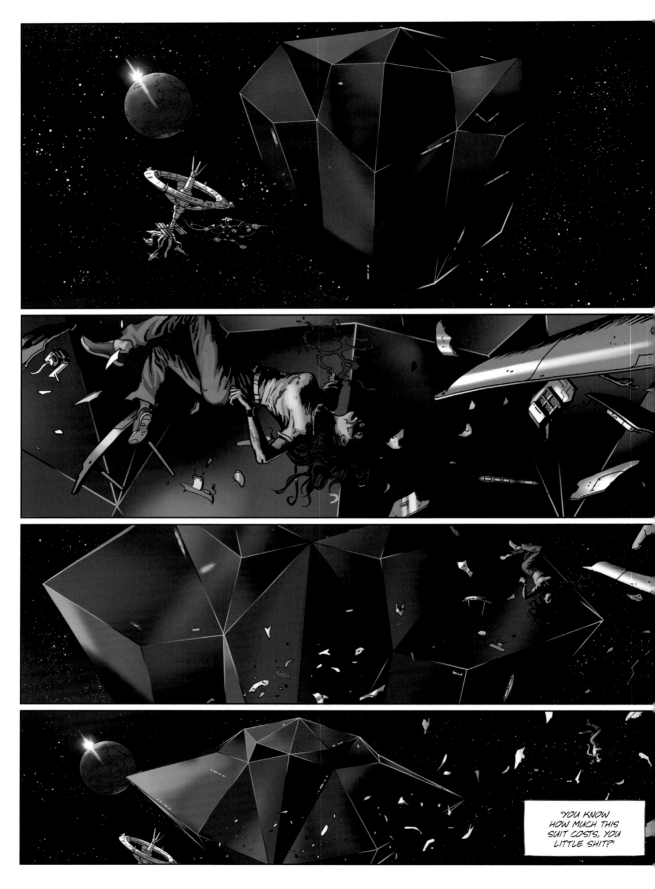

"YOU KNOW HOW MUCH THIS SUIT COSTS, YOU LITTLE SHIT?"

6

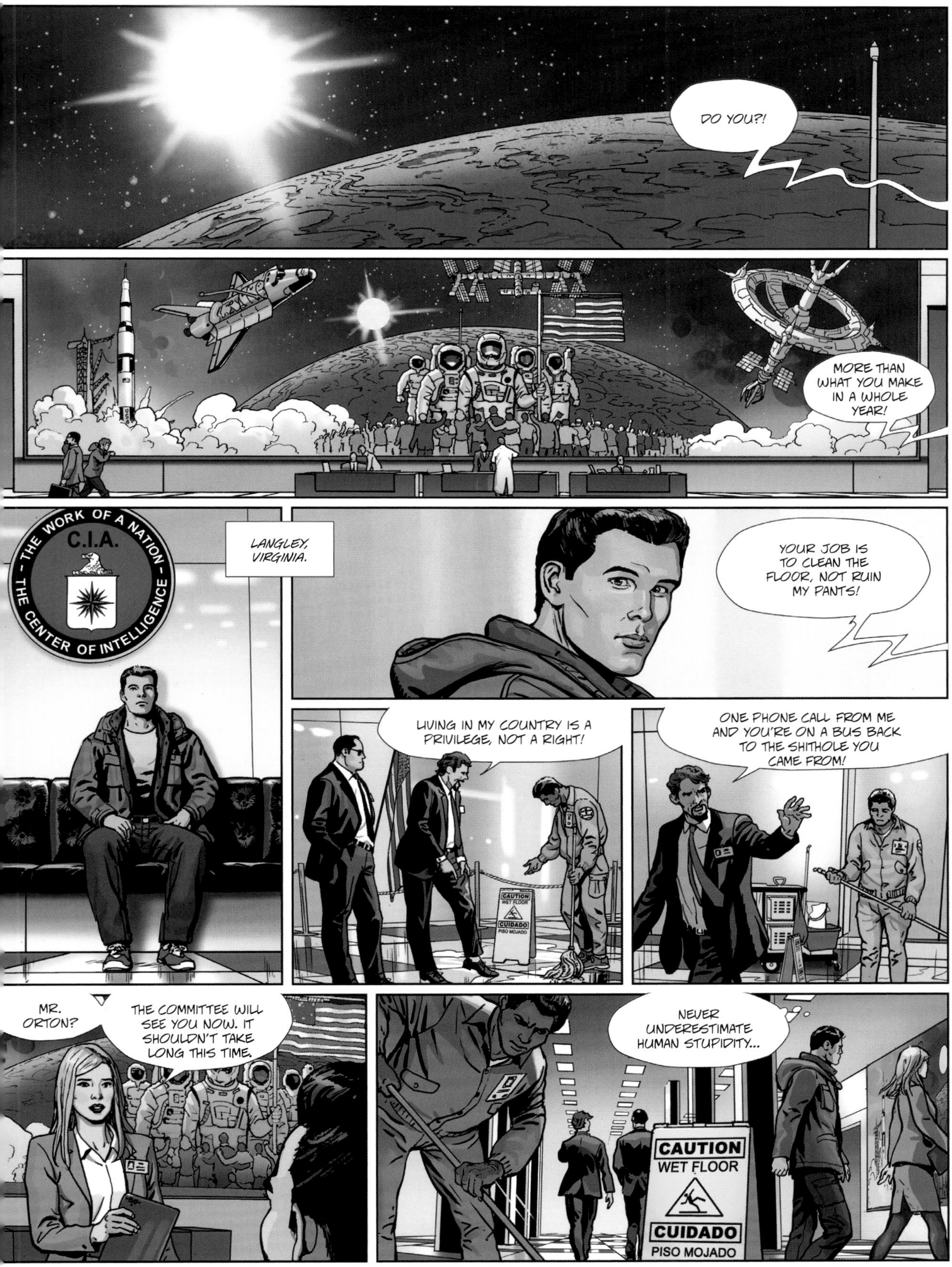
DO YOU?!
MORE THAN WHAT YOU MAKE IN A WHOLE YEAR!
C.I.A.
THE WORK OF A NATION
THE CENTER OF INTELLIGENCE
LANGLEY, VIRGINIA.
YOUR JOB IS TO CLEAN THE FLOOR, NOT RUIN MY PANTS!
LIVING IN MY COUNTRY IS A PRIVILEGE, NOT A RIGHT!
CAUTION WET FLOOR
CUIDADO PISO MOJADO
ONE PHONE CALL FROM ME AND YOU'RE ON A BUS BACK TO THE SHITHOLE YOU CAME FROM!
MR. ORTON?
THE COMMITTEE WILL SEE YOU NOW. IT SHOULDN'T TAKE LONG THIS TIME.
NEVER UNDERESTIMATE HUMAN STUPIDITY...
CAUTION
WET FLOOR
CUIDADO
PISO MOJADO

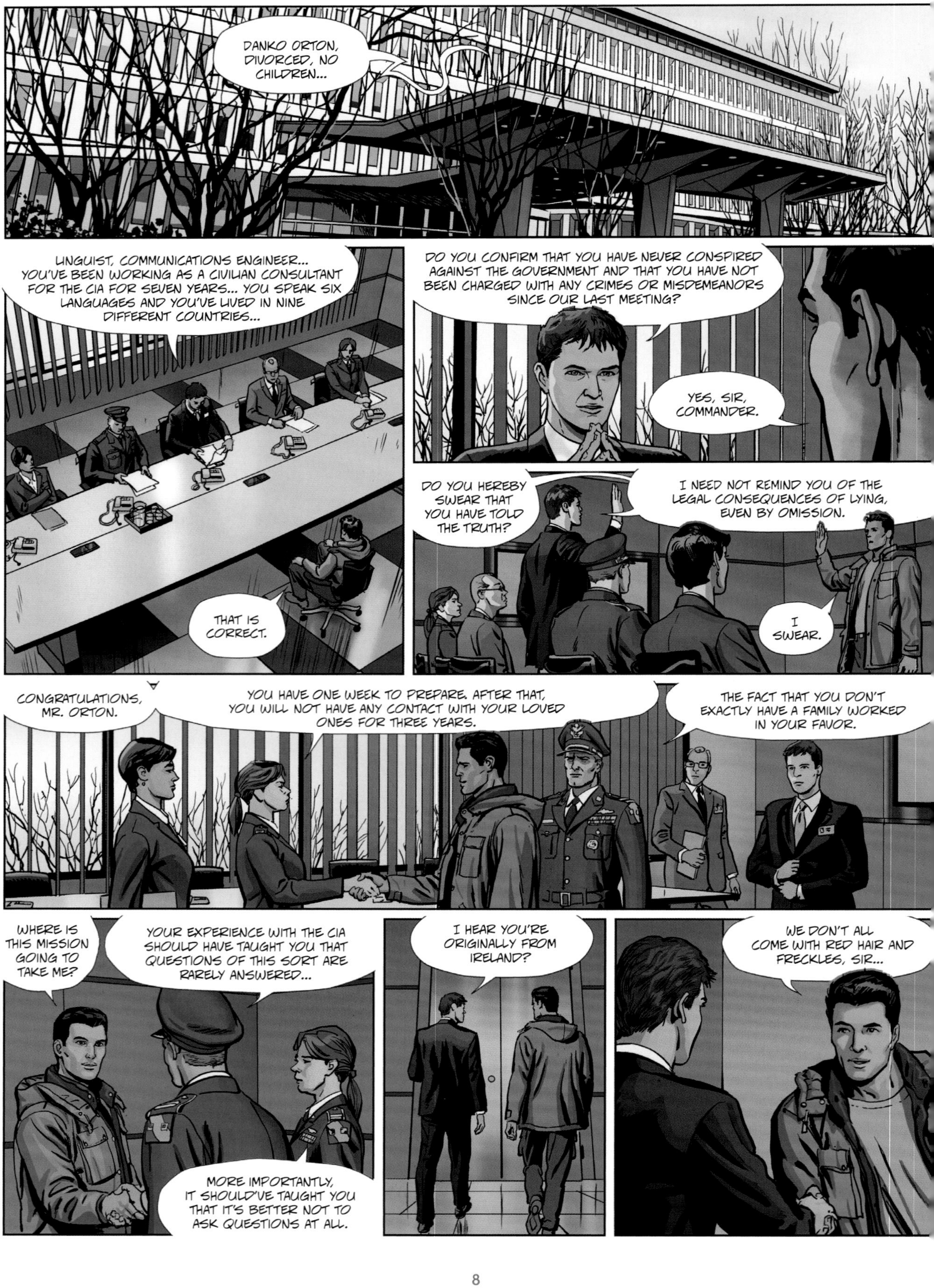
DANKO ORTON, DIVORCED, NO CHILDREN...
LINGUIST, COMMUNICATIONS ENGINEER... YOU'VE BEEN WORKING AS A CIVILIAN CONSULTANT FOR THE CIA FOR SEVEN YEARS... YOU SPEAK SIX LANGUAGES AND YOU'VE LIVED IN NINE DIFFERENT COUNTRIES...
THAT IS CORRECT.
DO YOU CONFIRM THAT YOU HAVE NEVER CONSPIRED AGAINST THE GOVERNMENT AND THAT YOU HAVE NOT BEEN CHARGED WITH ANY CRIMES OR MISDEMEANORS SINCE OUR LAST MEETING?
YES, SIR, COMMANDER.
DO YOU HEREBY SWEAR THAT YOU HAVE TOLD THE TRUTH?
I NEED NOT REMIND YOU OF THE LEGAL CONSEQUENCES OF LYING, EVEN BY OMISSION.
I SWEAR.
CONGRATULATIONS, MR. ORTON.
YOU HAVE ONE WEEK TO PREPARE. AFTER THAT, YOU WILL NOT HAVE ANY CONTACT WITH YOUR LOVED ONES FOR THREE YEARS.
THE FACT THAT YOU DON'T EXACTLY HAVE A FAMILY WORKED IN YOUR FAVOR.
WHERE IS THIS MISSION GOING TO TAKE ME?
YOUR EXPERIENCE WITH THE CIA SHOULD HAVE TAUGHT YOU THAT QUESTIONS OF THIS SORT ARE RARELY ANSWERED...
MORE IMPORTANTLY, IT SHOULD'VE TAUGHT YOU THAT IT'S BETTER NOT TO ASK QUESTIONS AT ALL.
I HEAR YOU'RE ORIGINALLY FROM IRELAND?
WE DON'T ALL COME WITH RED HAIR AND FRECKLES, SIR...

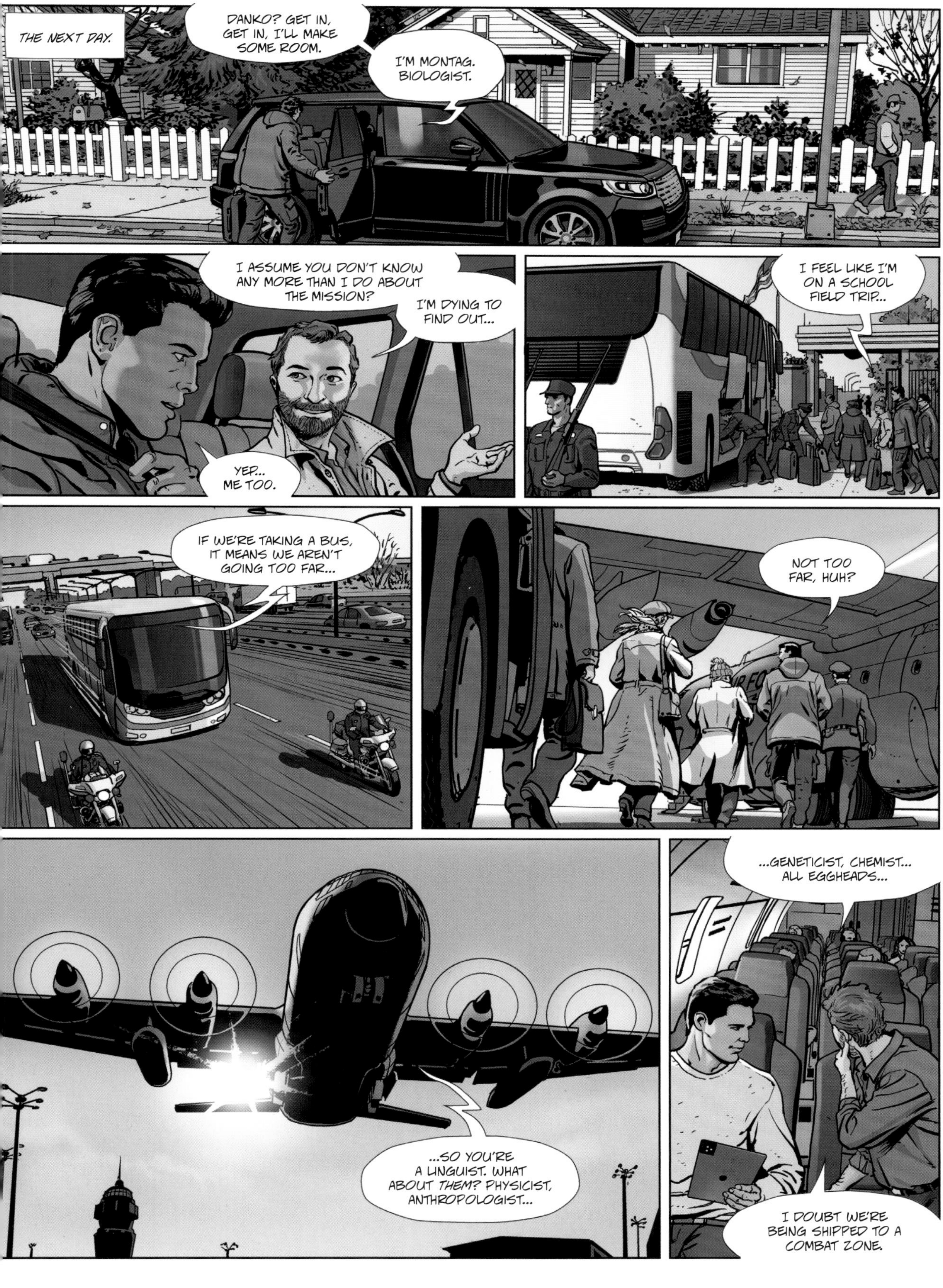
THE NEXT DAY.
DANKO? GET IN, GET IN, I'LL MAKE SOME ROOM.
I'M MONTAG. BIOLOGIST.
I ASSUME YOU DON'T KNOW ANY MORE THAN I DO ABOUT THE MISSION?
I'M DYING TO FIND OUT...
YEP... ME TOO.
I FEEL LIKE I'M ON A SCHOOL FIELD TRIP...
IF WE'RE TAKING A BUS, IT MEANS WE AREN'T GOING TOO FAR...
NOT TOO FAR, HUH?
...SO YOU'RE A LINGUIST. WHAT ABOUT *THEM*? PHYSICIST, ANTHROPOLOGIST...
...GENETICIST, CHEMIST... ALL EGGHEADS...
I DOUBT WE'RE BEING SHIPPED TO A COMBAT ZONE.

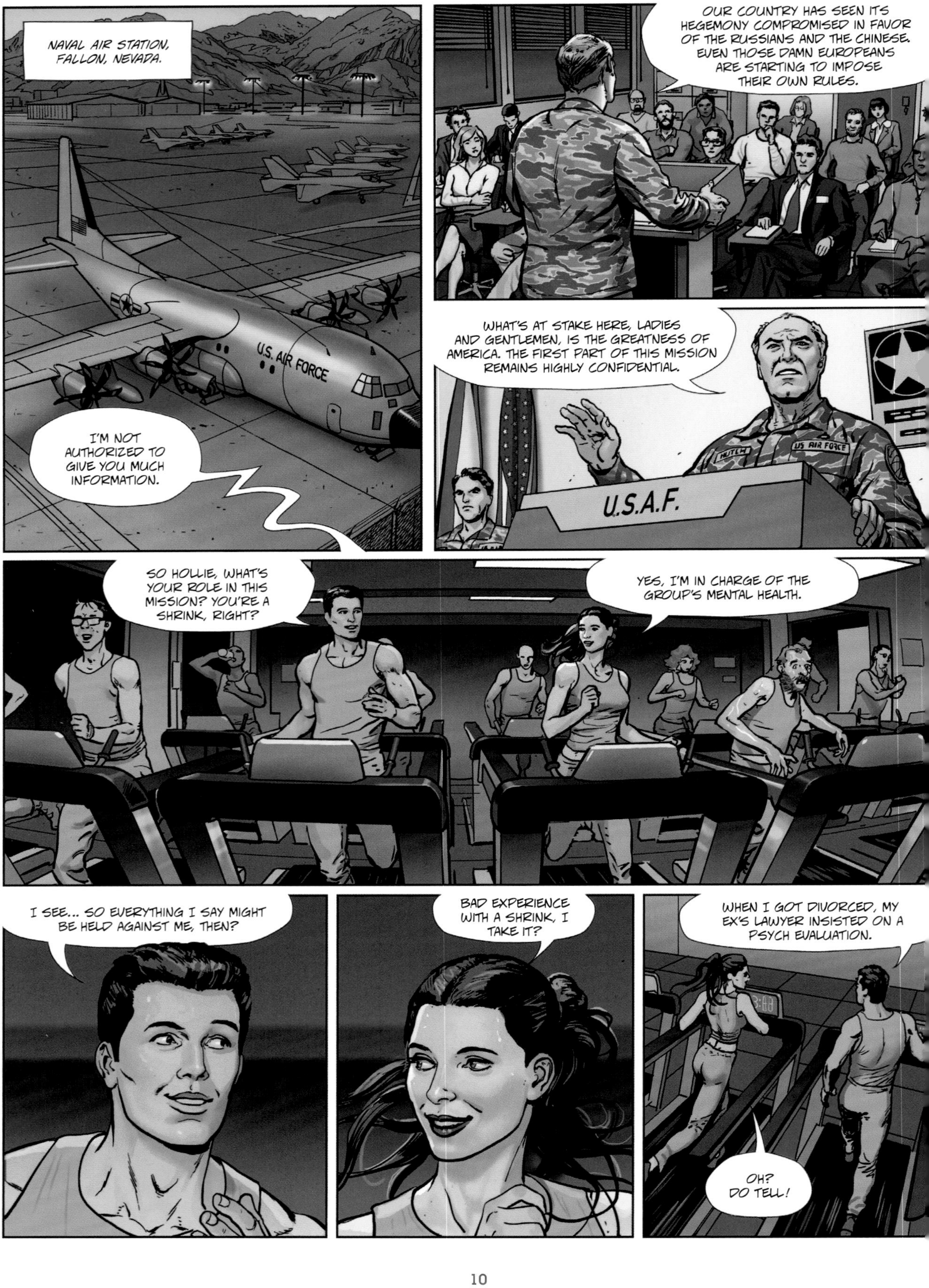
NAVAL AIR STATION, FALLON, NEVADA.
I'M NOT AUTHORIZED TO GIVE YOU MUCH INFORMATION.
U.S. AIR FORCE
OUR COUNTRY HAS SEEN ITS HEGEMONY COMPROMISED IN FAVOR OF THE RUSSIANS AND THE CHINESE. EVEN THOSE DAMN EUROPEANS ARE STARTING TO IMPOSE THEIR OWN RULES.
WHAT'S AT STAKE HERE, LADIES AND GENTLEMEN, IS THE GREATNESS OF AMERICA. THE FIRST PART OF THIS MISSION REMAINS HIGHLY CONFIDENTIAL.
U.S.A.F.
SO HOLLIE, WHAT'S YOUR ROLE IN THIS MISSION? YOU'RE A SHRINK, RIGHT?
YES, I'M IN CHARGE OF THE GROUP'S MENTAL HEALTH.
I SEE... SO EVERYTHING I SAY MIGHT BE HELD AGAINST ME, THEN?
BAD EXPERIENCE WITH A SHRINK, I TAKE IT?
WHEN I GOT DIVORCED, MY EX'S LAWYER INSISTED ON A PSYCH EVALUATION.
OH? DO TELL!

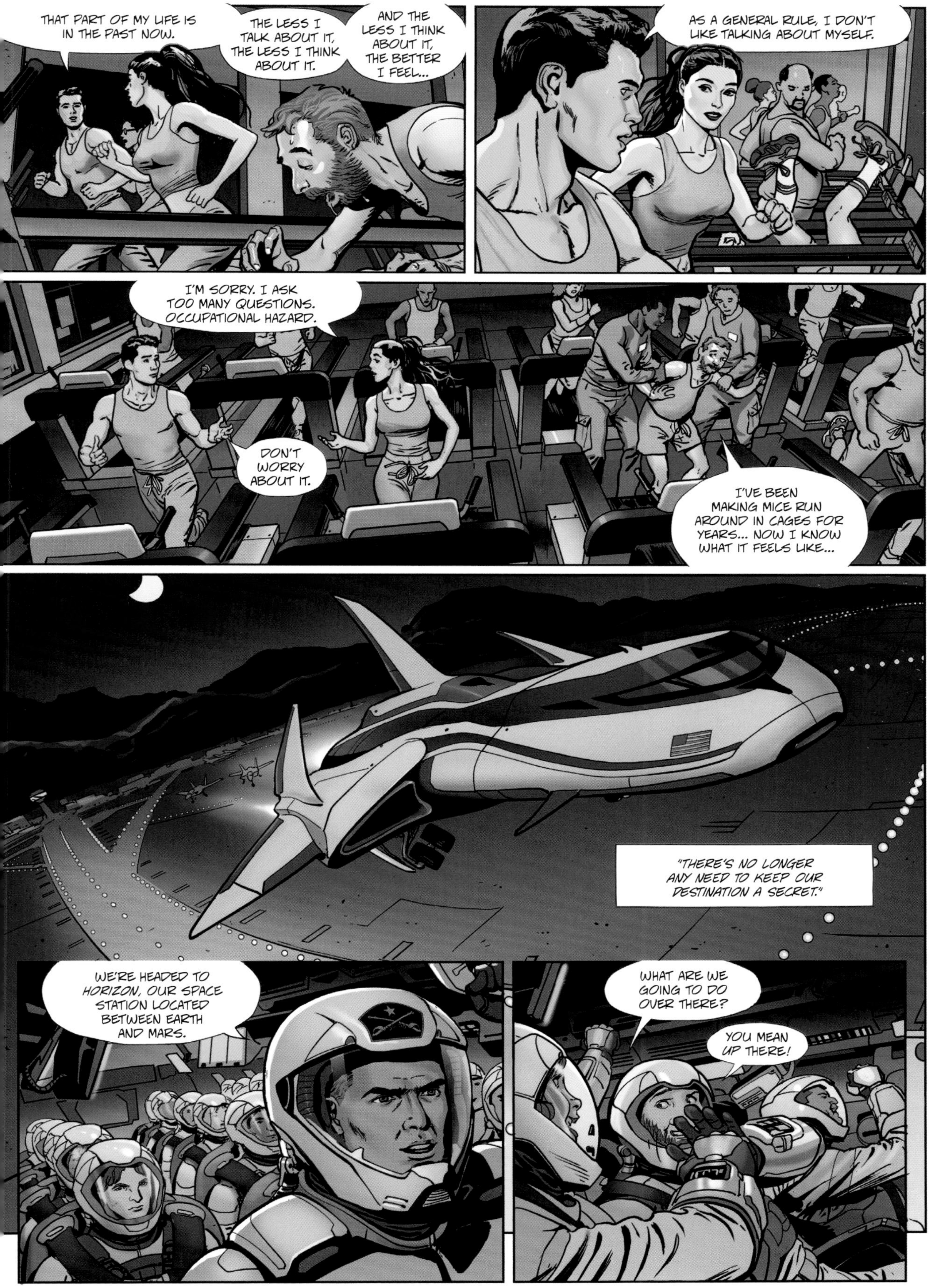
THAT PART OF MY LIFE IS IN THE PAST NOW.
THE LESS I TALK ABOUT IT, THE LESS I THINK ABOUT IT.
AND THE LESS I THINK ABOUT IT, THE BETTER I FEEL...
AS A GENERAL RULE, I DON'T LIKE TALKING ABOUT MYSELF.
I'M SORRY. I ASK TOO MANY QUESTIONS. OCCUPATIONAL HAZARD.
DON'T WORRY ABOUT IT.
I'VE BEEN MAKING MICE RUN AROUND IN CAGES FOR YEARS... NOW I KNOW WHAT IT FEELS LIKE...
"THERE'S NO LONGER ANY NEED TO KEEP OUR DESTINATION A SECRET."
WE'RE HEADED TO HORIZON, OUR SPACE STATION LOCATED BETWEEN EARTH AND MARS.
WHAT ARE WE GOING TO DO OVER THERE?
YOU MEAN UP THERE!

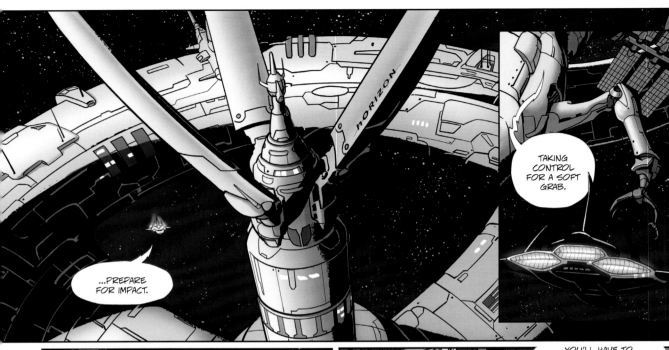

TAKING CONTROL FOR A SOFT GRAB.

...PREPARE FOR IMPACT.

CONFIRMED. GRAB SUCCESSFUL.

YOU'LL HAVE TO SQUEEZE IN. IT'S A TIGHT AIRLOCK

GRAVITY'S NOT AS STRONG HERE AS ON EARTH, BUT BE CAREFUL, THE TRANSITION CAN BE TOUGH ON THE SYSTEM.

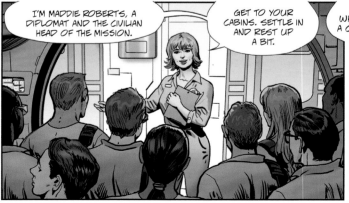

I'M MADDIE ROBERTS, A DIPLOMAT AND THE CIVILIAN HEAD OF THE MISSION.

GET TO YOUR CABINS. SETTLE IN AND REST UP A BIT.

THIS IS WHAT THEY CALL A CABIN AROUND HERE?

WHERE I COME FROM, IT'S CALLED A CLOSET.

A DRAWER, YOU MEAN...

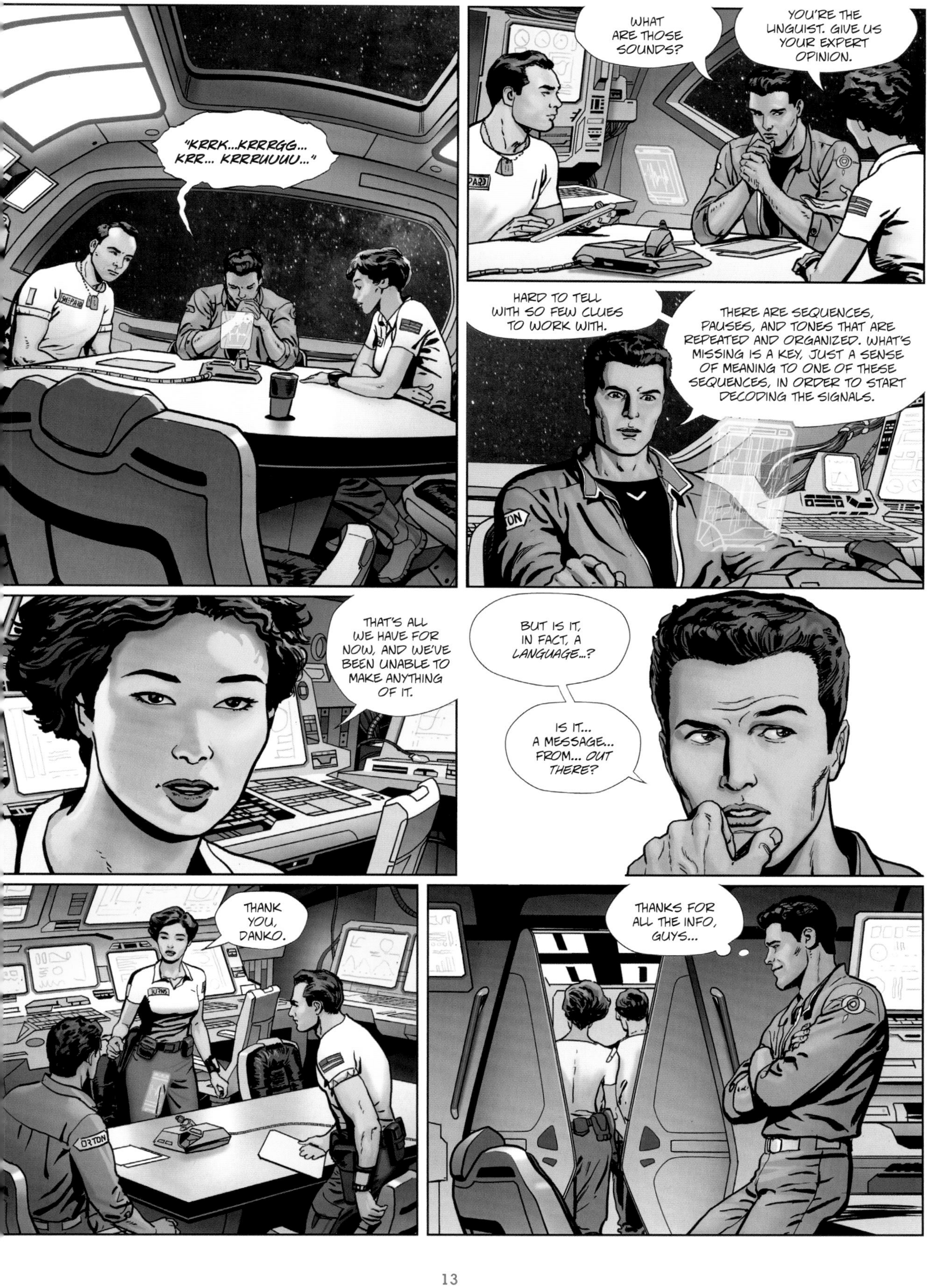
"KRRK...KRRRGG... KRR... KRRRUUUU..."
WHAT ARE THOSE SOUNDS?
YOU'RE THE LINGUIST. GIVE US YOUR EXPERT OPINION.
HARD TO TELL WITH SO FEW CLUES TO WORK WITH.
THERE ARE SEQUENCES, PAUSES, AND TONES THAT ARE REPEATED AND ORGANIZED. WHAT'S MISSING IS A KEY, JUST A SENSE OF MEANING TO ONE OF THESE SEQUENCES, IN ORDER TO START DECODING THE SIGNALS.
THAT'S ALL WE HAVE FOR NOW, AND WE'VE BEEN UNABLE TO MAKE ANYTHING OF IT.
BUT IS IT, IN FACT, A *LANGUAGE*...?
IS IT... A MESSAGE... FROM... *OUT THERE?*
THANK YOU, DANKO.
THANKS FOR ALL THE INFO, GUYS...

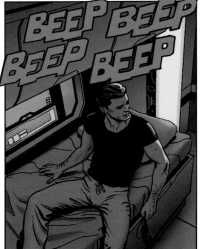

BEEP
BEEP
BEEP
BEEP

...PUT ON YOUR SURVIVAL SUITS AND REPORT TO YOUR EMERGENCY POSTS IMMEDIATELY...

WHAT'S GOING ON?

NO IDEA.

MOVE IT! MOVE IT! NO TIME FOR SLACKING. SUIT UP LIKE YOU DID IN TRAINING.

"...ALL SPACE FORCES MUST REPORT TO THEIR POSTS..."

HURRY UP, TOBIN! WE SHOUL ALREADY BE IN POSISITON!

I DON'T SEE ANYTHING.

FALSE ALARM?

PROBABLY.

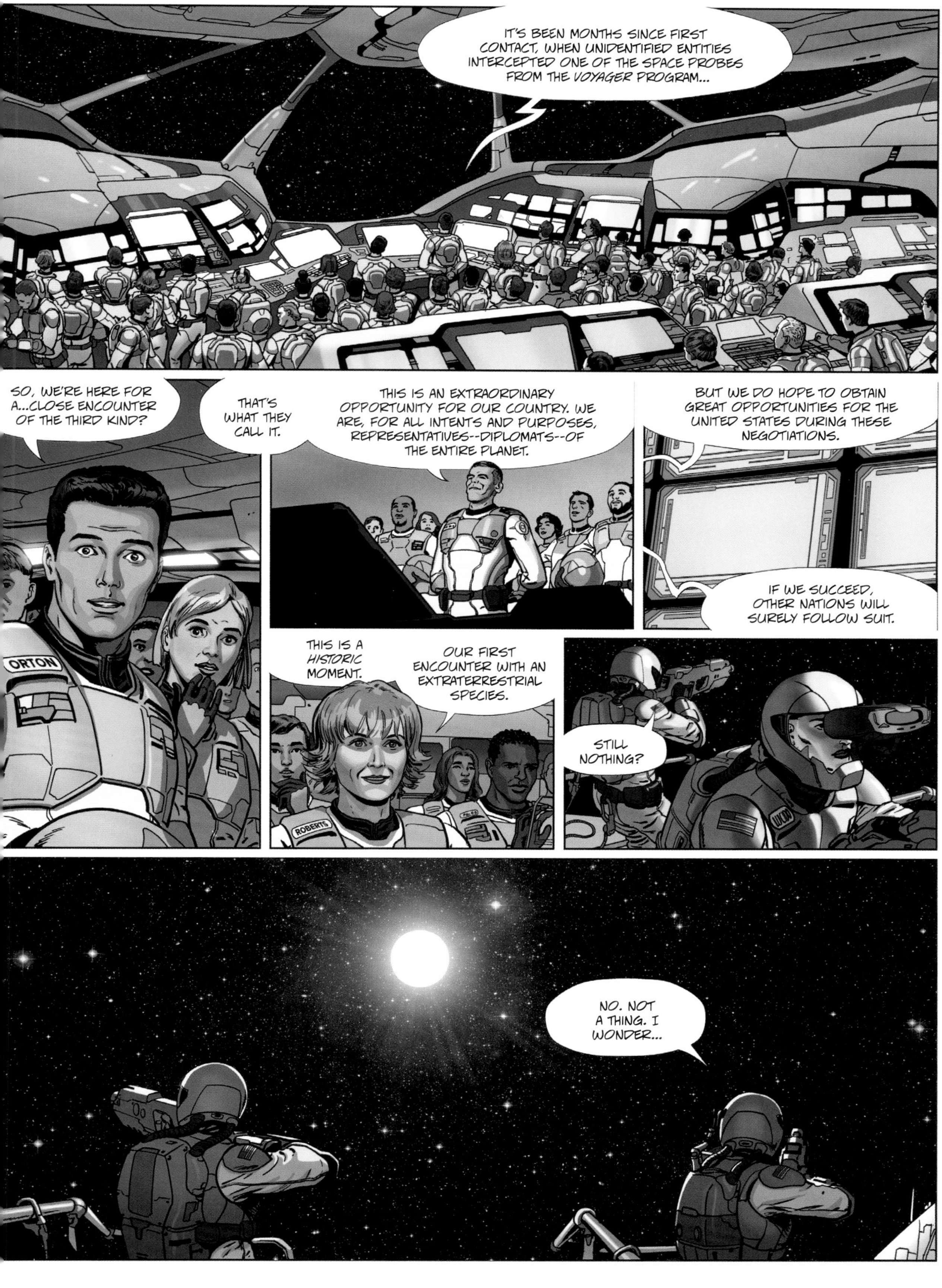

IT'S BEEN MONTHS SINCE FIRST CONTACT, WHEN UNIDENTIFIED ENTITIES INTERCEPTED ONE OF THE SPACE PROBES FROM THE *VOYAGER* PROGRAM...
SO, WE'RE HERE FOR A...CLOSE ENCOUNTER OF THE THIRD KIND?
THAT'S WHAT THEY CALL IT.
ORTON
THIS IS AN EXTRAORDINARY OPPORTUNITY FOR OUR COUNTRY. WE ARE, FOR ALL INTENTS AND PURPOSES, REPRESENTATIVES--DIPLOMATS--OF THE ENTIRE PLANET.
BUT WE DO HOPE TO OBTAIN GREAT OPPORTUNITIES FOR THE UNITED STATES DURING THESE NEGOTIATIONS.
IF WE SUCCEED, OTHER NATIONS WILL SURELY FOLLOW SUIT.
THIS IS A *HISTORIC* MOMENT.
OUR FIRST ENCOUNTER WITH AN EXTRATERRESTRIAL SPECIES.
ROBERTS
STILL NOTHING?
NO. NOT A THING. I WONDER...

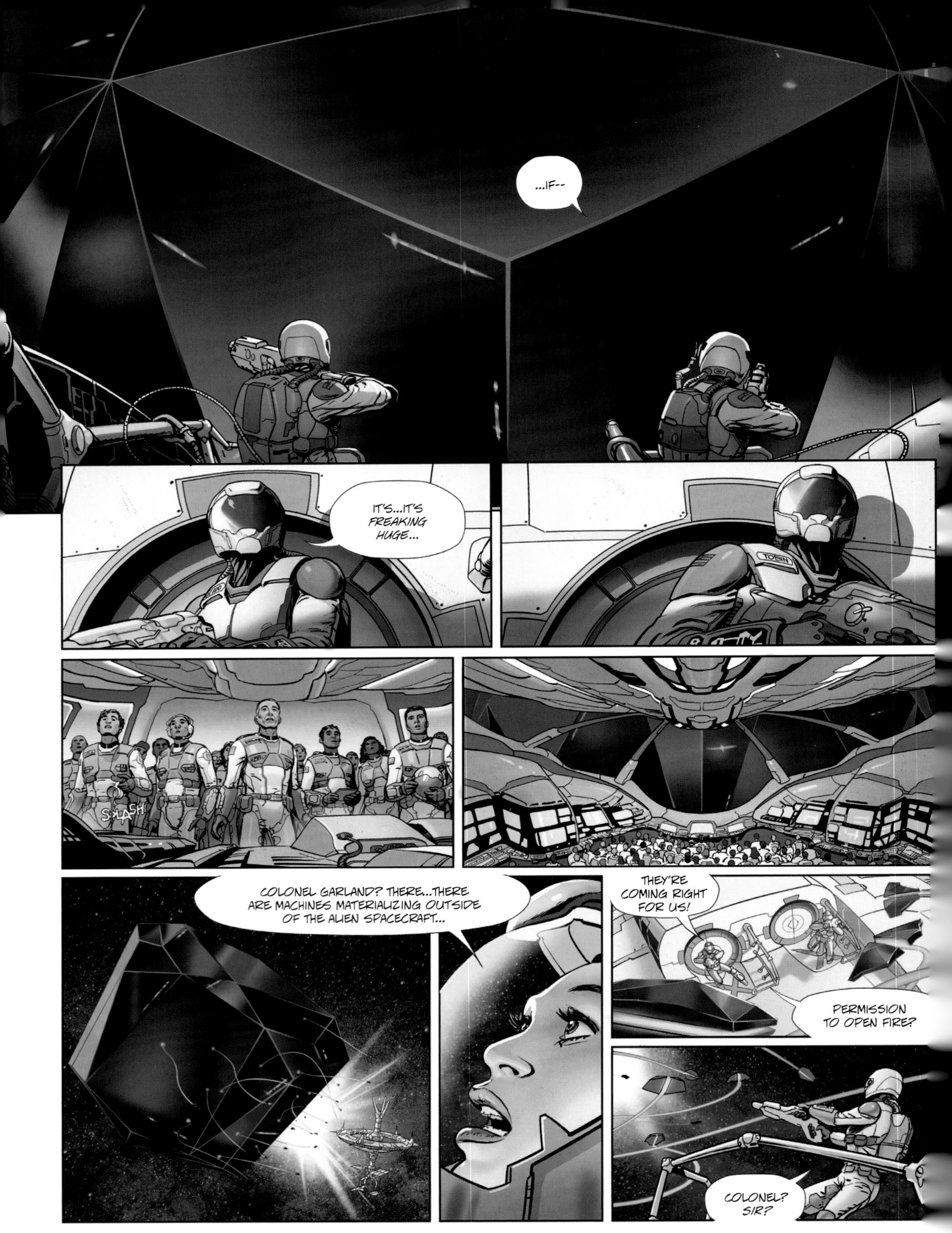

...IF--
IT'S...IT'S FREAKING HUGE...
TOBIN
SPLASH
COLONEL GARLAND? THERE...THERE ARE MACHINES MATERIALIZING OUTSIDE OF THE ALIEN SPACECRAFT...
THEY'RE COMING RIGHT FOR US!
PERMISSION TO OPEN FIRE?
COLONEL? SIR?

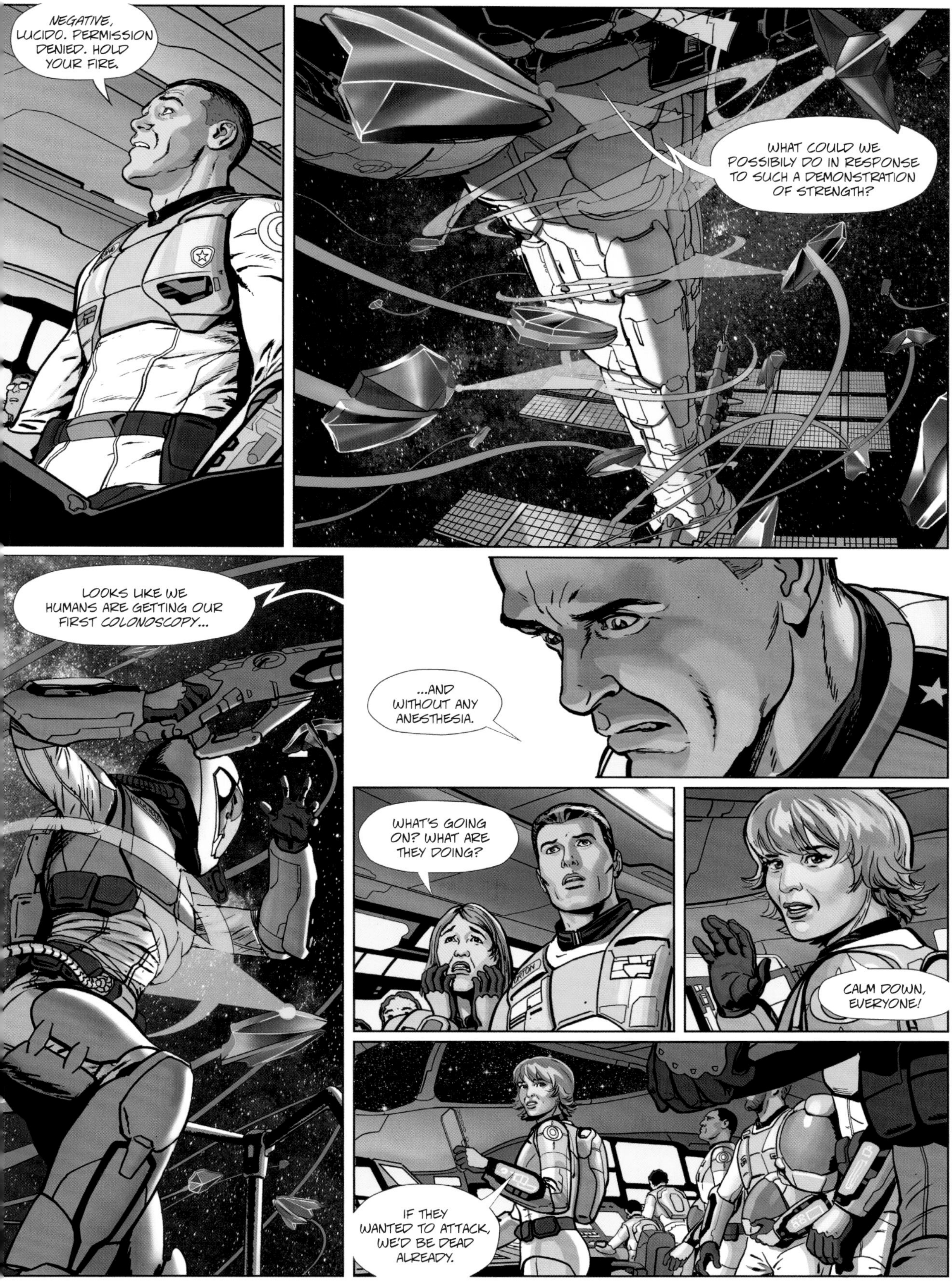
NEGATIVE, LUCIDO. PERMISSION DENIED. HOLD YOUR FIRE.
WHAT COULD WE POSSIBLY DO IN RESPONSE TO SUCH A DEMONSTRATION OF STRENGTH?
LOOKS LIKE WE HUMANS ARE GETTING OUR FIRST COLONOSCOPY...
...AND WITHOUT ANY ANESTHESIA.
WHAT'S GOING ON? WHAT ARE THEY DOING?
CALM DOWN, EVERYONE!
IF THEY WANTED TO ATTACK, WE'D BE DEAD ALREADY.

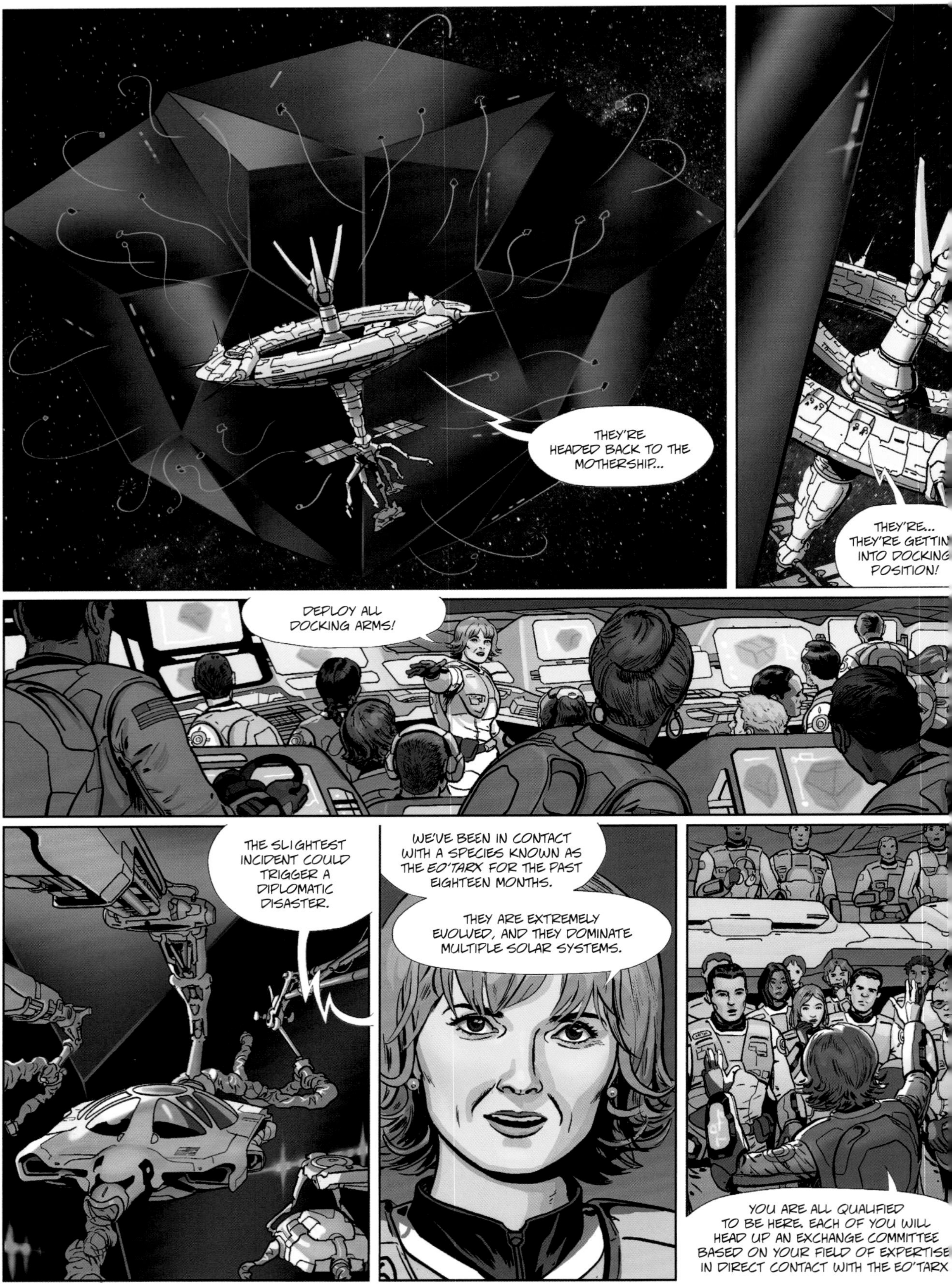
THEY'RE HEADED BACK TO THE MOTHERSHIP...
THEY'RE... THEY'RE GETTIN INTO DOCKING POSITION!
DEPLOY ALL DOCKING ARMS!
THE SLIGHTEST INCIDENT COULD TRIGGER A DIPLOMATIC DISASTER.
WE'VE BEEN IN CONTACT WITH A SPECIES KNOWN AS THE EO'TARX FOR THE PAST EIGHTEEN MONTHS.
THEY ARE EXTREMELY EVOLVED, AND THEY DOMINATE MULTIPLE SOLAR SYSTEMS.
YOU ARE ALL QUALIFIED TO BE HERE. EACH OF YOU WILL HEAD UP AN EXCHANGE COMMITTEE BASED ON YOUR FIELD OF EXPERTISE IN DIRECT CONTACT WITH THE EO'TARX

MEETINGS WITH THE EO'TARX MUST FOLLOW A VERY SPECIFIC PROTOCOL.

PRIORITY MEETINGS WILL TAKE PLACE BETWEEN DIPLOMATS...

...ALL OF WHICH--

--WILL BE *MONITORED* BY MILITARY AUTHORITIES.

THE ARMY ALSO HAS A PROTOCOL TO FOLLOW SO AS TO NOT PUT EARTH IN DANGER.

THERE IS NOTHING TO INDICATE THAT THE INTENTIONS OF THE EO'TARX ARE ANTAGONISTIC, BUT THERE IS NOTHING TO PROVE THAT THEY'RE PACIFISTS EITHER.

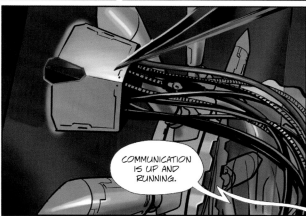

COMMUNICATION IS UP AND RUNNING.

THIS IS SPACE STATION *HORIZON*. WE WELCOME OUR EO'TARX FRIENDS.

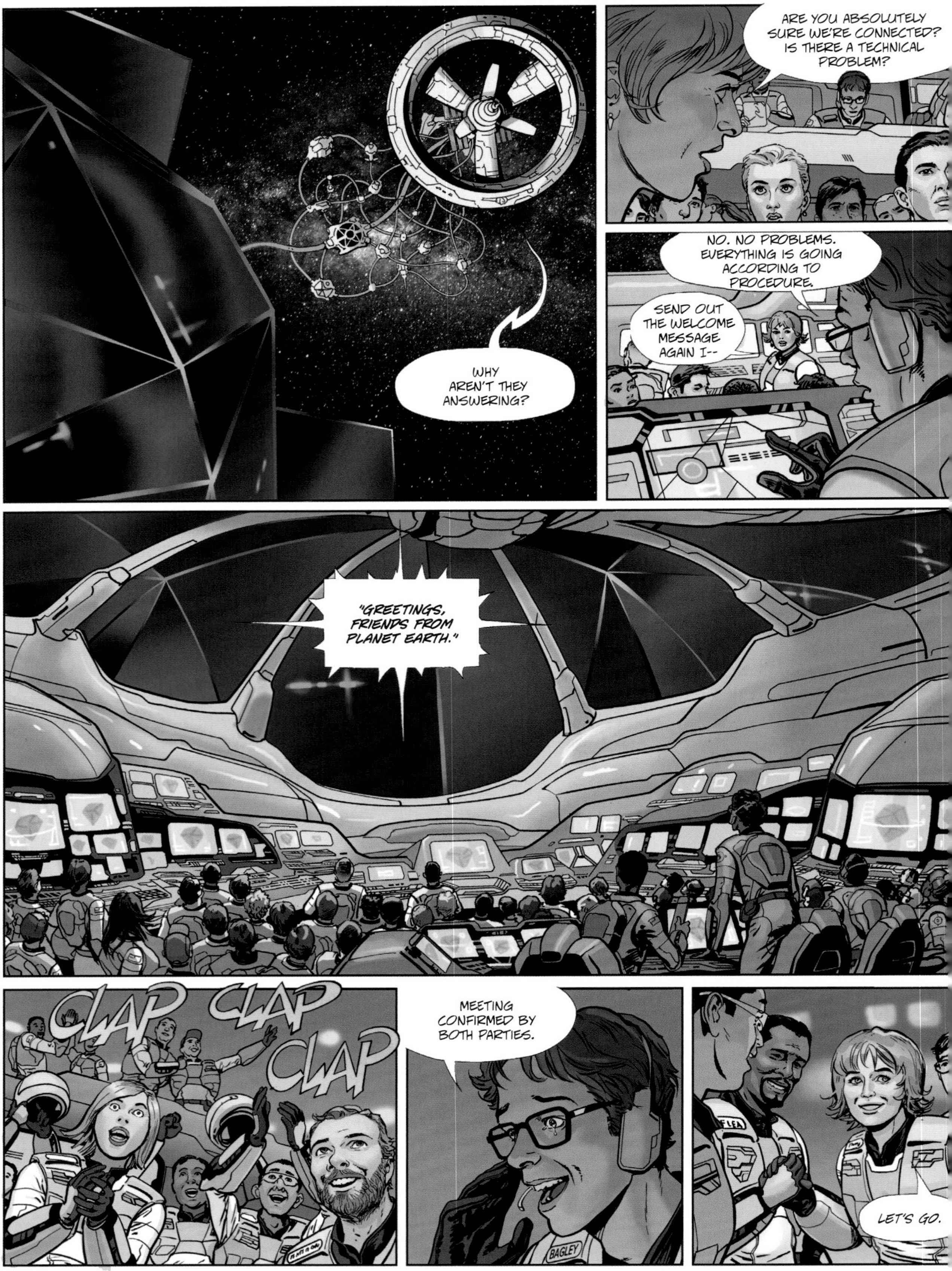
WHY AREN'T THEY ANSWERING?
ARE YOU ABSOLUTELY SURE WE'RE CONNECTED? IS THERE A TECHNICAL PROBLEM?
NO. NO PROBLEMS. EVERYTHING IS GOING ACCORDING TO PROCEDURE.
SEND OUT THE WELCOME MESSAGE AGAIN I--
"GREETINGS, FRIENDS FROM PLANET EARTH."
CLAP CLAP CLAP
MEETING CONFIRMED BY BOTH PARTIES.
BAGLEY
LET'S GO.

THE FIRST EXCHANGE IS RESTRICTED TO GREETINGS. NOTHING MORE.

THE PROTOCOL MUST BE FOLLOWED TO A T.

THE CLASHING OF CULTURES IS CITED AS THE NUMBER ONE THREAT TO DIPLOMACY.

STAY ON YOUR GUARD AND REPORT EVEN THE SLIGHTEST ISSUE.

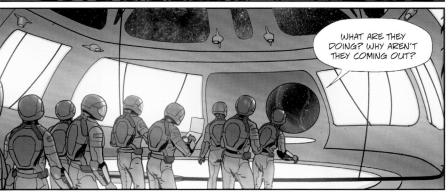

WHAT ARE THEY DOING? WHY AREN'T THEY COMING OUT?

LOOK! THE DOOR'S OPENING!

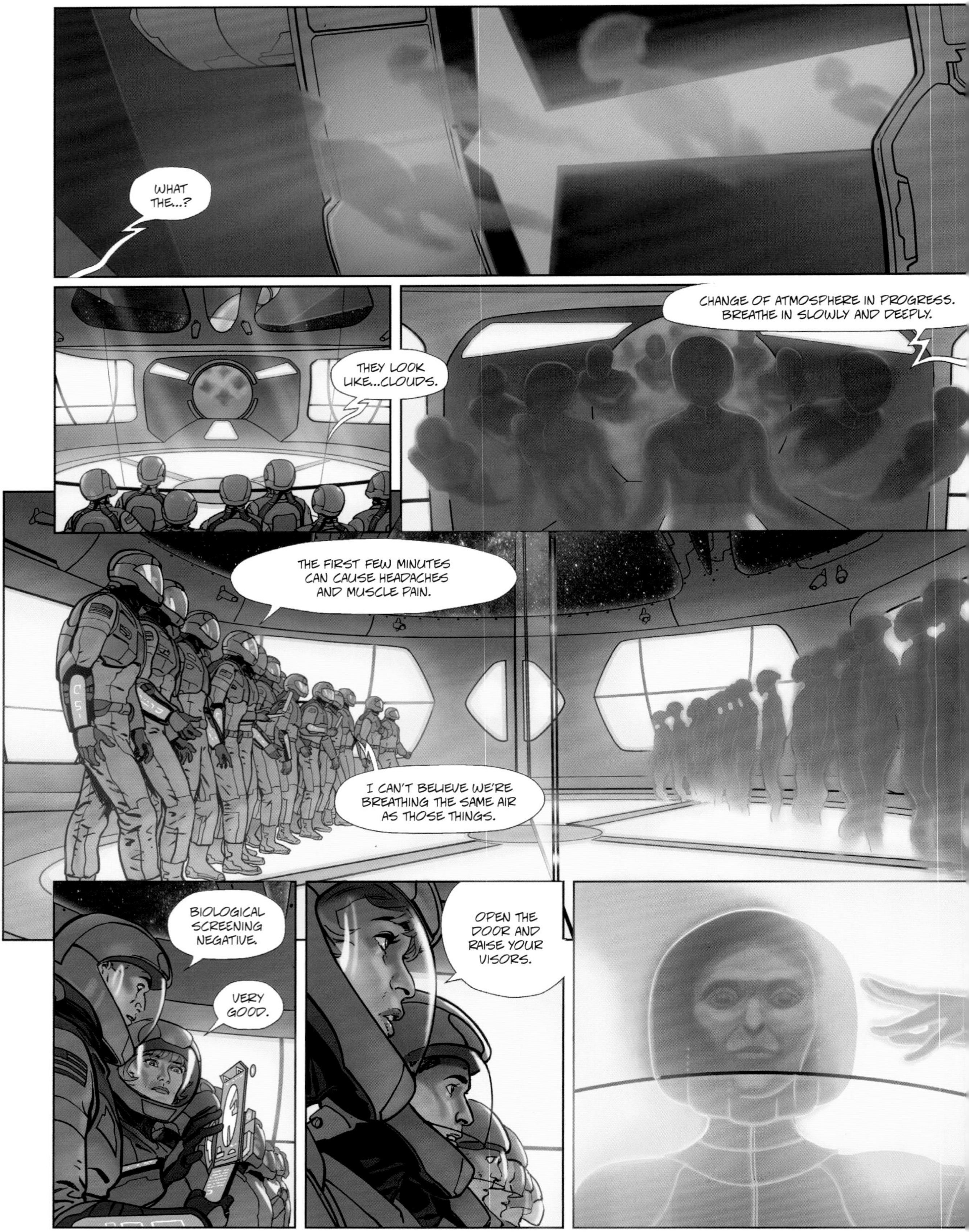
WHAT THE...?
THEY LOOK LIKE...CLOUDS.
CHANGE OF ATMOSPHERE IN PROGRESS. BREATHE IN SLOWLY AND DEEPLY.
THE FIRST FEW MINUTES CAN CAUSE HEADACHES AND MUSCLE PAIN.
I CAN'T BELIEVE WE'RE BREATHING THE SAME AIR AS THOSE THINGS.
BIOLOGICAL SCREENING NEGATIVE.
VERY GOOD.
OPEN THE DOOR AND RAISE YOUR VISORS.

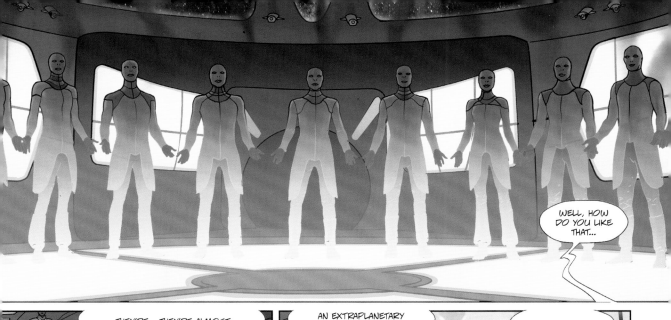

WELL, HOW DO YOU LIKE THAT...

THEY'RE... THEY'RE ALMOST TOO HUMAN TO BE REAL!

AN EXTRAPLANETARY SPECIES THAT LOOKS LIKE US...

WE HAVE PROOF NOW, RIGHT BEFORE OUR EYES!

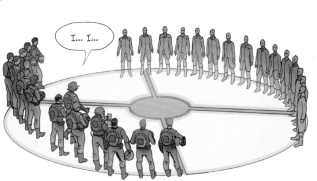

I... I...

H... HELLO.

HE-LLO.

STRANGE VOICE...

...AND A LITTLE SCARY TOO...

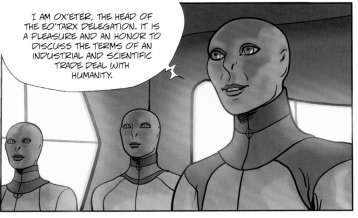

I AM OX'ETER, THE HEAD OF THE EO'TARX DELEGATION. IT IS A PLEASURE AND AN HONOR TO DISCUSS THE TERMS OF AN INDUSTRIAL AND SCIENTIFIC TRADE DEAL WITH HUMANITY.

ALLOW ME TO PROCEED WITH OUR PLAN: THE GIVING OF THE GIFTS.

THIS IS A PORTABLE PARTICLE ACCELERATOR AND A DETECTOR OF CELLS WITH DAMAGE.

AND NOW, ALLOW ME TO PRESENT TO YOU, IN THE NAME OF ALL OF HUMANITY, THE GIFTS YOU REQUESTED.

THEY GIVE US ADVANCED TECHNOLOGY AND WE GIVE THEM MONKEYS...?

THEY SEEM TO LIKE 'EM.

THESE ARE MY ASSOCIATES. MICHAEL BARETS, ETHNOLOGIST, HARRY SHECKLEY, GENETICIST...

...AND, LASTLY, DANKO ORTON, LINGUIST.

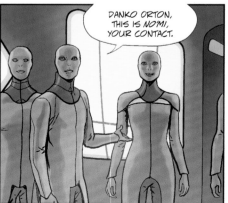

DANKO ORTON, THIS IS NO'MI, YOUR CONTACT.

GREETINGS, DANKO.

HELLO, NO'MI.

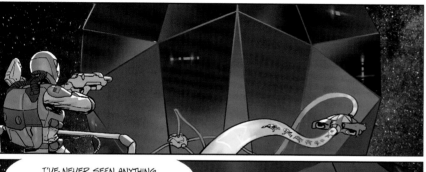

IN ANY CASE, THERE'S NOTHING THAT RESEMBLES A WEAPON. THEN AGAIN, HOW CAN WE BE SURE? THEIR SHIP DOESN'T LOOK LIKE A SHIP EITHER.

I'VE NEVER SEEN ANYTHING LIKE IT. IT'S LIKE THEIR VESSEL IS BOTH SOLID AND LIQUID.

IT'S INTERESTING TO NOTE THAT ONE OF THE MOST INTELLIGENT LIFE FORMS IN THE UNIVERSE UNDERWENT A MORPHOLOGICAL EVOLUTION THAT IS SYMMETRICAL TO OUR OWN.

THIS CERTAINLY OPENS UP NEW AVENUES WITH WHICH TO VIEW EXOBIOLOGY.

...PERSONALLY, WHAT I FIND ASTONISHING IS THE SIMPLICITY AND RESPECT IN THEIR SPEECH.

I LIKE IT A LOT.

PLEASE, I BEG YOU, DON'T TAKE WHAT OX'ETER SAYS AT FACE VALUE.

I, LIKE YOU, AM OVERWHELMED BY THIS FIRST CONTACT WITH THEM...

...BUT...

...THIS DOES NOT ELIMINATE ANY DOUBTS PERTAINING TO THE INTENTIONS OF THE EO'TARX. IT'S IMPORTANT TO KEEP THE DIALOGUE GOING, OF COURSE...

...BUT WE MUST ALSO REMAIN CAUTIOUS.

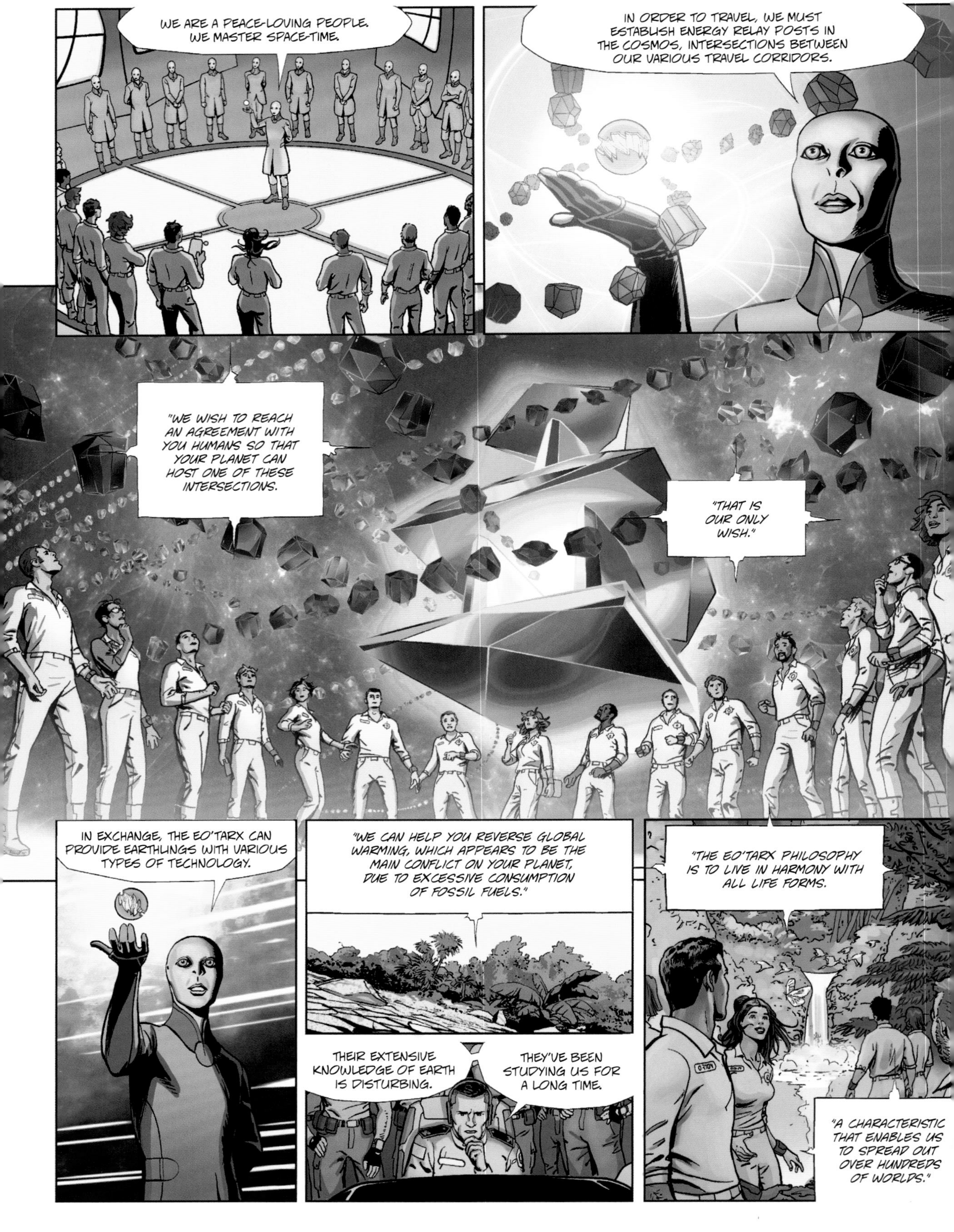
WE ARE A PEACE-LOVING PEOPLE. WE MASTER SPACE-TIME.
IN ORDER TO TRAVEL, WE MUST ESTABLISH ENERGY RELAY POSTS IN THE COSMOS, INTERSECTIONS BETWEEN OUR VARIOUS TRAVEL CORRIDORS.
"WE WISH TO REACH AN AGREEMENT WITH YOU HUMANS SO THAT YOUR PLANET CAN HOST ONE OF THESE INTERSECTIONS.
"THAT IS OUR ONLY WISH."
IN EXCHANGE, THE EO'TARX CAN PROVIDE EARTHLINGS WITH VARIOUS TYPES OF TECHNOLOGY.
"WE CAN HELP YOU REVERSE GLOBAL WARMING, WHICH APPEARS TO BE THE MAIN CONFLICT ON YOUR PLANET, DUE TO EXCESSIVE CONSUMPTION OF FOSSIL FUELS."
THEIR EXTENSIVE KNOWLEDGE OF EARTH IS DISTURBING.
THEY'VE BEEN STUDYING US FOR A LONG TIME.
"THE EO'TARX PHILOSOPHY IS TO LIVE IN HARMONY WITH ALL LIFE FORMS.
"A CHARACTERISTIC THAT ENABLES US TO SPREAD OUT OVER HUNDREDS OF WORLDS."

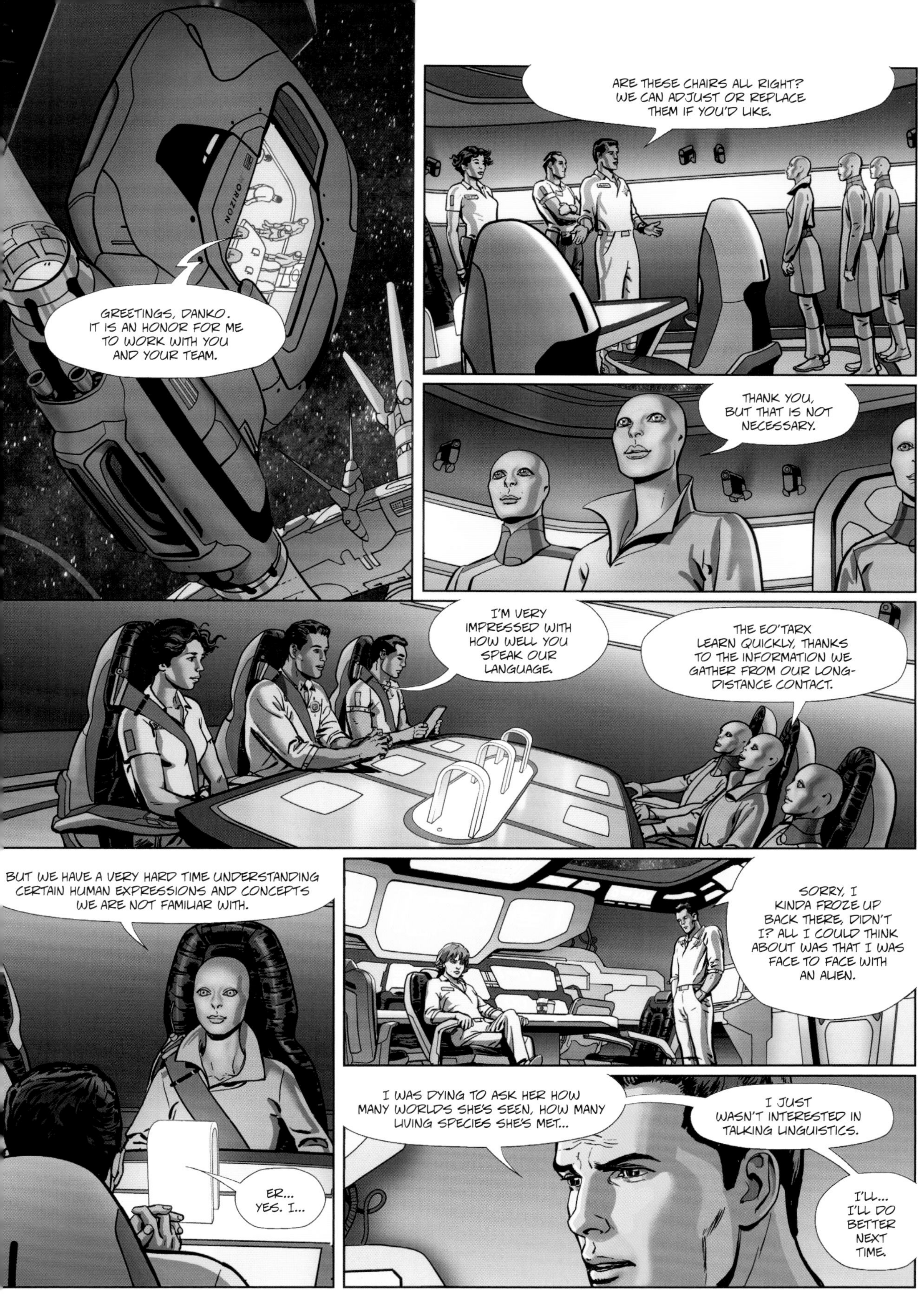
GREETINGS, DANKO. IT IS AN HONOR FOR ME TO WORK WITH YOU AND YOUR TEAM.
ARE THESE CHAIRS ALL RIGHT? WE CAN ADJUST OR REPLACE THEM IF YOU'D LIKE.
THANK YOU, BUT THAT IS NOT NECESSARY.
I'M VERY IMPRESSED WITH HOW WELL YOU SPEAK OUR LANGUAGE.
THE EO'TARX LEARN QUICKLY, THANKS TO THE INFORMATION WE GATHER FROM OUR LONG-DISTANCE CONTACT.
BUT WE HAVE A VERY HARD TIME UNDERSTANDING CERTAIN HUMAN EXPRESSIONS AND CONCEPTS WE ARE NOT FAMILIAR WITH.
ER... YES. I...
SORRY, I KINDA FROZE UP BACK THERE, DIDN'T I? ALL I COULD THINK ABOUT WAS THAT I WAS FACE TO FACE WITH AN ALIEN.
I WAS DYING TO ASK HER HOW MANY WORLDS SHE'S SEEN, HOW MANY LIVING SPECIES SHE'S MET...
I JUST WASN'T INTERESTED IN TALKING LINGUISTICS.
I'LL... I'LL DO BETTER NEXT TIME.

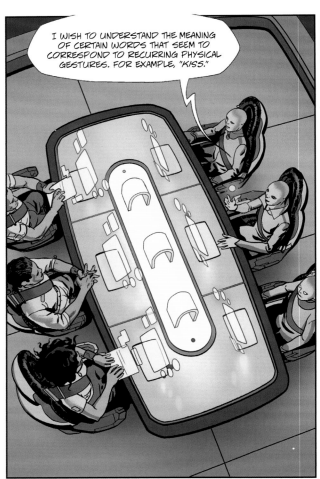

I WISH TO UNDERSTAND THE MEANING OF CERTAIN WORDS THAT SEEM TO CORRESPOND TO RECURRING PHYSICAL GESTURES. FOR EXAMPLE, "KISS."

HUH?

UH...IT'S A GESTURE OF AFFECTION THAT YOU EXCHANGE WITH...PEOPLE CLOSE TO YOU. HUMANS DO IT WITH THEIR MOUTHS.

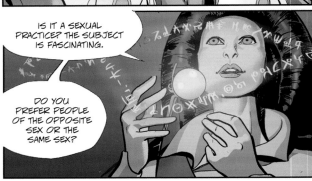

WITH THEIR MOUTHS... IS THIS A COMMON GESTURE? DO YOU KISS A LOT?

I...

IS IT A SEXUAL PRACTICE? THE SUBJECT IS FASCINATING.

DO YOU PREFER PEOPLE OF THE OPPOSITE SEX OR THE SAME SEX?

I...I DON'T REALLY LIKE TALKING ABOUT MYSELF...

YOU DO NOT WISH TO ANSWER? IS IT CUSTOMARY FOR HUMANS NOT TO ANSWER QUESTIONS?

"NO, NO... IT'S NOT THAT..."

I...LIKE PEOPLE OF THE OPPOSITE SEX. AND I DO KISS THEM...

...WHEN THEY'RE OKAY WITH IT, OF COURSE.

I UNDERSTAND.

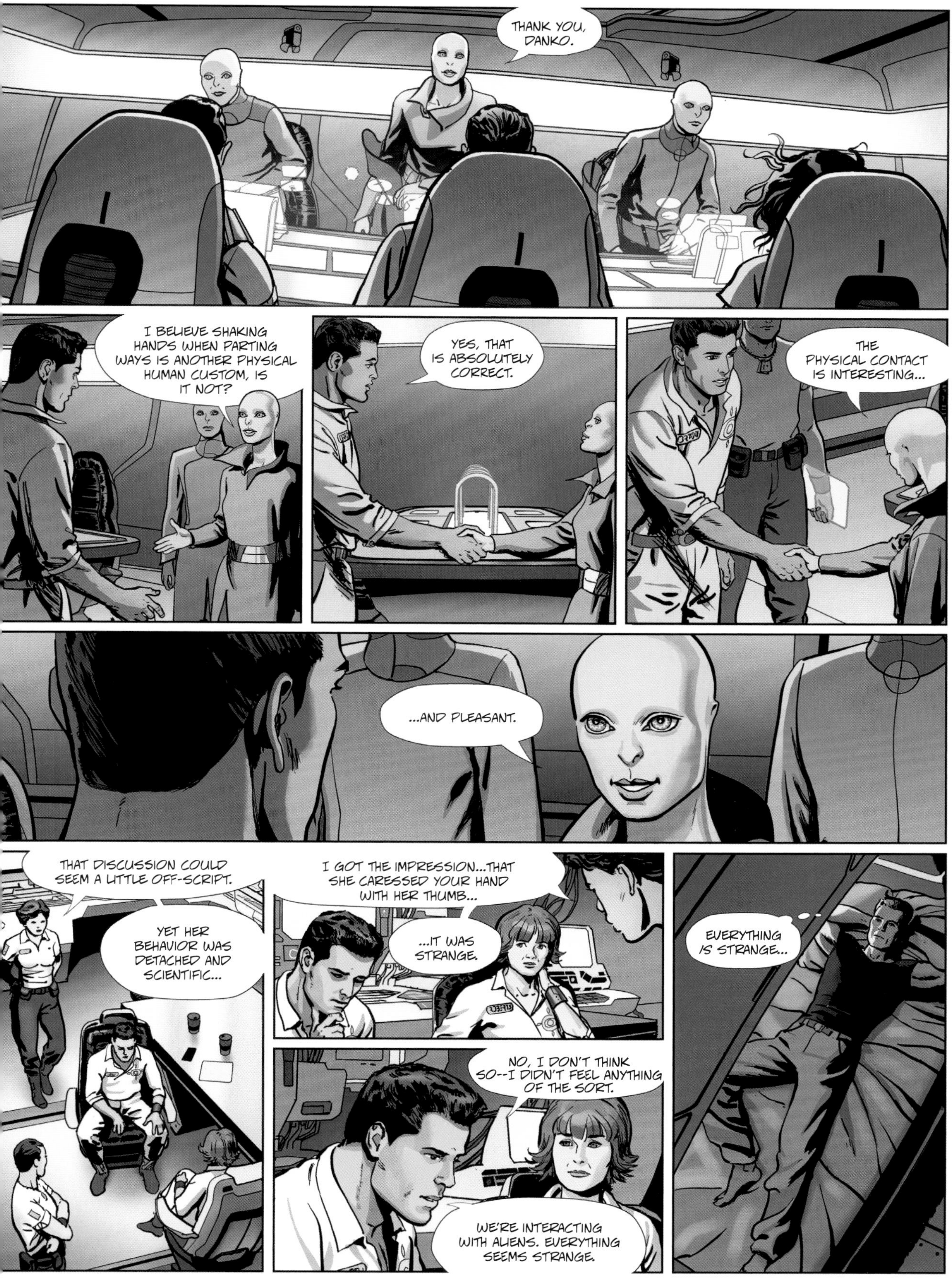
THANK YOU, DANKO.
I BELIEVE SHAKING HANDS WHEN PARTING WAYS IS ANOTHER PHYSICAL HUMAN CUSTOM, IS IT NOT?
YES, THAT IS ABSOLUTELY CORRECT.
THE PHYSICAL CONTACT IS INTERESTING...
...AND PLEASANT.
THAT DISCUSSION COULD SEEM A LITTLE OFF-SCRIPT.
YET HER BEHAVIOR WAS DETACHED AND SCIENTIFIC...
I GOT THE IMPRESSION...THAT SHE CARESSED YOUR HAND WITH HER THUMB...
...IT WAS STRANGE.
NO, I DON'T THINK SO--I DIDN'T FEEL ANYTHING OF THE SORT.
WE'RE INTERACTING WITH ALIENS. EVERYTHING SEEMS STRANGE.
EVERYTHING IS STRANGE...

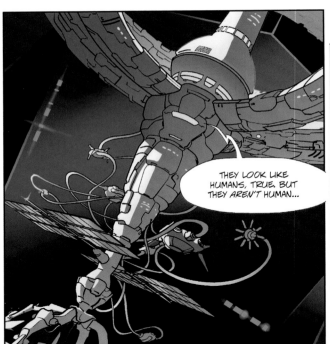

THEY LOOK LIKE HUMANS, TRUE. BUT THEY AREN'T HUMAN...

YOU'RE RIGHT, COLONEL, BUT THE EO'TARX COME FROM ANOTHER CULTURE, SO HOW CAN WE DRAW CONCLUSIONS ABOUT THEIR ABILITY OR TENDENCIES TO LIE?

WE CAN'T. BUT IF THEY'RE NOT HUMAN, THEY MAY NOT SHARE OUR MORAL COMPASS, LIMITING OUR ABILITY TO TRUST THEM IN ANY WAY.

DO YOU THINK HOLLIE'S HOT?

I THINK SHE'S SUPER HOT...

ANYONE WAITING FOR YOU BACK ON EARTH? DON'T YOU MISS GETTING LAID?

IT'S GETTING TO ME--BEING STUCK UP HERE WITHOUT ANY ACTION...

I'M STARTING TO SERIOUSLY CONSIDER TAKING ONE OF THOSE INHIBITORS THEY SUGGESTED.

HEY, YOU LISTENING TO ME?

DANKO?

"ANYONE WAITING FOR YOU BACK ON EARTH? DON'T YOU MISS GETTING LAID?"

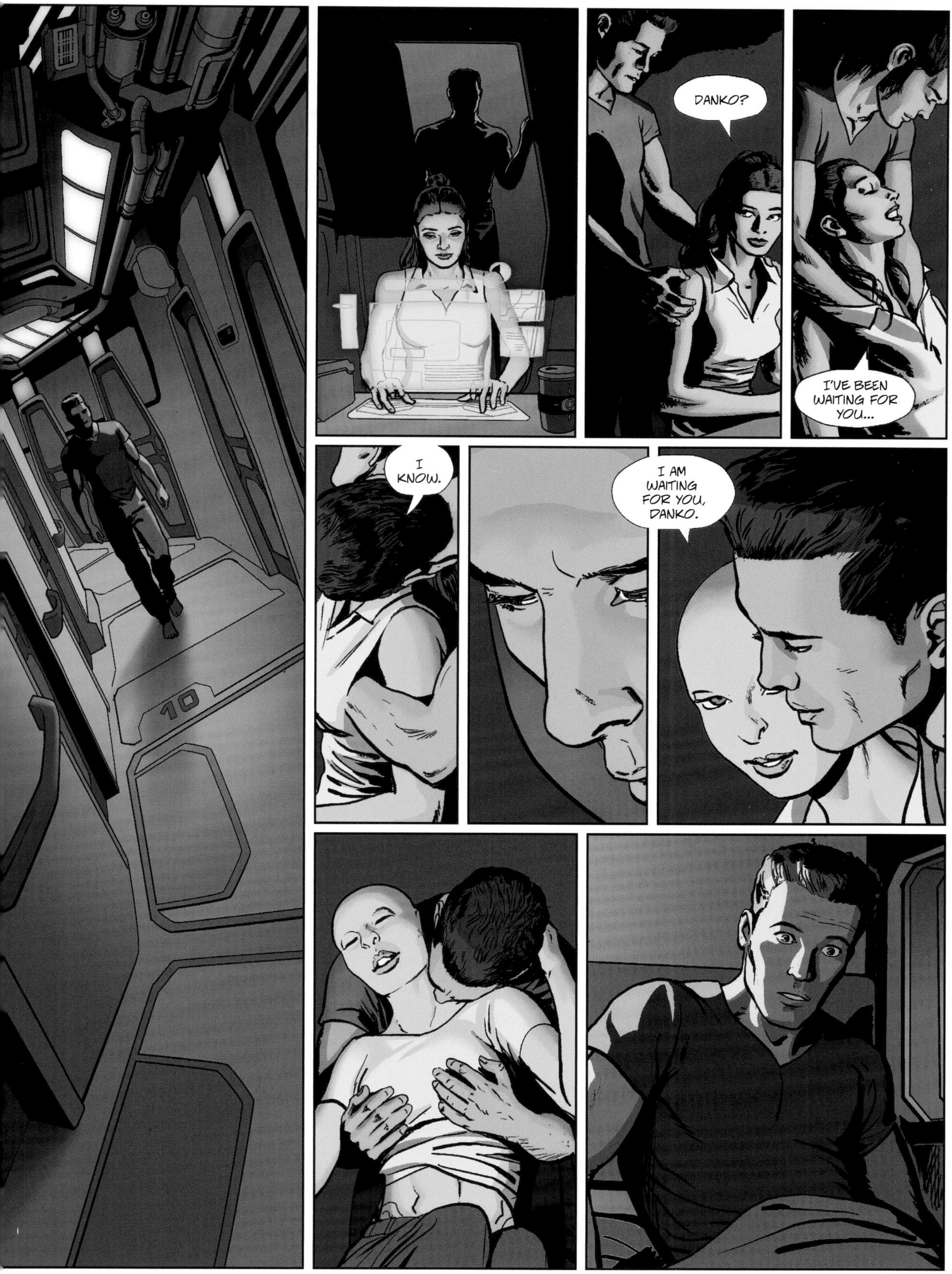
DANKO?
I'VE BEEN WAITING FOR YOU...
I KNOW.
I AM WAITING FOR YOU, DANKO.

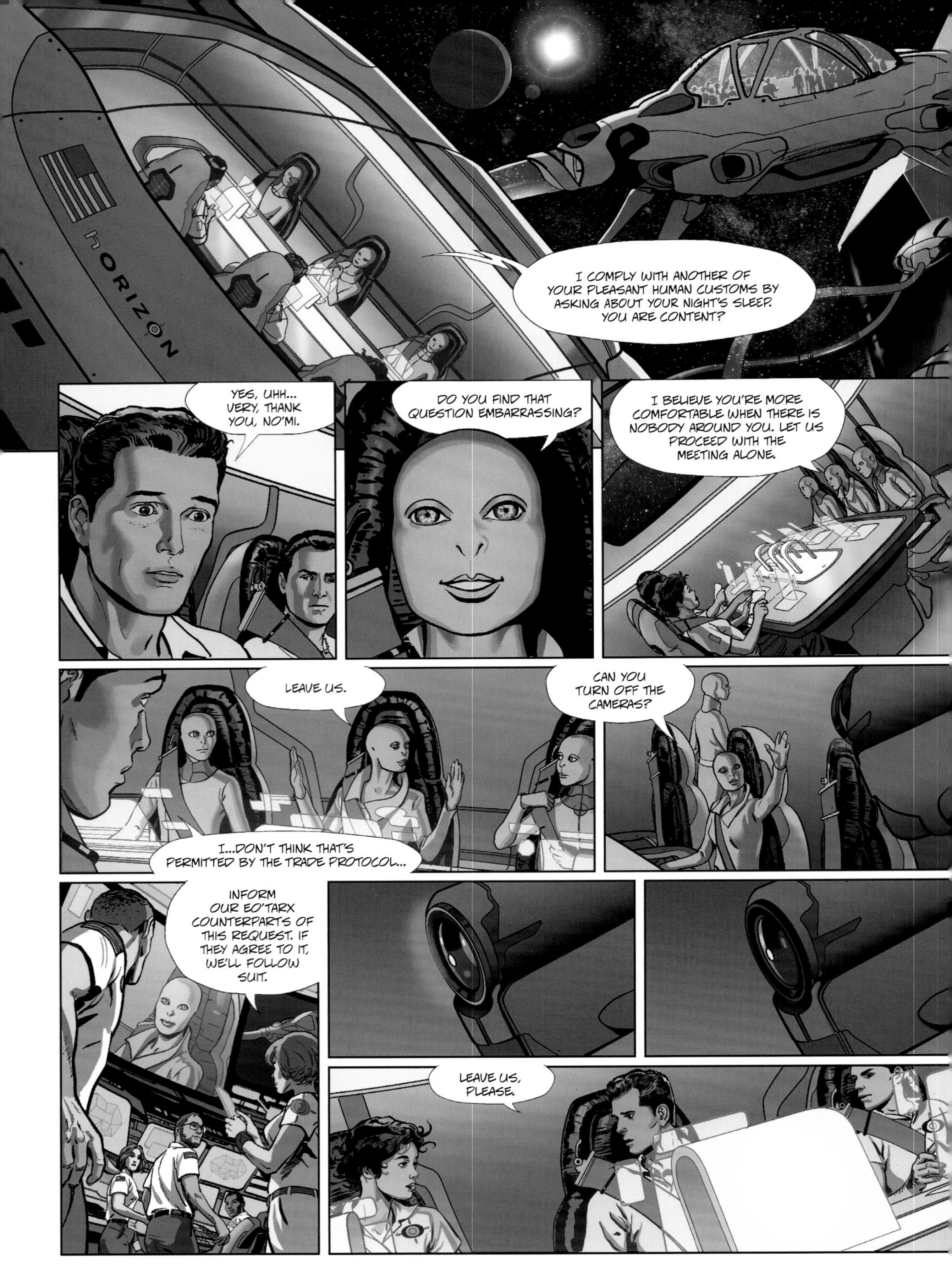
I COMPLY WITH ANOTHER OF YOUR PLEASANT HUMAN CUSTOMS BY ASKING ABOUT YOUR NIGHT'S SLEEP. YOU ARE CONTENT?
YES, UHH... VERY, THANK YOU, NO'MI.
DO YOU FIND THAT QUESTION EMBARRASSING?
I BELIEVE YOU'RE MORE COMFORTABLE WHEN THERE IS NOBODY AROUND YOU. LET US PROCEED WITH THE MEETING ALONE.
LEAVE US.
I...DON'T THINK THAT'S PERMITTED BY THE TRADE PROTOCOL...
CAN YOU TURN OFF THE CAMERAS?
INFORM OUR EO'TARX COUNTERPARTS OF THIS REQUEST. IF THEY AGREE TO IT, WE'LL FOLLOW SUIT.
LEAVE US, PLEASE.

YES, THIS IS FAR MORE COMFORTABLE. I HATE THOSE CHAIRS.

OH, YES... I CERTAINLY DO...

DANKO. TELL ME ABOUT THIS TENDENCY HUMANS HAVE TO LIVE IN PAIRS.

IT IS NOT A CUSTOM WE SHARE.

WHERE ARE YOU WANTING TO GO, DANKO? WHAT ARE YOU WANTING TO SEE?

HERE?

WE CAN GO ANYWHERE. DO YOU LIKE THIS?

YOU KNOW...ASIDE FROM THE PURELY BIOLOGICAL ASPECT OF IT, I'M NOT SURE I'M THE BEST PERSON TO DESCRIBE HOW A COUPLE WORKS.

I ALSO TAKE INTEREST IN WHAT IS NOT CUSTOMARY. PLEASE TELL ME ABOUT YOUR EXPERIENCE.

VERY WELL, NO'MI...

IF YOU INSIST... BUT YOU SHOULD KNOW THAT WHAT I'M ABOUT TO TELL YOU IS USUALLY SOMETHING I KEEP TO MYSELF.

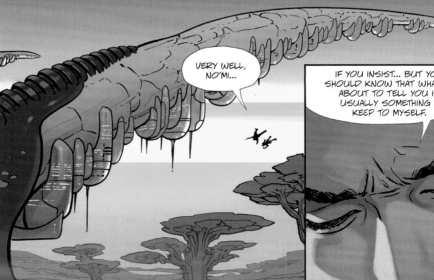

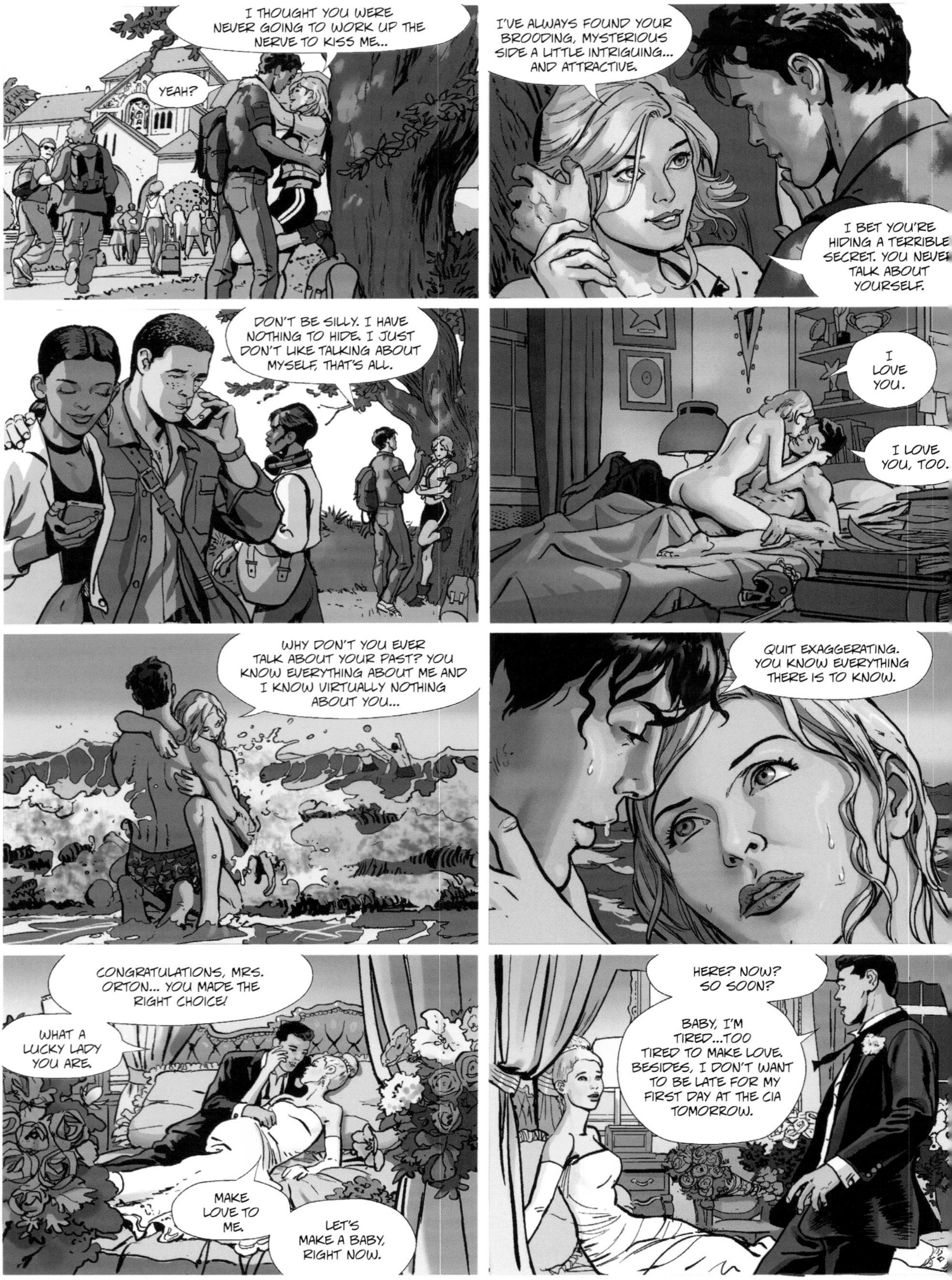
I THOUGHT YOU WERE NEVER GOING TO WORK UP THE NERVE TO KISS ME...
YEAH?
I'VE ALWAYS FOUND YOUR BROODING, MYSTERIOUS SIDE A LITTLE INTRIGUING... AND ATTRACTIVE.
I BET YOU'RE HIDING A TERRIBLE SECRET. YOU NEVER TALK ABOUT YOURSELF.
DON'T BE SILLY. I HAVE NOTHING TO HIDE. I JUST DON'T LIKE TALKING ABOUT MYSELF, THAT'S ALL.
I LOVE YOU.
I LOVE YOU, TOO.
WHY DON'T YOU EVER TALK ABOUT YOUR PAST? YOU KNOW EVERYTHING ABOUT ME AND I KNOW VIRTUALLY NOTHING ABOUT YOU...
QUIT EXAGGERATING. YOU KNOW EVERYTHING THERE IS TO KNOW.
CONGRATULATIONS, MRS. ORTON... YOU MADE THE RIGHT CHOICE!
WHAT A LUCKY LADY YOU ARE.
MAKE LOVE TO ME.
LET'S MAKE A BABY, RIGHT NOW.
HERE? NOW? SO SOON?
BABY, I'M TIRED...TOO TIRED TO MAKE LOVE. BESIDES, I DON'T WANT TO BE LATE FOR MY FIRST DAY AT THE CIA TOMORROW.

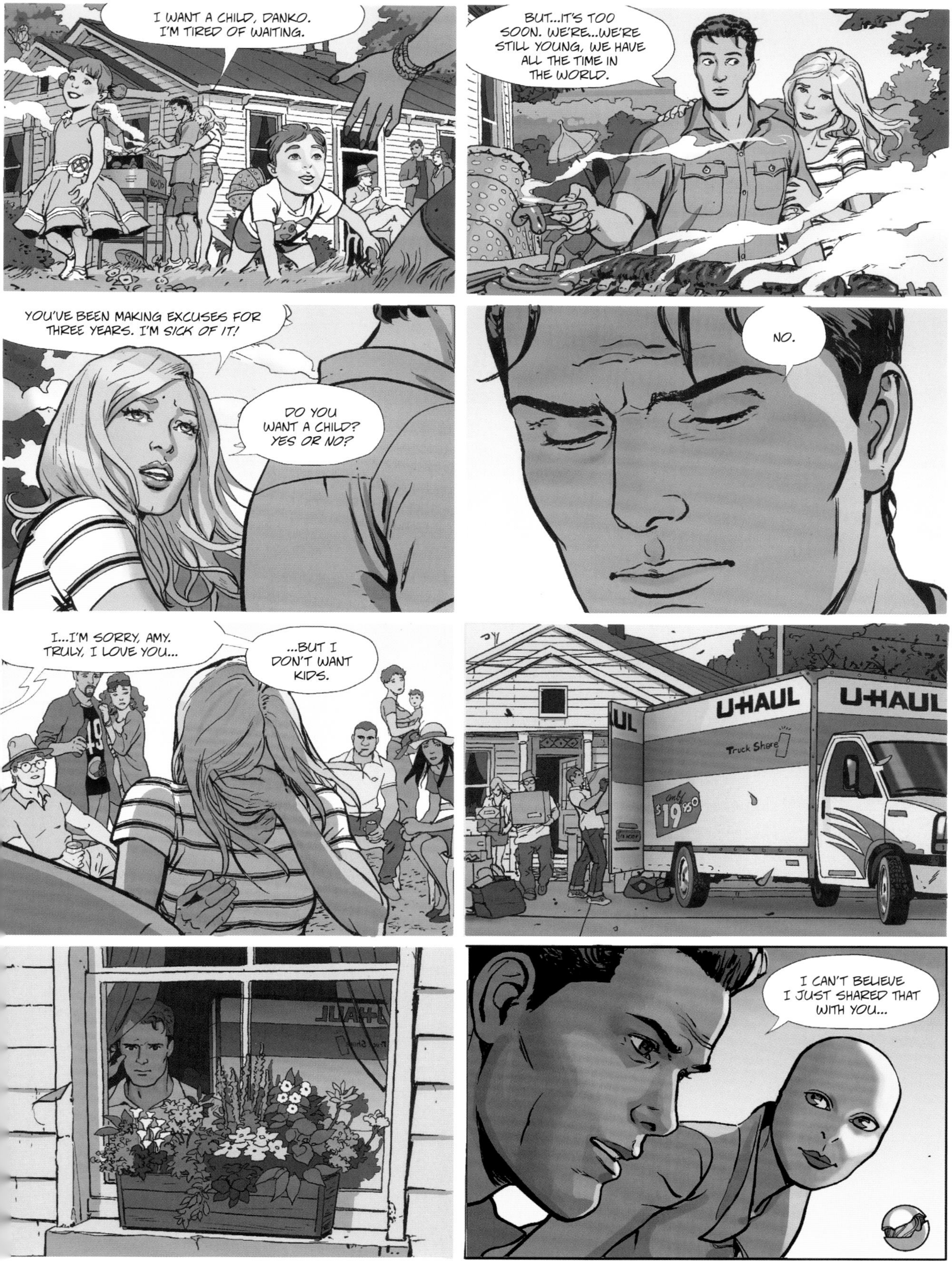
I WANT A CHILD, DANKO. I'M TIRED OF WAITING.
BUT...IT'S TOO SOON. WE'RE...WE'RE STILL YOUNG. WE HAVE ALL THE TIME IN THE WORLD.
YOU'VE BEEN MAKING EXCUSES FOR THREE YEARS. I'M *SICK OF IT!*
DO YOU WANT A CHILD? *YES OR NO?*
NO.
I...I'M SORRY, AMY. TRULY, I LOVE YOU...
...BUT I DON'T WANT KIDS.
U-HAUL
U-HAUL
Truck Share
I CAN'T BELIEVE I JUST SHARED THAT WITH YOU...

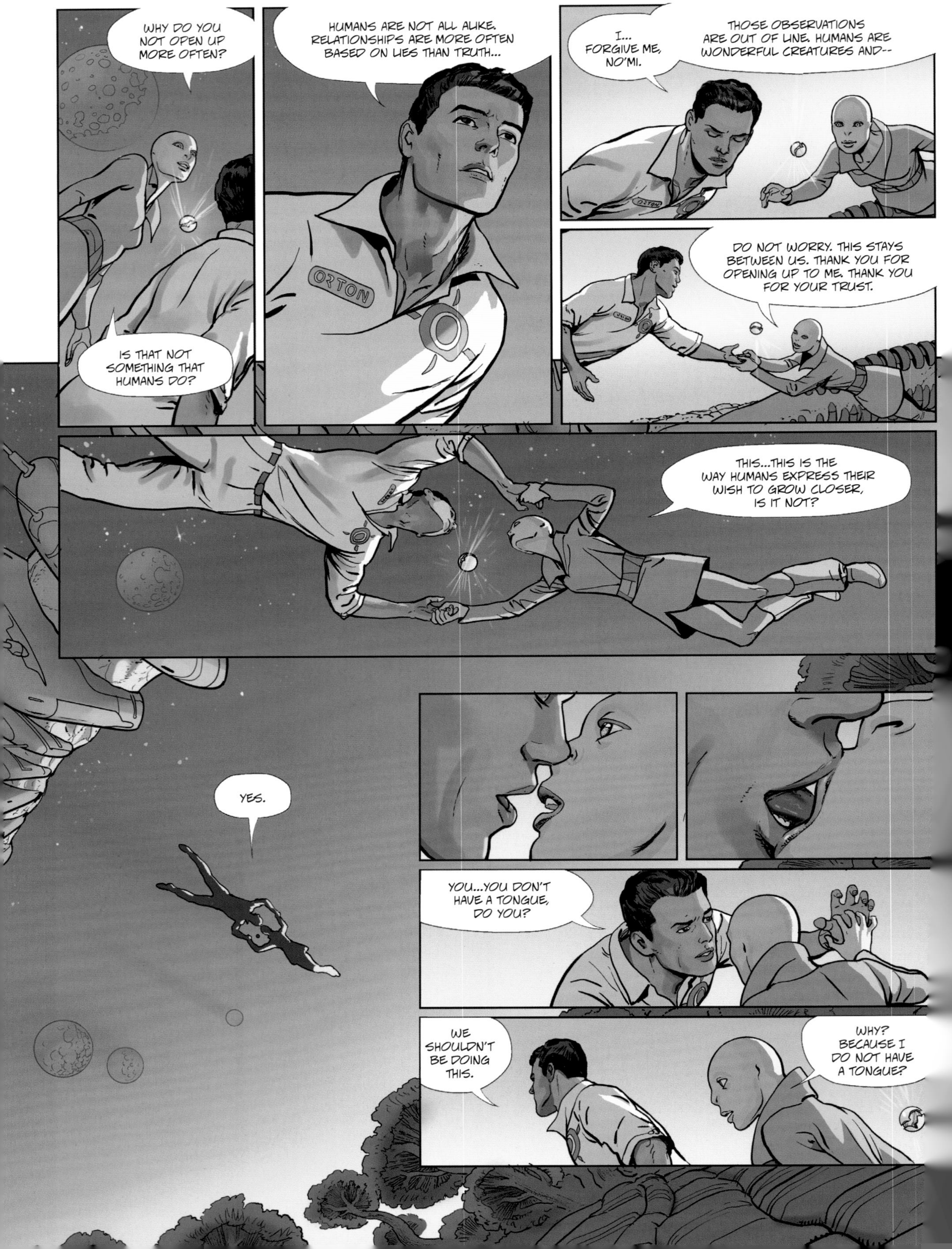
WHY DO YOU NOT OPEN UP MORE OFTEN?
IS THAT NOT SOMETHING THAT HUMANS DO?
HUMANS ARE NOT ALL ALIKE. RELATIONSHIPS ARE MORE OFTEN BASED ON LIES THAN TRUTH...
ORTON
I... FORGIVE ME, NO'MI.
THOSE OBSERVATIONS ARE OUT OF LINE. HUMANS ARE WONDERFUL CREATURES AND--
DO NOT WORRY. THIS STAYS BETWEEN US. THANK YOU FOR OPENING UP TO ME. THANK YOU FOR YOUR TRUST.
THIS...THIS IS THE WAY HUMANS EXPRESS THEIR WISH TO GROW CLOSER, IS IT NOT?
YES.
YOU...YOU DON'T HAVE A TONGUE, DO YOU?
WE SHOULDN'T BE DOING THIS.
WHY? BECAUSE I DO NOT HAVE A TONGUE?

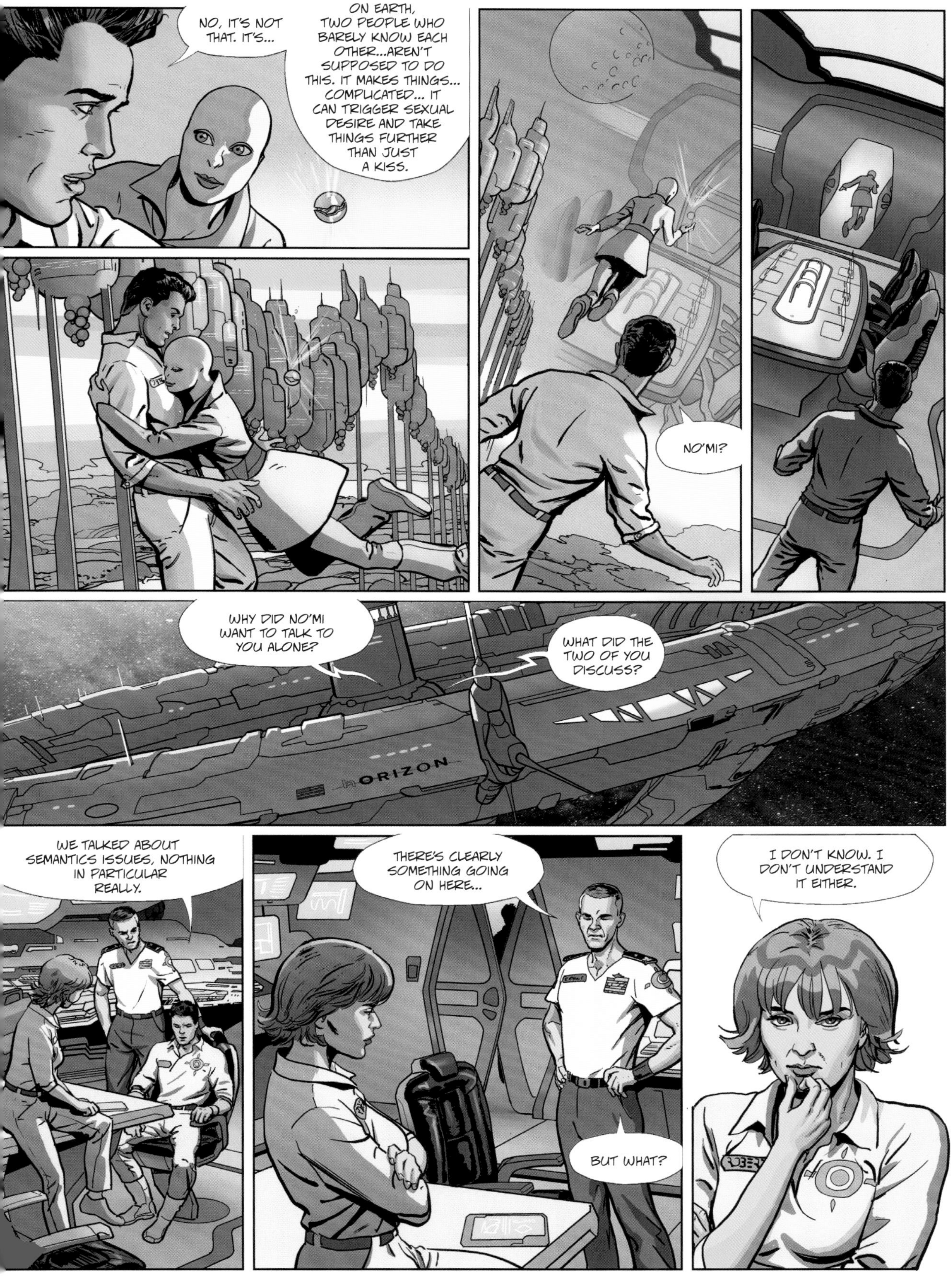
NO, IT'S NOT THAT. IT'S...
ON EARTH, TWO PEOPLE WHO BARELY KNOW EACH OTHER...AREN'T SUPPOSED TO DO THIS. IT MAKES THINGS... COMPLICATED... IT CAN TRIGGER SEXUAL DESIRE AND TAKE THINGS FURTHER THAN JUST A KISS.
NO'MI?
WHY DID NO'MI WANT TO TALK TO YOU ALONE?
WHAT DID THE TWO OF YOU DISCUSS?
HORIZON
WE TALKED ABOUT SEMANTICS ISSUES, NOTHING IN PARTICULAR REALLY.
THERE'S CLEARLY SOMETHING GOING ON HERE...
BUT WHAT?
I DON'T KNOW. I DON'T UNDERSTAND IT EITHER.

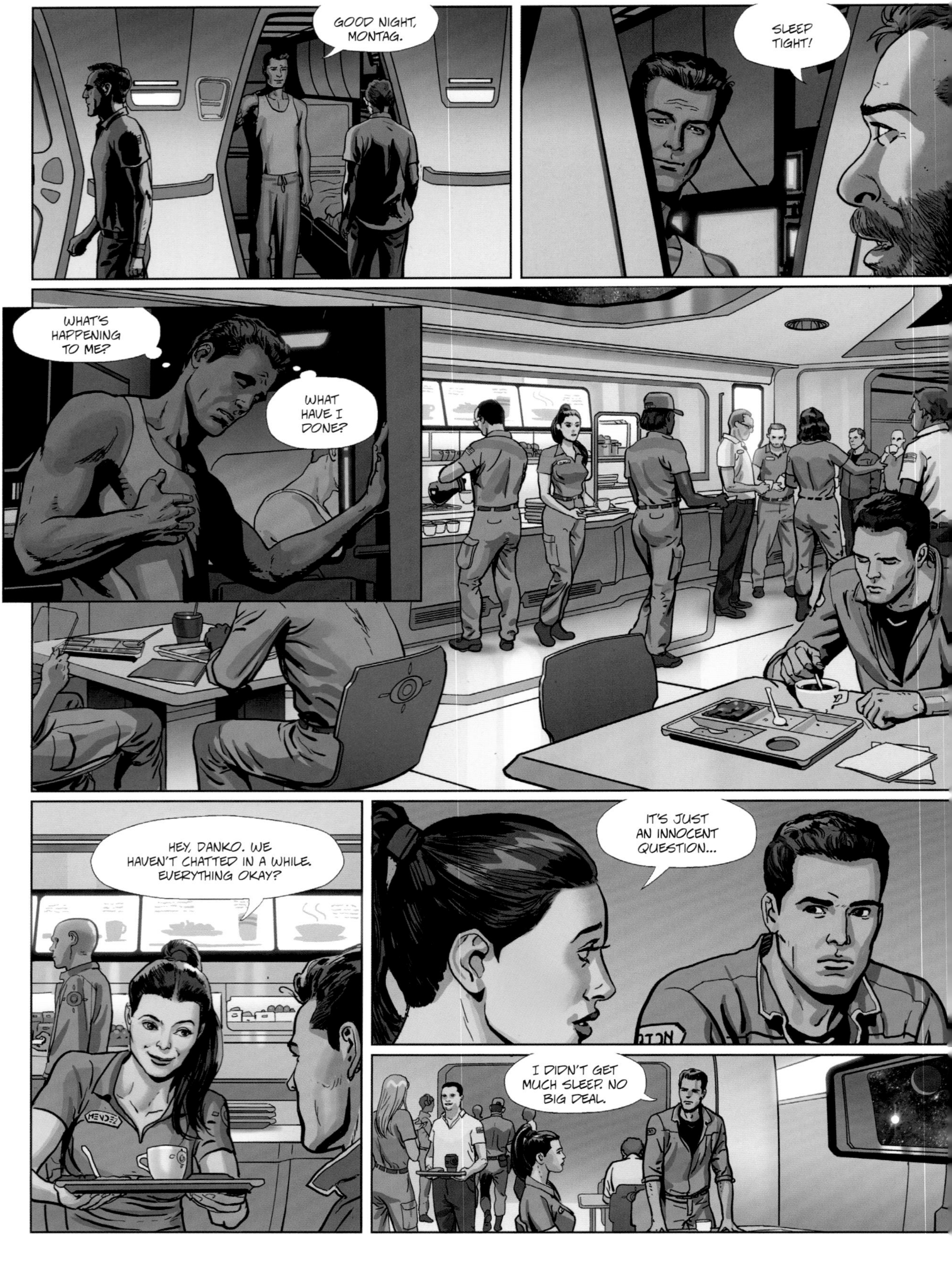
GOOD NIGHT, MONTAG.
SLEEP TIGHT!
WHAT'S HAPPENING TO ME?
WHAT HAVE I DONE?
HEY, DANKO. WE HAVEN'T CHATTED IN A WHILE. EVERYTHING OKAY?
IT'S JUST AN INNOCENT QUESTION...
I DIDN'T GET MUCH SLEEP. NO BIG DEAL.

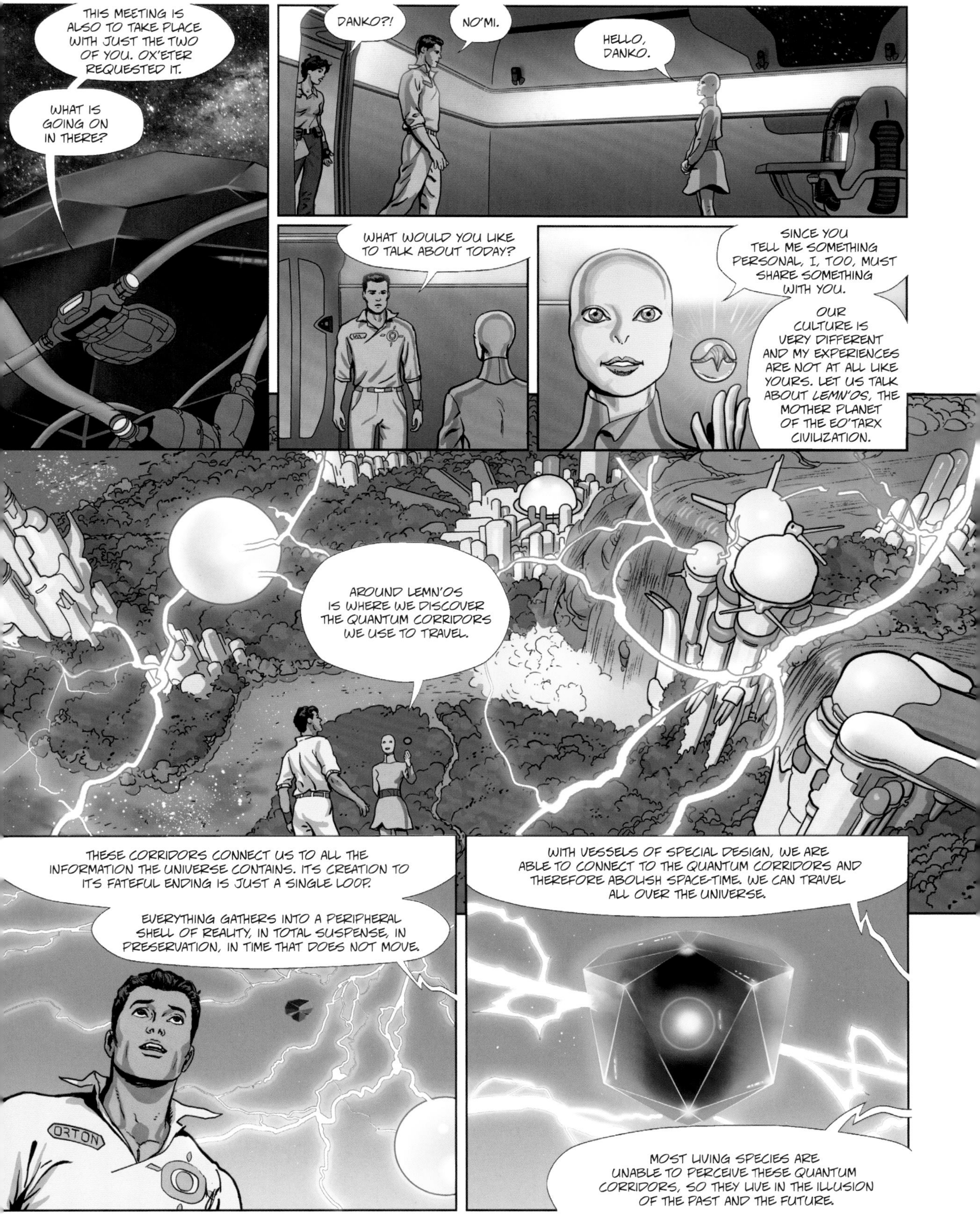
THIS MEETING IS ALSO TO TAKE PLACE WITH JUST THE TWO OF YOU. OX'ETER REQUESTED IT.
WHAT IS GOING ON IN THERE?
DANKO?!
NO'MI.
HELLO, DANKO.
WHAT WOULD YOU LIKE TO TALK ABOUT TODAY?
SINCE YOU TELL ME SOMETHING PERSONAL, I, TOO, MUST SHARE SOMETHING WITH YOU.
OUR CULTURE IS VERY DIFFERENT AND MY EXPERIENCES ARE NOT AT ALL LIKE YOURS. LET US TALK ABOUT LEMN'OS, THE MOTHER PLANET OF THE EO'TARX CIVILIZATION.
AROUND LEMN'OS IS WHERE WE DISCOVER THE QUANTUM CORRIDORS WE USE TO TRAVEL.
THESE CORRIDORS CONNECT US TO ALL THE INFORMATION THE UNIVERSE CONTAINS. ITS CREATION TO ITS FATEFUL ENDING IS JUST A SINGLE LOOP.
EVERYTHING GATHERS INTO A PERIPHERAL SHELL OF REALITY, IN TOTAL SUSPENSE, IN PRESERVATION, IN TIME THAT DOES NOT MOVE.
ORTON
WITH VESSELS OF SPECIAL DESIGN, WE ARE ABLE TO CONNECT TO THE QUANTUM CORRIDORS AND THEREFORE ABOLISH SPACE-TIME. WE CAN TRAVEL ALL OVER THE UNIVERSE.
MOST LIVING SPECIES ARE UNABLE TO PERCEIVE THESE QUANTUM CORRIDORS, SO THEY LIVE IN THE ILLUSION OF THE PAST AND THE FUTURE.

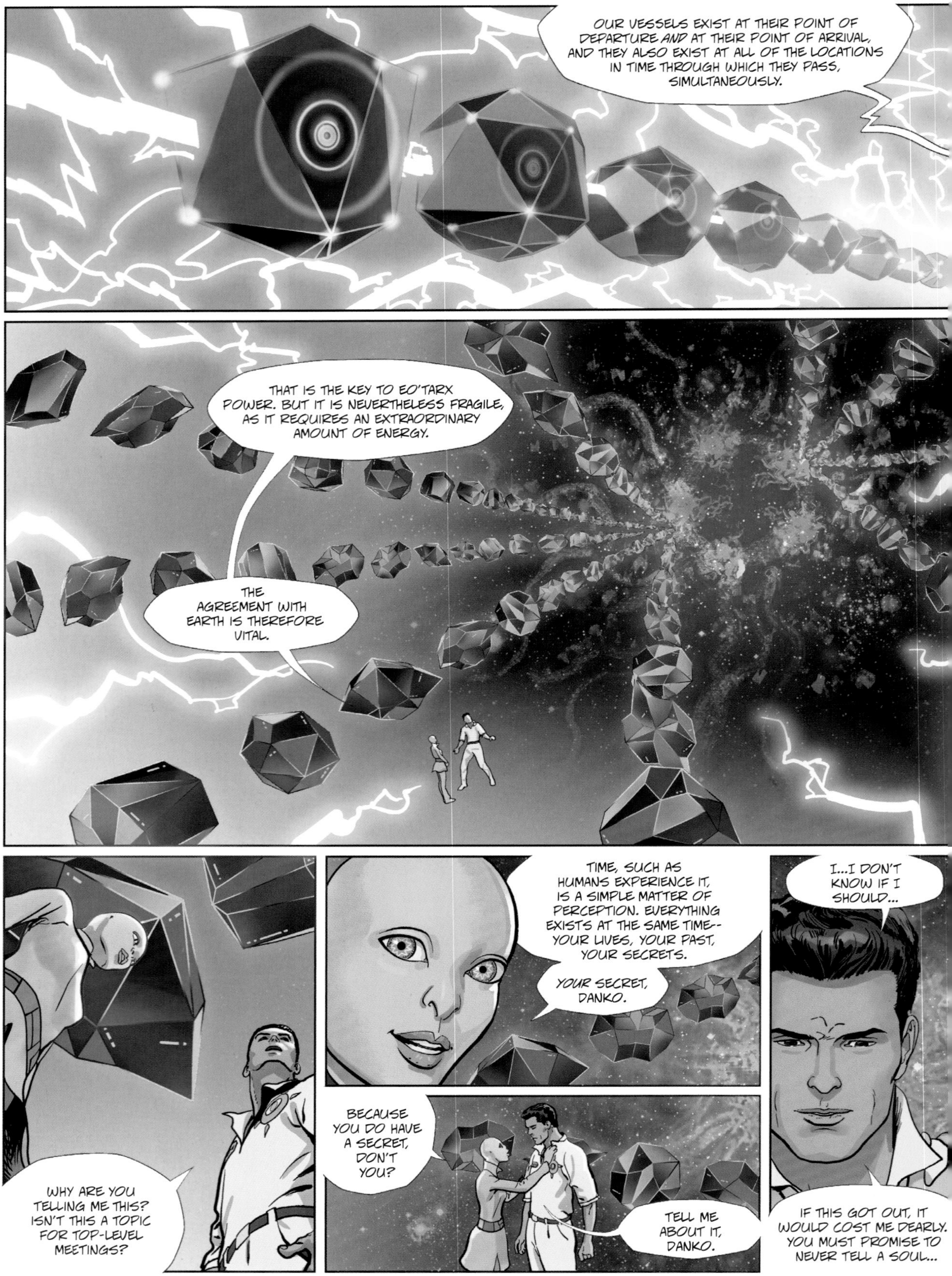
OUR VESSELS EXIST AT THEIR POINT OF DEPARTURE *AND* AT THEIR POINT OF ARRIVAL, AND THEY ALSO EXIST AT ALL OF THE LOCATIONS IN TIME THROUGH WHICH THEY PASS, SIMULTANEOUSLY.
THAT IS THE KEY TO EO'TARX POWER. BUT IT IS NEVERTHELESS FRAGILE, AS IT REQUIRES AN EXTRAORDINARY AMOUNT OF ENERGY.
THE AGREEMENT WITH EARTH IS THEREFORE VITAL.
WHY ARE YOU TELLING ME THIS? ISN'T THIS A TOPIC FOR TOP-LEVEL MEETINGS?
TIME, SUCH AS HUMANS EXPERIENCE IT, IS A SIMPLE MATTER OF PERCEPTION. EVERYTHING EXISTS AT THE SAME TIME-- YOUR LIVES, YOUR PAST, YOUR SECRETS.
YOUR SECRET, DANKO.
BECAUSE YOU DO HAVE A SECRET, DON'T YOU?
TELL ME ABOUT IT, DANKO.
I...I DON'T KNOW IF I SHOULD...
IF THIS GOT OUT, IT WOULD COST ME DEARLY. YOU MUST PROMISE TO NEVER TELL A SOUL...

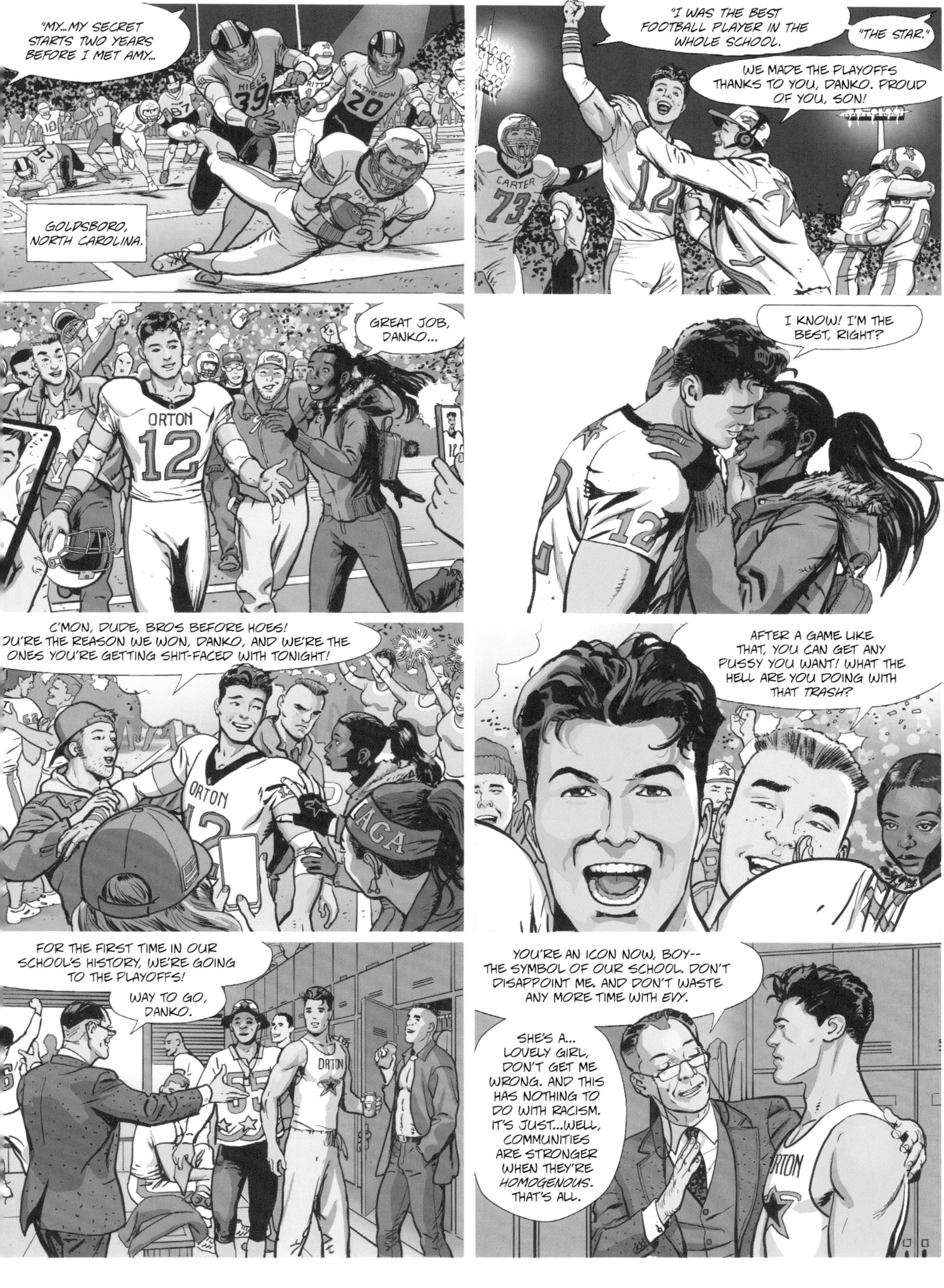
"MY...MY SECRET STARTS TWO YEARS BEFORE I MET AMY...
GOLDSBORO, NORTH CAROLINA.
"I WAS THE BEST FOOTBALL PLAYER IN THE WHOLE SCHOOL.
"THE STAR."
WE MADE THE PLAYOFFS THANKS TO YOU, DANKO. PROUD OF YOU, SON!
GREAT JOB, DANKO...
I KNOW! I'M THE BEST, RIGHT?
C'MON, DUDE, BROS BEFORE HOES! YOU'RE THE REASON WE WON, DANKO, AND WE'RE THE ONES YOU'RE GETTING SHIT-FACED WITH TONIGHT!
AFTER A GAME LIKE THAT, YOU CAN GET ANY PUSSY YOU WANT! WHAT THE HELL ARE YOU DOING WITH THAT *TRASH*?
FOR THE FIRST TIME IN OUR SCHOOL'S HISTORY, WE'RE GOING TO THE PLAYOFFS!
WAY TO GO, DANKO.
YOU'RE AN ICON NOW, BOY-- THE SYMBOL OF OUR SCHOOL. DON'T DISAPPOINT ME. AND DON'T WASTE ANY MORE TIME WITH EVY.
SHE'S A... LOVELY GIRL, DON'T GET ME WRONG. AND THIS HAS NOTHING TO DO WITH RACISM. IT'S JUST...WELL, COMMUNITIES ARE STRONGER WHEN THEY'RE *HOMOGENOUS*. THAT'S ALL.

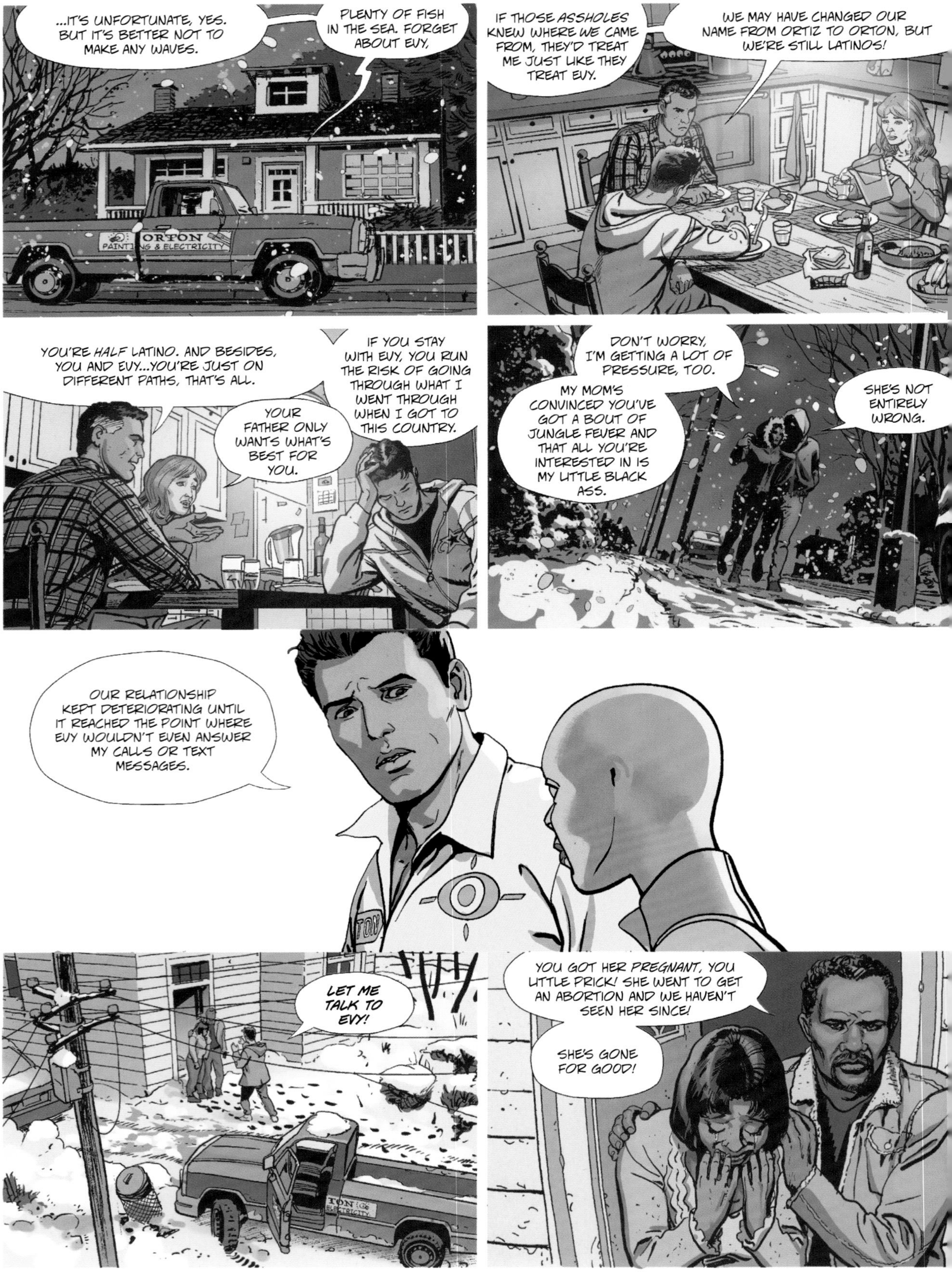
...IT'S UNFORTUNATE, YES. BUT IT'S BETTER NOT TO MAKE ANY WAVES.
PLENTY OF FISH IN THE SEA. FORGET ABOUT EVY.
ORTON
PAINTING & ELECTRICITY
IF THOSE *ASSHOLES* KNEW WHERE *WE* CAME FROM, THEY'D TREAT ME JUST LIKE THEY TREAT EVY.
WE MAY HAVE CHANGED OUR NAME FROM ORTIZ TO ORTON, BUT WE'RE STILL LATINOS!
YOU'RE *HALF* LATINO. AND BESIDES, YOU AND EVY...YOU'RE JUST ON DIFFERENT PATHS, THAT'S ALL.
YOUR FATHER ONLY WANTS WHAT'S BEST FOR YOU.
IF YOU STAY WITH EVY, YOU RUN THE RISK OF GOING THROUGH WHAT I WENT THROUGH WHEN I GOT TO THIS COUNTRY.
DON'T WORRY, I'M GETTING A LOT OF PRESSURE, TOO.
MY MOM'S CONVINCED YOU'VE GOT A BOUT OF JUNGLE FEVER AND THAT ALL YOU'RE INTERESTED IN IS MY LITTLE BLACK ASS.
SHE'S NOT ENTIRELY WRONG.
OUR RELATIONSHIP KEPT DETERIORATING UNTIL IT REACHED THE POINT WHERE EVY WOULDN'T EVEN ANSWER MY CALLS OR TEXT MESSAGES.
LET ME TALK TO EVY!
YOU GOT HER *PREGNANT*, YOU LITTLE PRICK! SHE WENT TO GET AN ABORTION AND WE HAVEN'T SEEN HER SINCE!
SHE'S GONE FOR GOOD!

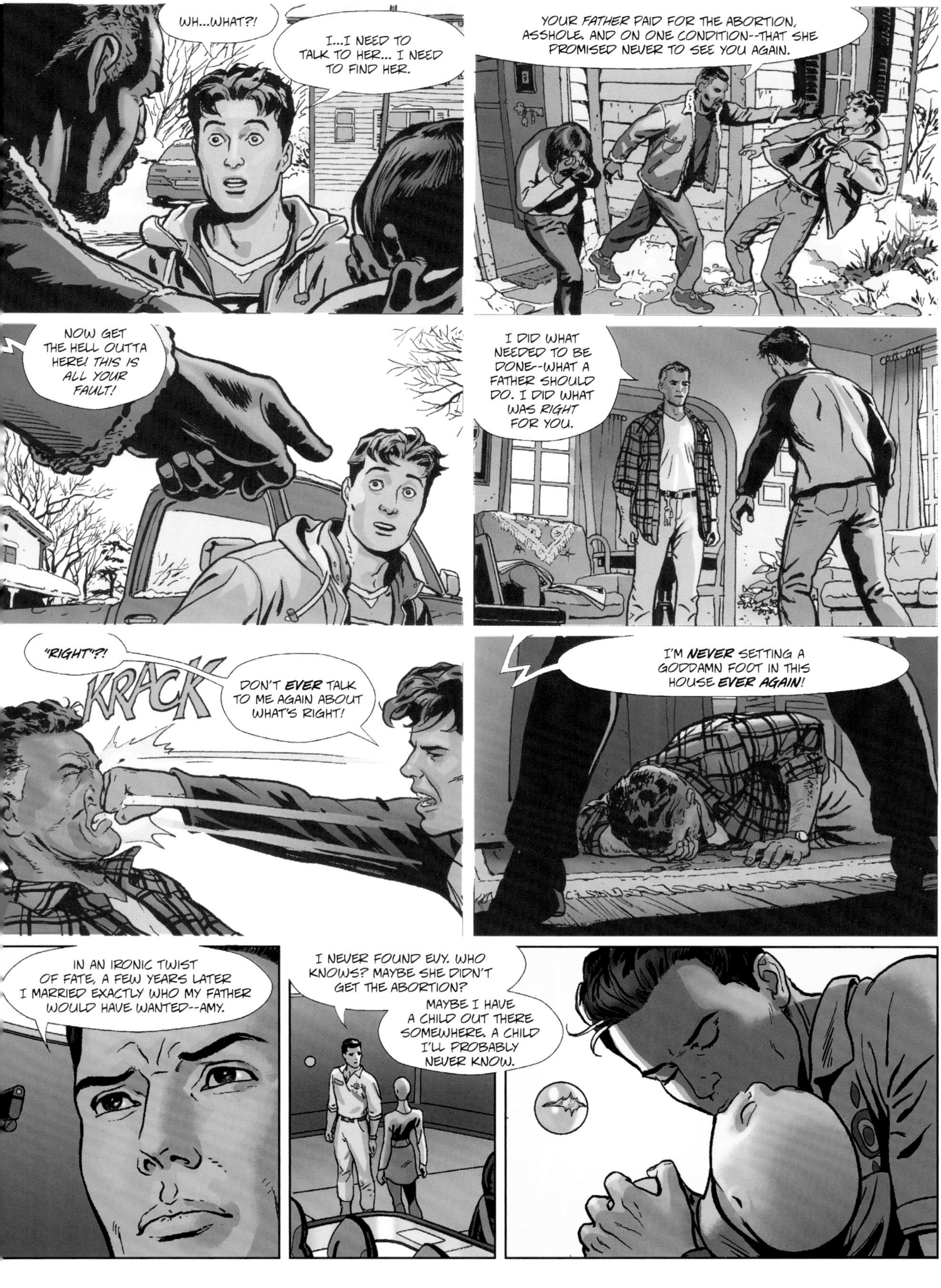
WH...WHAT?!
I...I NEED TO TALK TO HER... I NEED TO FIND HER.
YOUR FATHER PAID FOR THE ABORTION, ASSHOLE. AND ON ONE CONDITION--THAT SHE PROMISED NEVER TO SEE YOU AGAIN.
NOW GET THE HELL OUTTA HERE! THIS IS ALL YOUR FAULT!
I DID WHAT NEEDED TO BE DONE--WHAT A FATHER SHOULD DO. I DID WHAT WAS RIGHT FOR YOU.
"RIGHT"?!
KRACK
DON'T EVER TALK TO ME AGAIN ABOUT WHAT'S RIGHT!
I'M NEVER SETTING A GODDAMN FOOT IN THIS HOUSE EVER AGAIN!
IN AN IRONIC TWIST OF FATE, A FEW YEARS LATER I MARRIED EXACTLY WHO MY FATHER WOULD HAVE WANTED--AMY.
I NEVER FOUND EVY. WHO KNOWS? MAYBE SHE DIDN'T GET THE ABORTION?
MAYBE I HAVE A CHILD OUT THERE SOMEWHERE. A CHILD I'LL PROBABLY NEVER KNOW.

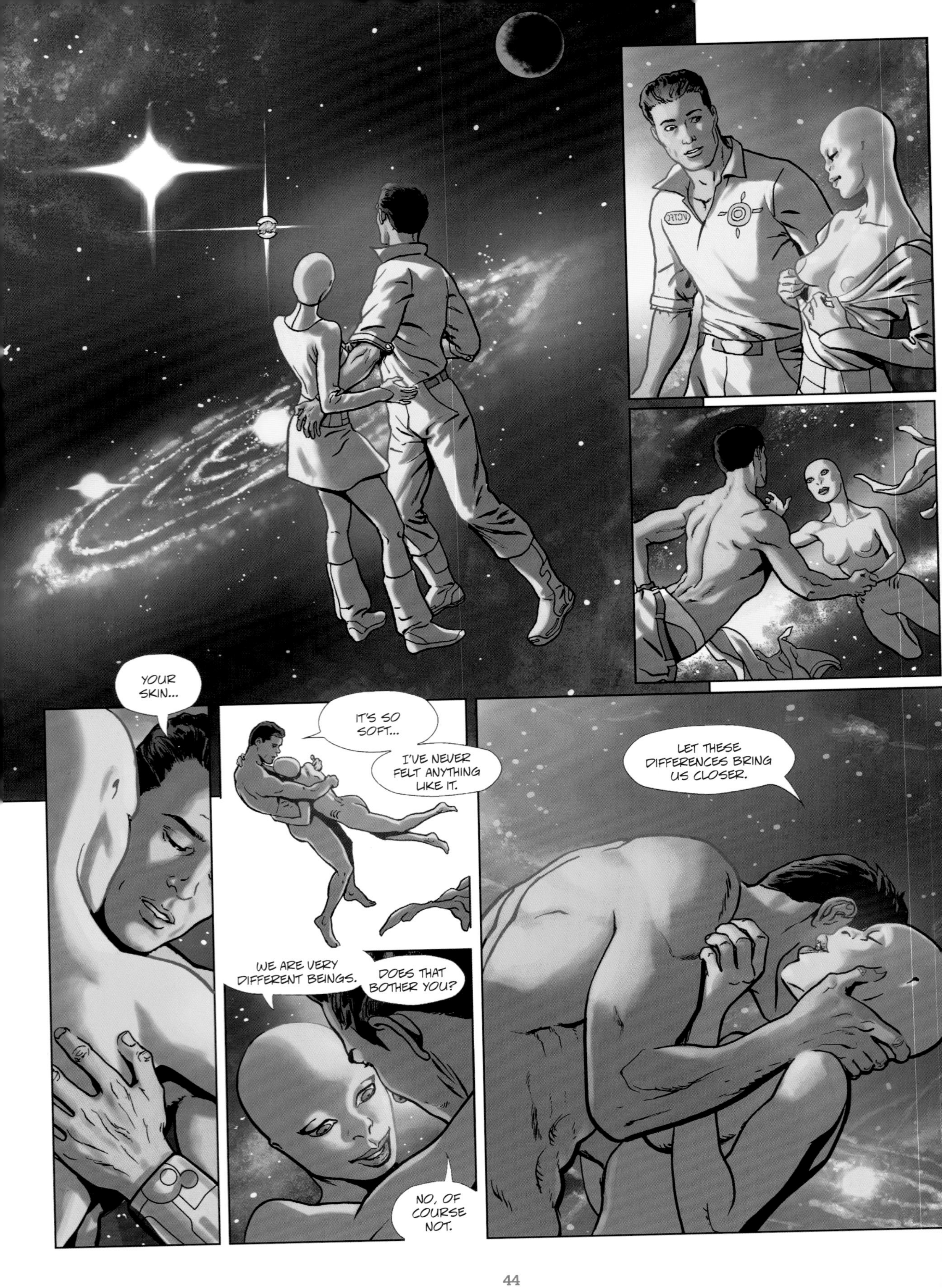
VCTF
YOUR SKIN...
IT'S SO SOFT...
I'VE NEVER FELT ANYTHING LIKE IT.
WE ARE VERY DIFFERENT BEINGS.
DOES THAT BOTHER YOU?
NO, OF COURSE NOT.
LET THESE DIFFERENCES BRING US CLOSER.

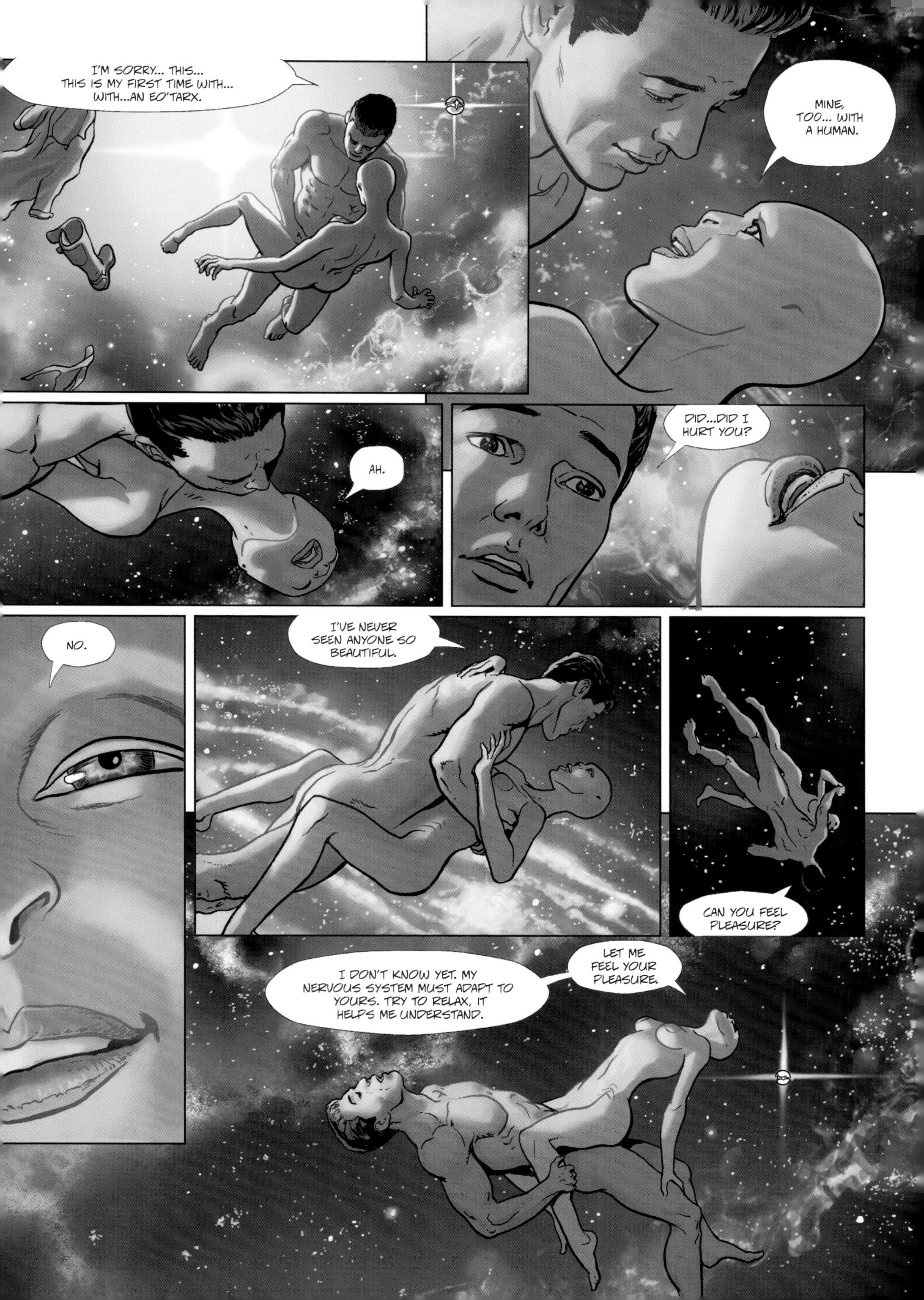
I'M SORRY... THIS... THIS IS MY FIRST TIME WITH... WITH...AN EO'TARX.
MINE, TOO... WITH A HUMAN.
AH.
DID...DID I HURT YOU?
NO.
I'VE NEVER SEEN ANYONE SO BEAUTIFUL.
CAN YOU FEEL PLEASURE?
I DON'T KNOW YET. MY NERVOUS SYSTEM MUST ADAPT TO YOURS. TRY TO RELAX, IT HELPS ME UNDERSTAND.
LET ME FEEL YOUR PLEASURE.

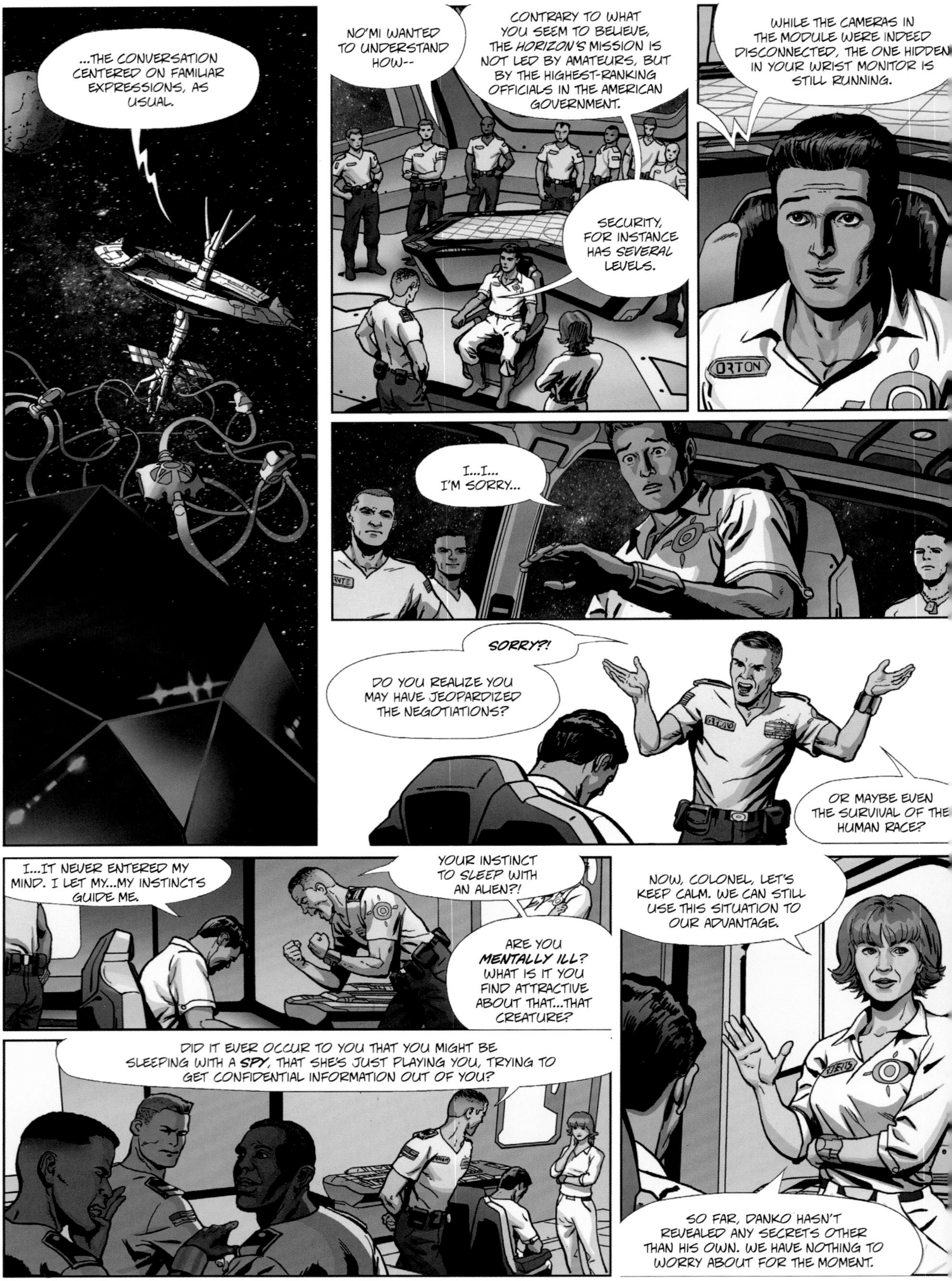
...THE CONVERSATION CENTERED ON FAMILIAR EXPRESSIONS, AS USUAL.
NO'MI WANTED TO UNDERSTAND HOW--
CONTRARY TO WHAT YOU SEEM TO BELIEVE, THE HORIZON'S MISSION IS NOT LED BY AMATEURS, BUT BY THE HIGHEST-RANKING OFFICIALS IN THE AMERICAN GOVERNMENT.
SECURITY, FOR INSTANCE HAS SEVERAL LEVELS.
WHILE THE CAMERAS IN THE MODULE WERE INDEED DISCONNECTED, THE ONE HIDDEN IN YOUR WRIST MONITOR IS STILL RUNNING.
ORTON
I...I... I'M SORRY...
SORRY?!
DO YOU REALIZE YOU MAY HAVE JEOPARDIZED THE NEGOTIATIONS?
OR MAYBE EVEN THE SURVIVAL OF THE HUMAN RACE?
I...IT NEVER ENTERED MY MIND. I LET MY...MY INSTINCTS GUIDE ME.
YOUR INSTINCT TO SLEEP WITH AN ALIEN?!
ARE YOU MENTALLY ILL? WHAT IS IT YOU FIND ATTRACTIVE ABOUT THAT...THAT CREATURE?
DID IT EVER OCCUR TO YOU THAT YOU MIGHT BE SLEEPING WITH A SPY, THAT SHE'S JUST PLAYING YOU, TRYING TO GET CONFIDENTIAL INFORMATION OUT OF YOU?
NOW, COLONEL, LET'S KEEP CALM. WE CAN STILL USE THIS SITUATION TO OUR ADVANTAGE.
SO FAR, DANKO HASN'T REVEALED ANY SECRETS OTHER THAN HIS OWN. WE HAVE NOTHING TO WORRY ABOUT FOR THE MOMENT.

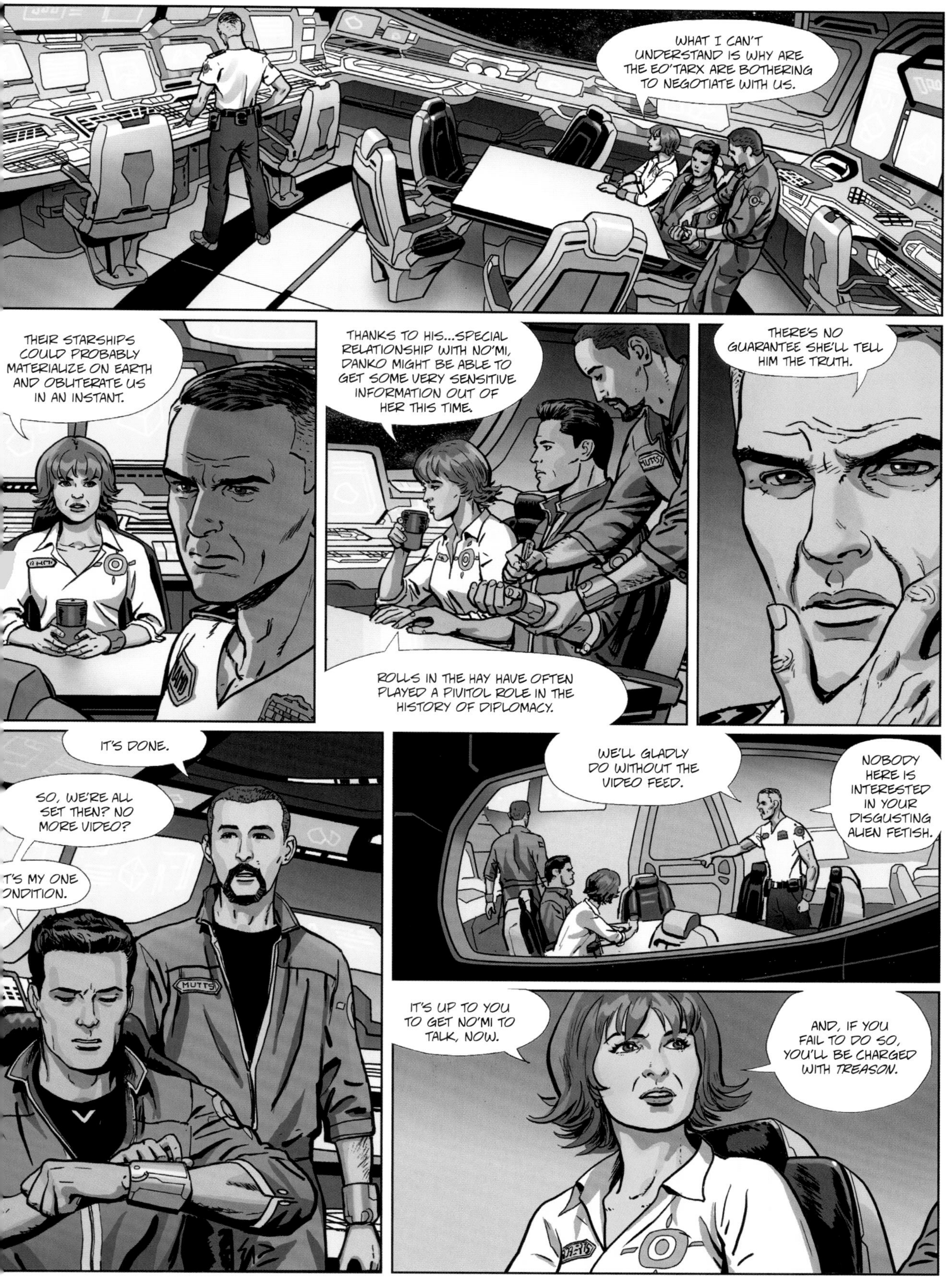

WHAT I CAN'T UNDERSTAND IS WHY ARE THE EO'TARX ARE BOTHERING TO NEGOTIATE WITH US.
THEIR STARSHIPS COULD PROBABLY MATERIALIZE ON EARTH AND OBLITERATE US IN AN INSTANT.
THANKS TO HIS...SPECIAL RELATIONSHIP WITH NO'MI, DANKO MIGHT BE ABLE TO GET SOME VERY SENSITIVE INFORMATION OUT OF HER THIS TIME.
ROLLS IN THE HAY HAVE OFTEN PLAYED A PIVITOL ROLE IN THE HISTORY OF DIPLOMACY.
THERE'S NO GUARANTEE SHE'LL TELL HIM THE TRUTH.
IT'S DONE.
SO, WE'RE ALL SET THEN? NO MORE VIDEO?
T'S MY ONE ONDITION.
MUTTS
WE'LL GLADLY DO WITHOUT THE VIDEO FEED.
NOBODY HERE IS INTERESTED IN YOUR DISGUSTING ALIEN FETISH.
IT'S UP TO YOU TO GET NO'MI TO TALK, NOW.
AND, IF YOU FAIL TO DO SO, YOU'LL BE CHARGED WITH *TREASON*.

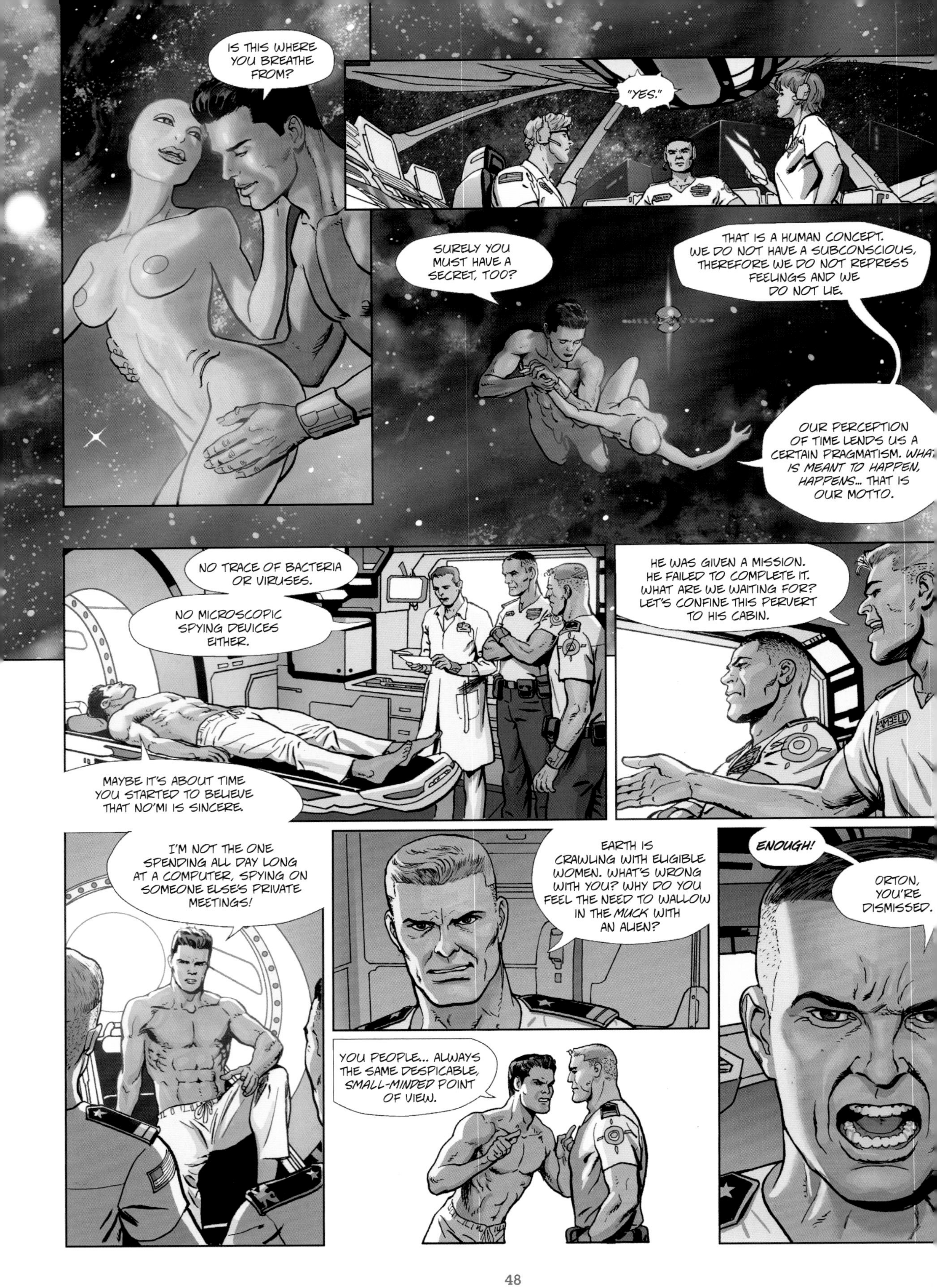
IS THIS WHERE YOU BREATHE FROM?
"YES."
SURELY YOU MUST HAVE A SECRET, TOO?
THAT IS A HUMAN CONCEPT. WE DO NOT HAVE A SUBCONSCIOUS, THEREFORE WE DO NOT REPRESS FEELINGS AND WE DO NOT LIE.
OUR PERCEPTION OF TIME LENDS US A CERTAIN PRAGMATISM. *WHAT IS MEANT TO HAPPEN, HAPPENS*... THAT IS OUR MOTTO.
NO TRACE OF BACTERIA OR VIRUSES.
NO MICROSCOPIC SPYING DEVICES EITHER.
MAYBE IT'S ABOUT TIME YOU STARTED TO BELIEVE THAT NO'MI IS SINCERE.
HE WAS GIVEN A MISSION. HE FAILED TO COMPLETE IT. WHAT ARE WE WAITING FOR? LET'S CONFINE THIS PERVERT TO HIS CABIN.
I'M NOT THE ONE SPENDING ALL DAY LONG AT A COMPUTER, SPYING ON SOMEONE ELSE'S PRIVATE MEETINGS!
EARTH IS CRAWLING WITH ELIGIBLE WOMEN. WHAT'S WRONG WITH YOU? WHY DO YOU FEEL THE NEED TO WALLOW IN THE *MUCK* WITH AN ALIEN?
YOU PEOPLE... ALWAYS THE SAME DESPICABLE, *SMALL-MINDED* POINT OF VIEW.
ENOUGH!
ORTON, YOU'RE DISMISSED.

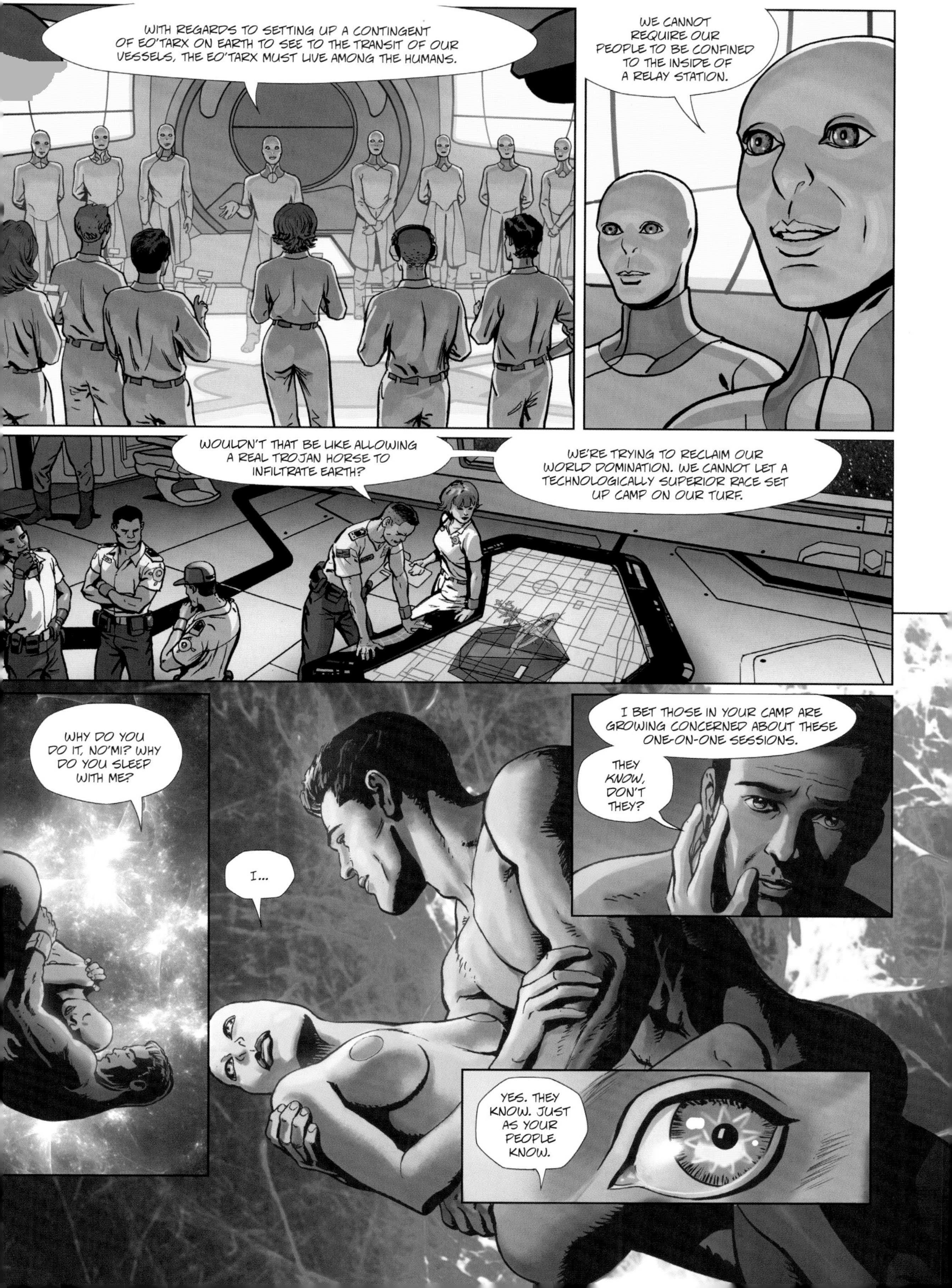
WITH REGARDS TO SETTING UP A CONTINGENT OF EO'TARX ON EARTH TO SEE TO THE TRANSIT OF OUR VESSELS, THE EO'TARX MUST LIVE AMONG THE HUMANS.
WE CANNOT REQUIRE OUR PEOPLE TO BE CONFINED TO THE INSIDE OF A RELAY STATION.
WOULDN'T THAT BE LIKE ALLOWING A REAL TROJAN HORSE TO INFILTRATE EARTH?
WE'RE TRYING TO RECLAIM OUR WORLD DOMINATION. WE CANNOT LET A TECHNOLOGICALLY SUPERIOR RACE SET UP CAMP ON OUR TURF.
WHY DO YOU DO IT, NO'MI? WHY DO YOU SLEEP WITH ME?
I...
I BET THOSE IN YOUR CAMP ARE GROWING CONCERNED ABOUT THESE ONE-ON-ONE SESSIONS.
THEY KNOW, DON'T THEY?
YES. THEY KNOW. JUST AS YOUR PEOPLE KNOW.

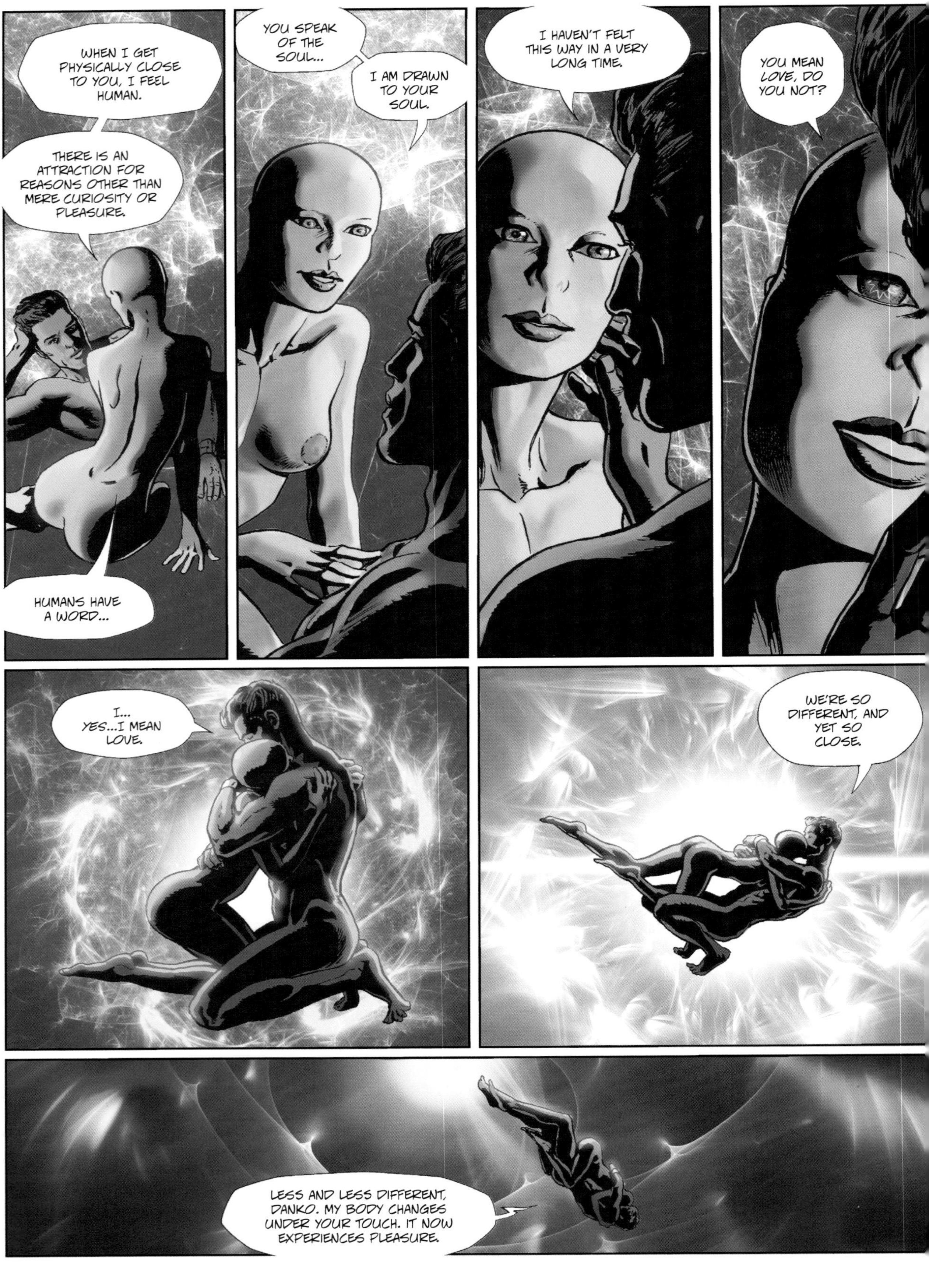
WHEN I GET PHYSICALLY CLOSE TO YOU, I FEEL HUMAN.
THERE IS AN ATTRACTION FOR REASONS OTHER THAN MERE CURIOSITY OR PLEASURE.
HUMANS HAVE A WORD...
YOU SPEAK OF THE SOUL...
I AM DRAWN TO YOUR SOUL.
I HAVEN'T FELT THIS WAY IN A VERY LONG TIME.
YOU MEAN LOVE, DO YOU NOT?
I... YES...I MEAN LOVE.
WE'RE SO DIFFERENT, AND YET SO CLOSE.
LESS AND LESS DIFFERENT, DANKO. MY BODY CHANGES UNDER YOUR TOUCH. IT NOW EXPERIENCES PLEASURE.

LEAVING WITH EMPTY HOLDS IS AN ACT OF FOLLY THAT WILL COST MY EMPLOYER A FORTUNE... IT WILL PROBABLY RUIN HIM!

ORBIT OF IO, MOON OF JUPITER.

YOUR COMMENTS ARE UNACCEPTABLE AND UNWORTHY OF A CITIZEN OF OUR GREAT REPUBLIC.

THE SAFETY OF THE HUMAN RACE IS MORE IMPORTANT THAN MAKING MONEY FOR THAT COMPANY YOU WORK FOR!

YOUR CARGO SHIP IS THE ONLY WAY FOR US TO QUICKLY APPROACH *HORIZON*, WHERE THE AMERICANS ARE CLEARLY PLANNING SOMETHING MAJOR.

YOU SHOULD BE PROUD TO PLAY A ROLE IN A MISSION LIKE THIS, AND EVEN PROUDER TO SACRIFICE YOURSELF FOR THE PEOPLE'S REPUBLIC OF CHINA!

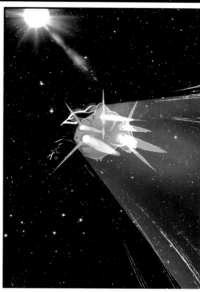

I AM NA'FER, YOUR NEW CONTACT PERSON.

THE EO'TARX MISSION NOW RESUMES ACCORDING TO PROTOCOL.

WHERE'S NO'MI? IS SHE COMING BACK? DID SOMETHING HAPPEN TO HER?

IT IS BEST YOU FORGET NO'MI. SIMPLY TELL YOURSELF SHE DOES NOT EXIST.

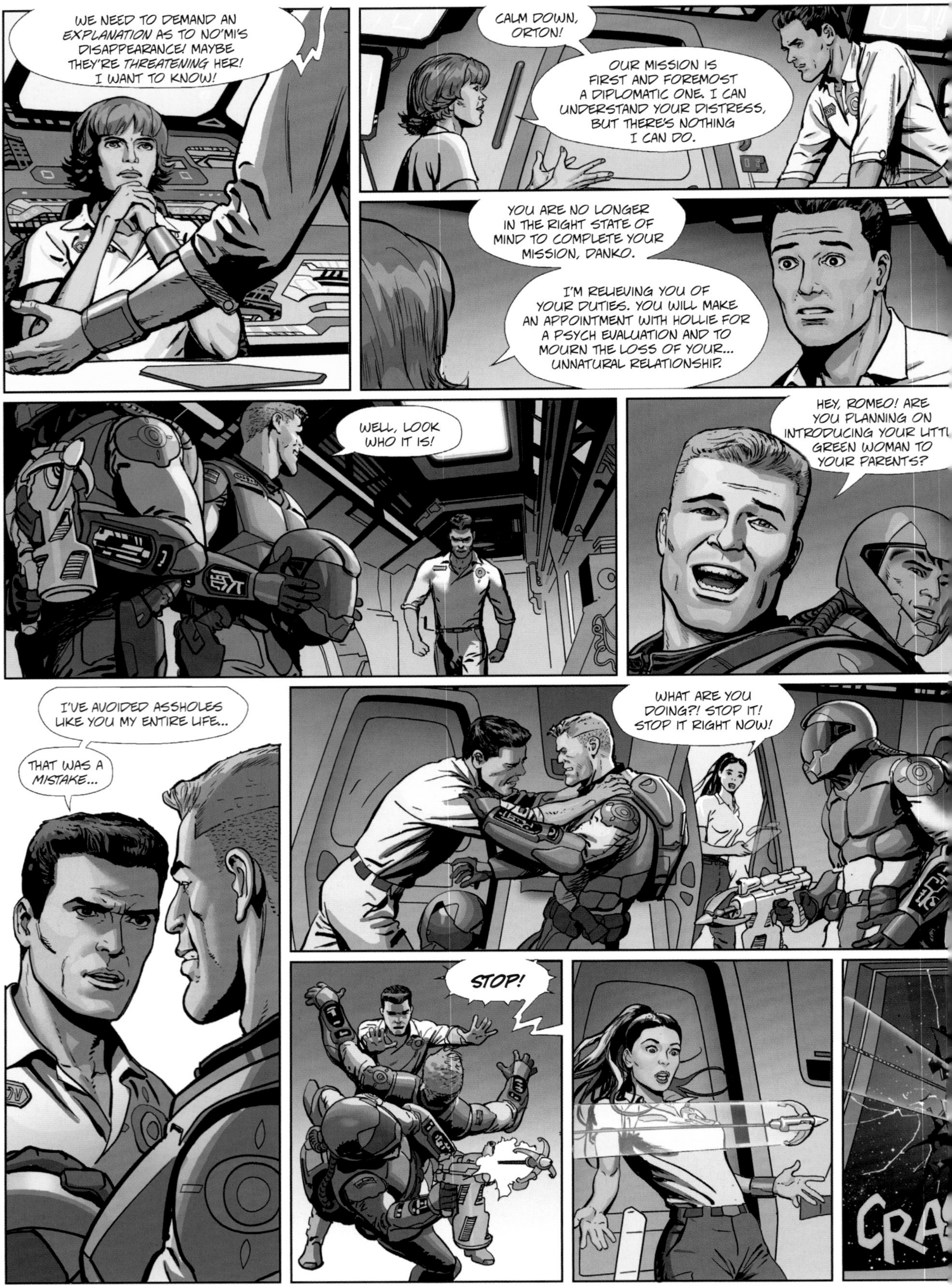
WE NEED TO DEMAND AN EXPLANATION AS TO NO'MI'S DISAPPEARANCE! MAYBE THEY'RE THREATENING HER! I WANT TO KNOW!
CALM DOWN, ORTON!
OUR MISSION IS FIRST AND FOREMOST A DIPLOMATIC ONE. I CAN UNDERSTAND YOUR DISTRESS, BUT THERE'S NOTHING I CAN DO.
YOU ARE NO LONGER IN THE RIGHT STATE OF MIND TO COMPLETE YOUR MISSION, DANKO.
I'M RELIEVING YOU OF YOUR DUTIES. YOU WILL MAKE AN APPOINTMENT WITH HOLLIE FOR A PSYCH EVALUATION AND TO MOURN THE LOSS OF YOUR... UNNATURAL RELATIONSHIP.
WELL, LOOK WHO IT IS!
HEY, ROMEO! ARE YOU PLANNING ON INTRODUCING YOUR LITTL GREEN WOMAN TO YOUR PARENTS?
I'VE AVOIDED ASSHOLES LIKE YOU MY ENTIRE LIFE...
THAT WAS A MISTAKE...
WHAT ARE YOU DOING?! STOP IT! STOP IT RIGHT NOW!
STOP!
CRA

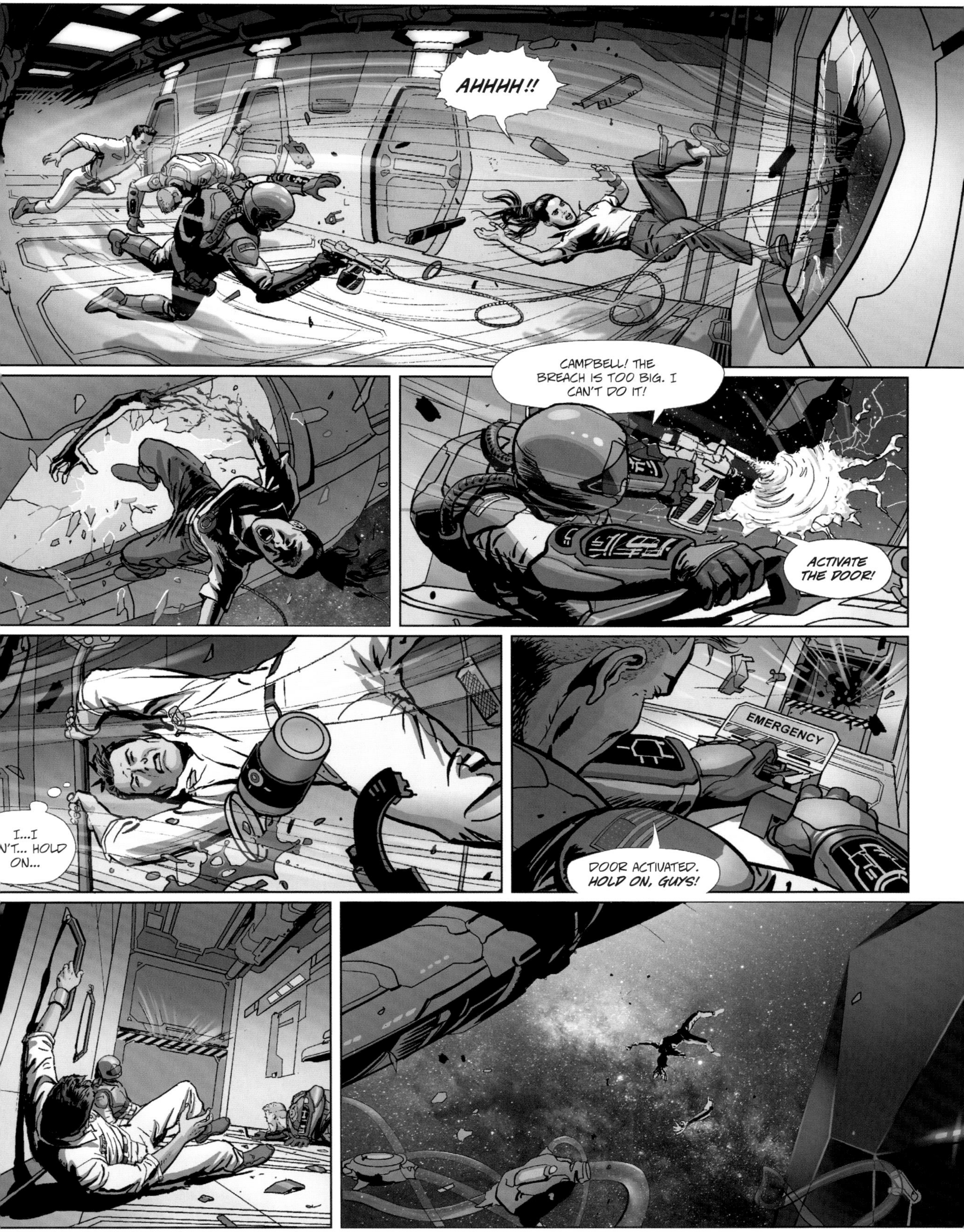
AHHHH!!
CAMPBELL! THE BREACH IS TOO BIG. I CAN'T DO IT!
ACTIVATE THE DOOR!
I...I 'T... HOLD ON...
EMERGENCY
DOOR ACTIVATED. HOLD ON, GUYS!

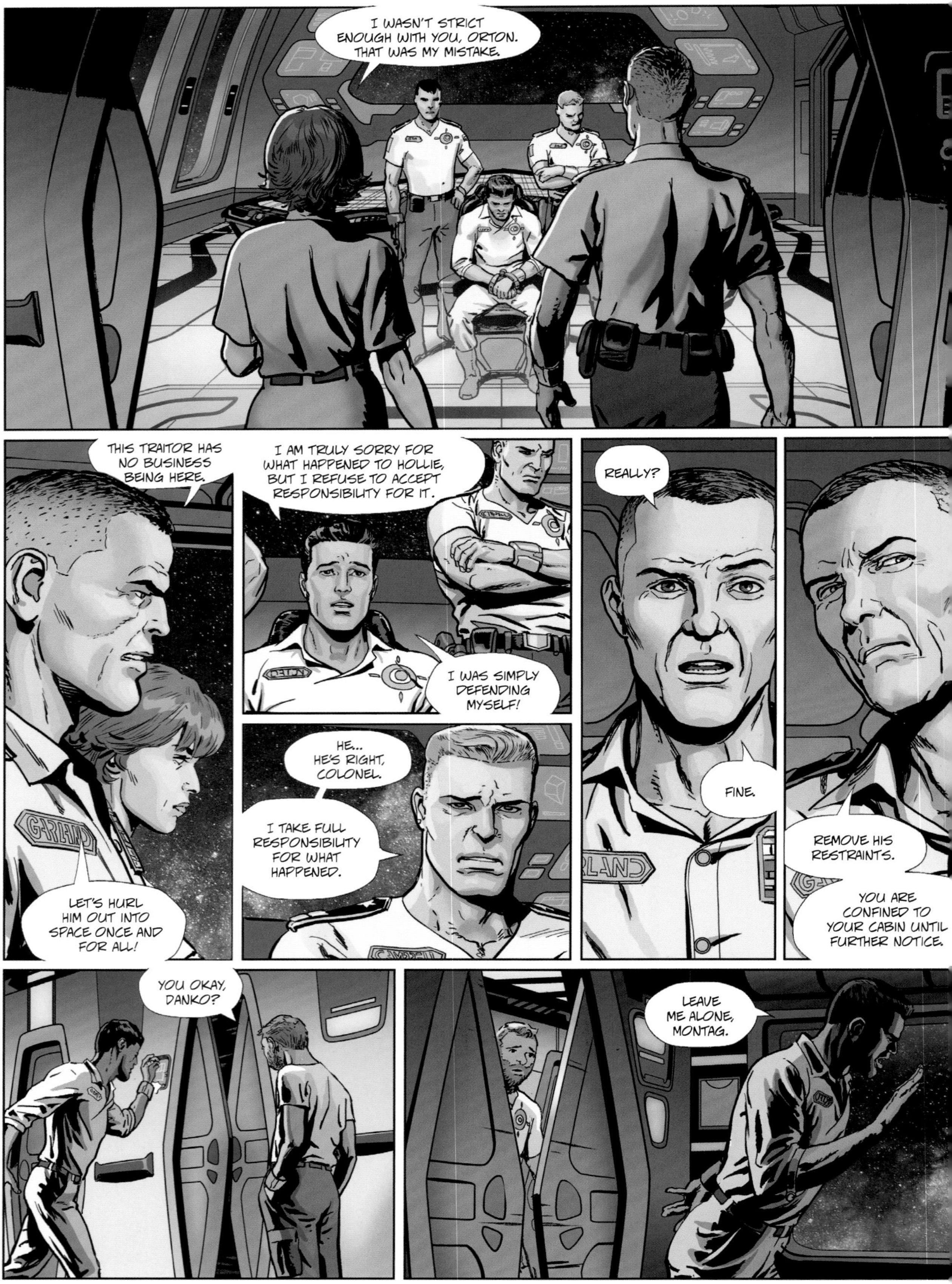
I WASN'T STRICT ENOUGH WITH YOU, ORTON. THAT WAS MY MISTAKE.
THIS TRAITOR HAS NO BUSINESS BEING HERE.
LET'S HURL HIM OUT INTO SPACE ONCE AND FOR ALL!
I AM TRULY SORRY FOR WHAT HAPPENED TO HOLLIE, BUT I REFUSE TO ACCEPT RESPONSIBILITY FOR IT.
I WAS SIMPLY DEFENDING MYSELF!
HE... HE'S RIGHT, COLONEL.
I TAKE FULL RESPONSIBILITY FOR WHAT HAPPENED.
REALLY?
FINE.
REMOVE HIS RESTRAINTS.
YOU ARE CONFINED TO YOUR CABIN UNTIL FURTHER NOTICE.
YOU OKAY, DANKO?
LEAVE ME ALONE, MONTAG.

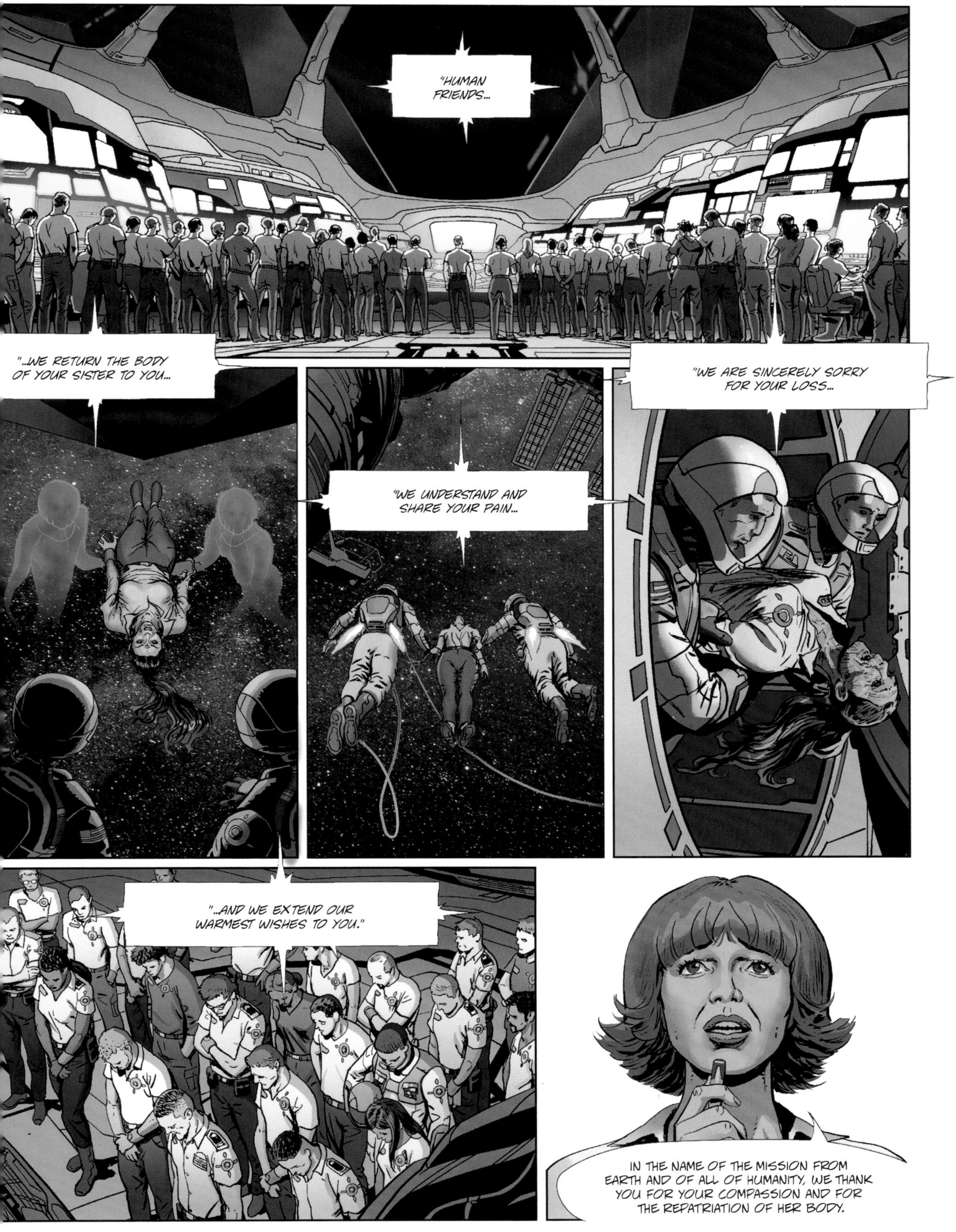
"HUMAN FRIENDS...
"...WE RETURN THE BODY OF YOUR SISTER TO YOU...
"WE UNDERSTAND AND SHARE YOUR PAIN...
"WE ARE SINCERELY SORRY FOR YOUR LOSS...
"...AND WE EXTEND OUR WARMEST WISHES TO YOU."
IN THE NAME OF THE MISSION FROM EARTH AND OF ALL OF HUMANITY, WE THANK YOU FOR YOUR COMPASSION AND FOR THE REPATRIATION OF HER BODY.

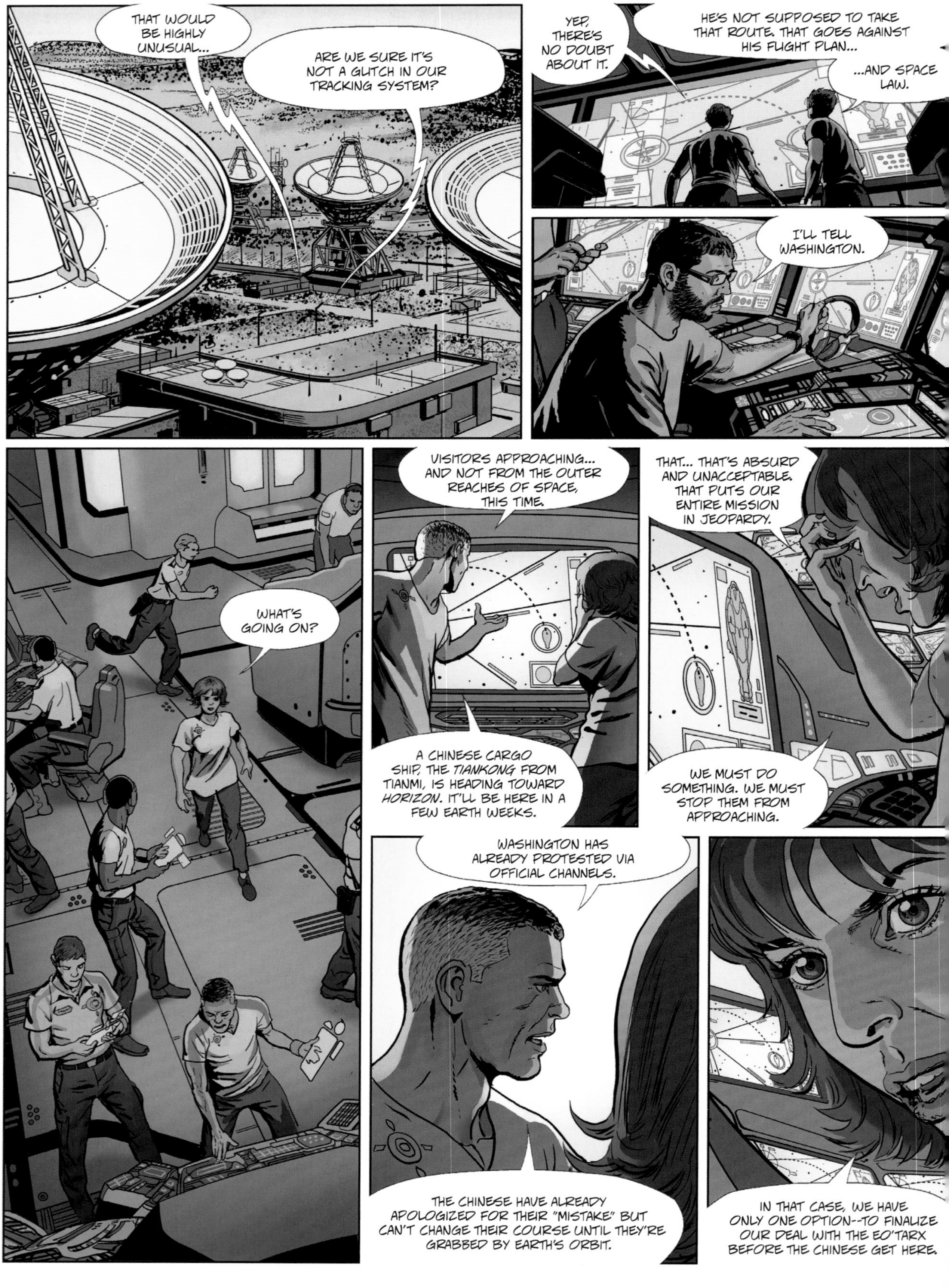

THAT WOULD BE HIGHLY UNUSUAL...
ARE WE SURE IT'S NOT A GLITCH IN OUR TRACKING SYSTEM?
YEP, THERE'S NO DOUBT ABOUT IT.
HE'S NOT SUPPOSED TO TAKE THAT ROUTE. THAT GOES AGAINST HIS FLIGHT PLAN...
...AND SPACE LAW.
I'LL TELL WASHINGTON.
WHAT'S GOING ON?
VISITORS APPROACHING... AND NOT FROM THE OUTER REACHES OF SPACE, THIS TIME.
A CHINESE CARGO SHIP, THE *TIANKONG* FROM TIANMI, IS HEADING TOWARD *HORIZON*. IT'LL BE HERE IN A FEW EARTH WEEKS.
THAT... THAT'S ABSURD AND UNACCEPTABLE. THAT PUTS OUR ENTIRE MISSION IN JEOPARDY.
WE MUST DO SOMETHING. WE MUST STOP THEM FROM APPROACHING.
WASHINGTON HAS ALREADY PROTESTED VIA OFFICIAL CHANNELS.
THE CHINESE HAVE ALREADY APOLOGIZED FOR THEIR "MISTAKE" BUT CAN'T CHANGE THEIR COURSE UNTIL THEY'RE GRABBED BY EARTH'S ORBIT.
IN THAT CASE, WE HAVE ONLY ONE OPTION--TO FINALIZE OUR DEAL WITH THE EO'TARX BEFORE THE CHINESE GET HERE.

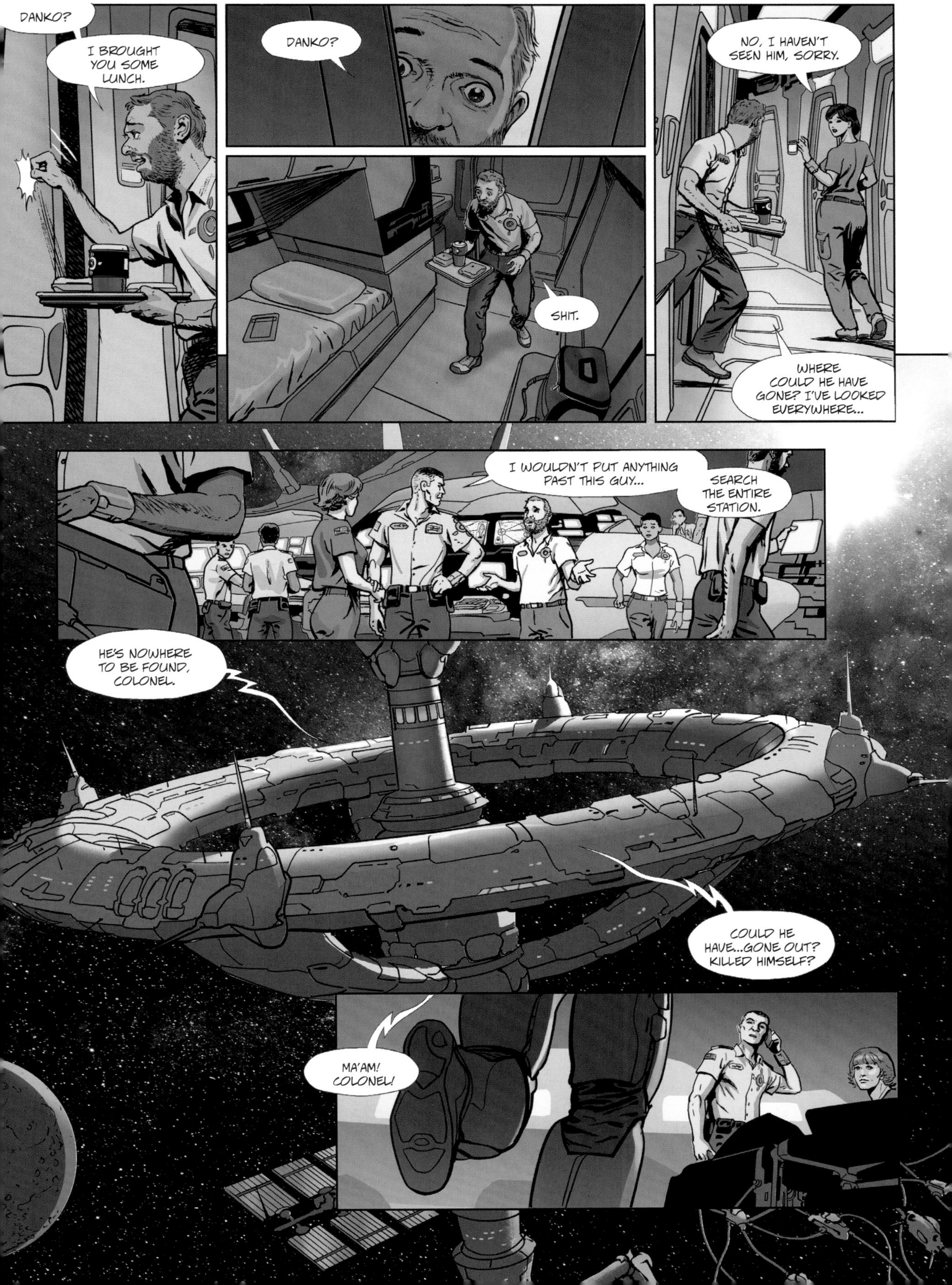
DANKO?
I BROUGHT YOU SOME LUNCH.
DANKO?
SHIT.
NO, I HAVEN'T SEEN HIM, SORRY.
WHERE COULD HE HAVE GONE? I'VE LOOKED EVERYWHERE...
I WOULDN'T PUT ANYTHING PAST THIS GUY...
SEARCH THE ENTIRE STATION.
HE'S NOWHERE TO BE FOUND, COLONEL.
COULD HE HAVE...GONE OUT? KILLED HIMSELF?
MA'AM! COLONEL!

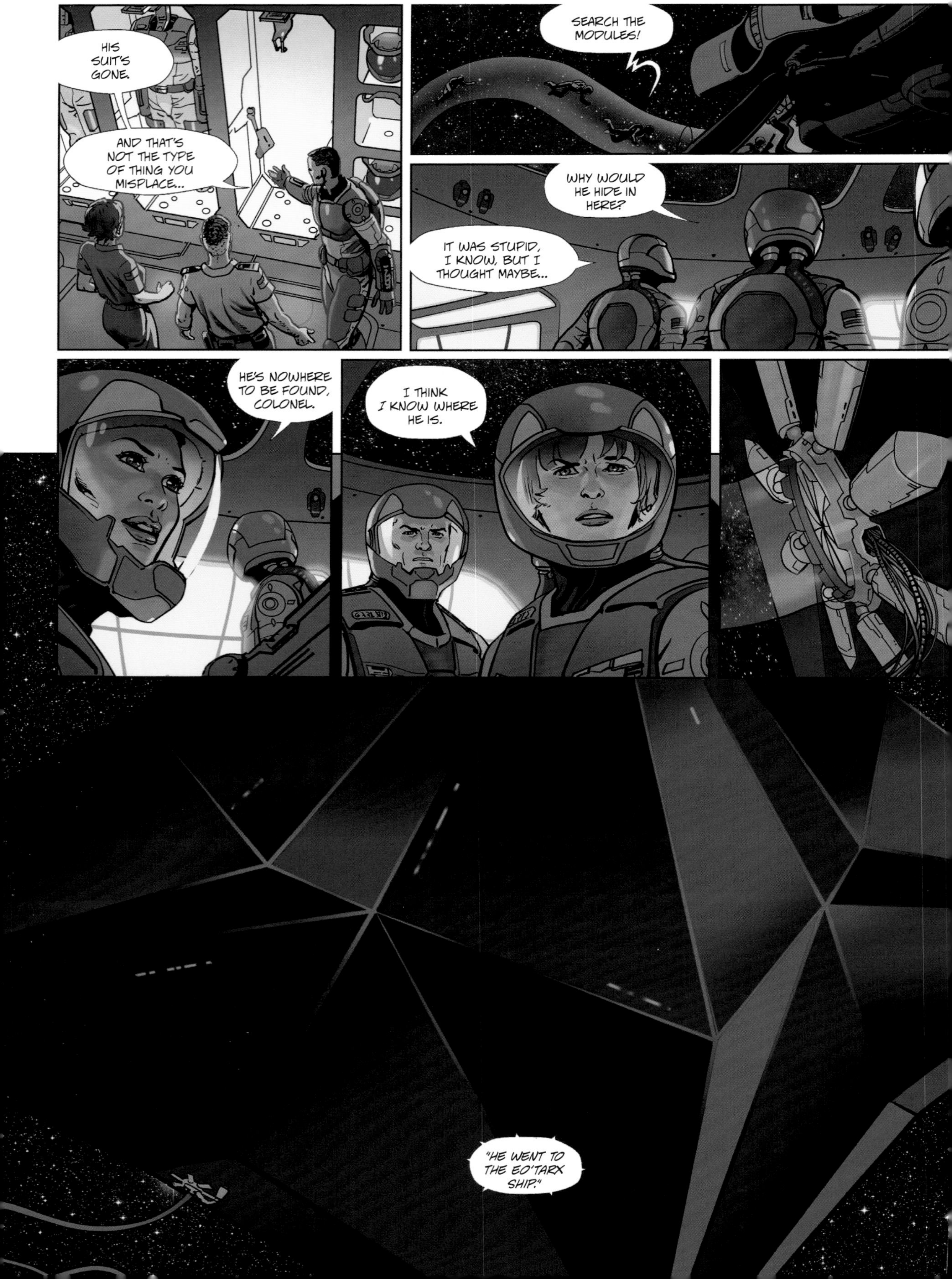
HIS SUIT'S GONE.
AND THAT'S NOT THE TYPE OF THING YOU MISPLACE...
SEARCH THE MODULES!
WHY WOULD HE HIDE IN HERE?
IT WAS STUPID, I KNOW, BUT I THOUGHT MAYBE...
HE'S NOWHERE TO BE FOUND, COLONEL.
I THINK I KNOW WHERE HE IS.
"HE WENT TO THE EO'TARX SHIP."

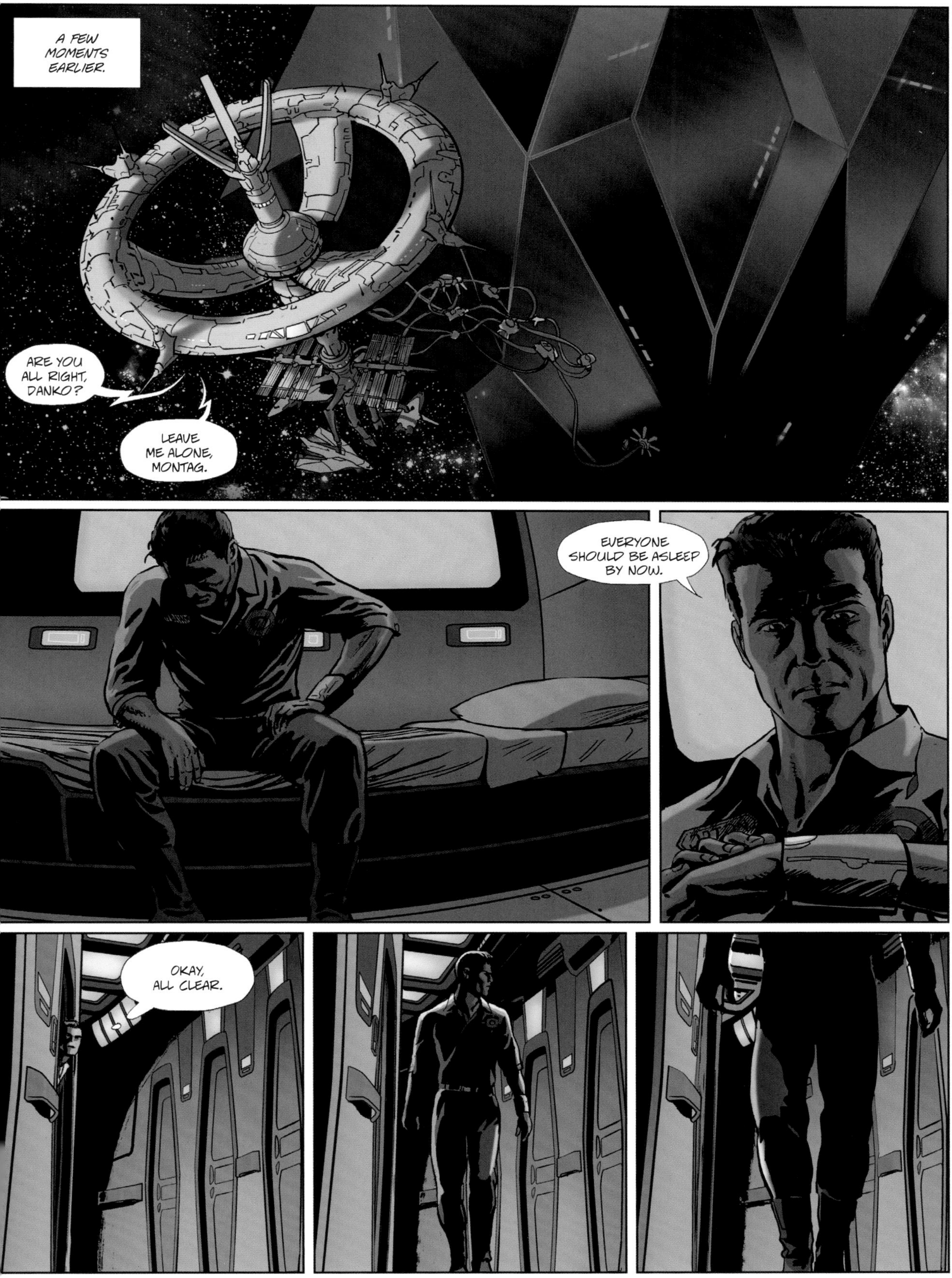
A FEW MOMENTS EARLIER.
ARE YOU ALL RIGHT, DANKO?
LEAVE ME ALONE, MONTAG.
EVERYONE SHOULD BE ASLEEP BY NOW.
OKAY, ALL CLEAR.

DATA COMPRESSION COMPLETE. I'LL TRANSFER IT TO THE SERVER.
GREAT.
TRANSFER COMPLETE IN SEVENTEEN MINUTES AND FORTY-FOUR SECONDS.
STILL WORKS.
MMMMMMMMMMMM
MMMMMMMMMMMM
LET'S HOPE THEY DIDN'T BLOCK MY ACCESS CARD.
OXYGEN LEVEL AT 20.95%...
20.95
AM I MAKING THE BIGGEST MISTAKE OF MY LIFE HERE?

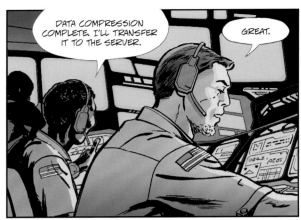

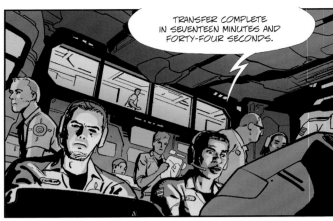

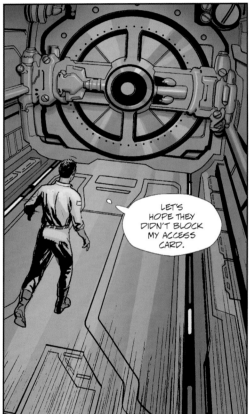

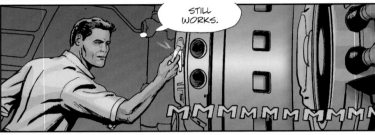

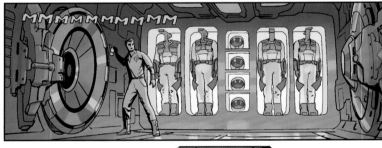

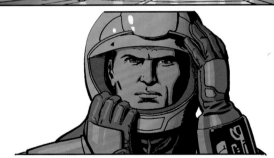

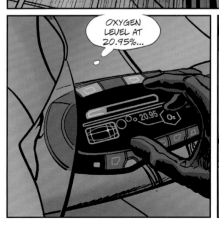

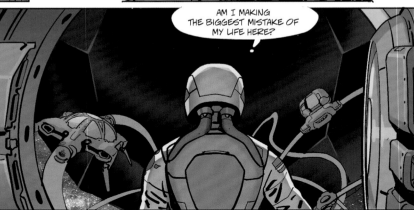

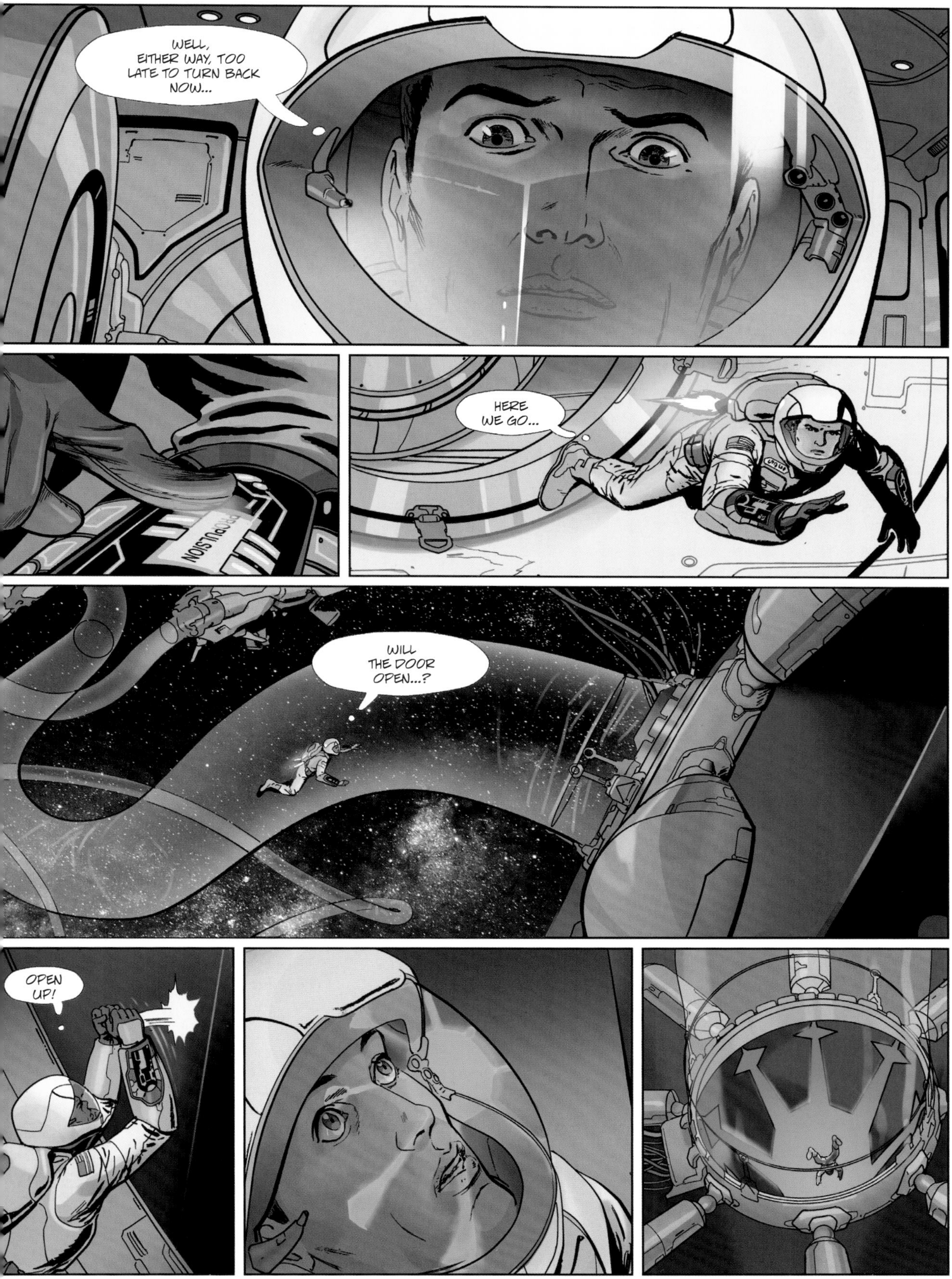
WELL, EITHER WAY, TOO LATE TO TURN BACK NOW...
PROPULSION
HERE WE GO...
WILL THE DOOR OPEN...?
OPEN UP!

WHAT THE--
WHAT THE HELL IS
THAT SMELL?!

IT SMELLS
LIKE...SOMETHING'S
ROTTING!

OUR MODULES
WERE DESIGNED AS NEUTRAL
TERRITORY BETWEEN THE TWO
SPECIES, BORROWING
EQUALLY FROM EACH
CULTURE.

BUT I DON'T
SEE ANY SIMILARITY
WHATSOEVER BETWEEN
THE MODULES AND
THIS PLACE....

HOW DO
THE EO'TARX NAVIGATE
THESE WALKWAYS?

THEY MUST BE RESTING RIGHT
NOW, JUST AS THE
HUMANS ARE.

AH,
FINALLY,
A LIGHT.

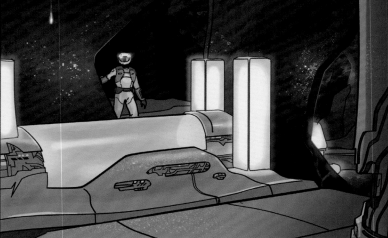

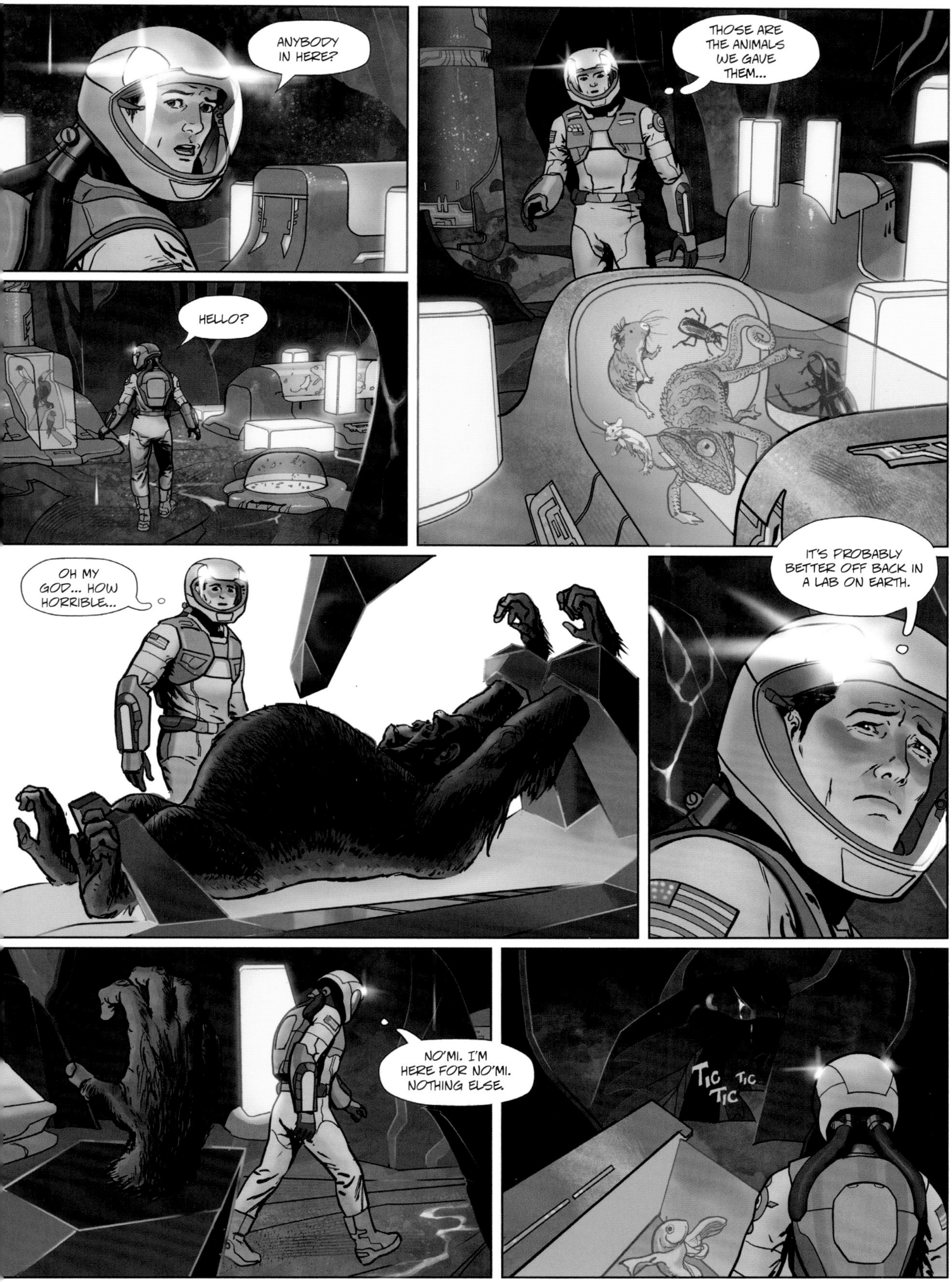
ANYBODY IN HERE?
THOSE ARE THE ANIMALS WE GAVE THEM...
HELLO?
OH MY GOD... HOW HORRIBLE...
IT'S PROBABLY BETTER OFF BACK IN A LAB ON EARTH.
NO'MI. I'M HERE FOR NO'MI. NOTHING ELSE.
TIC TIC TIC

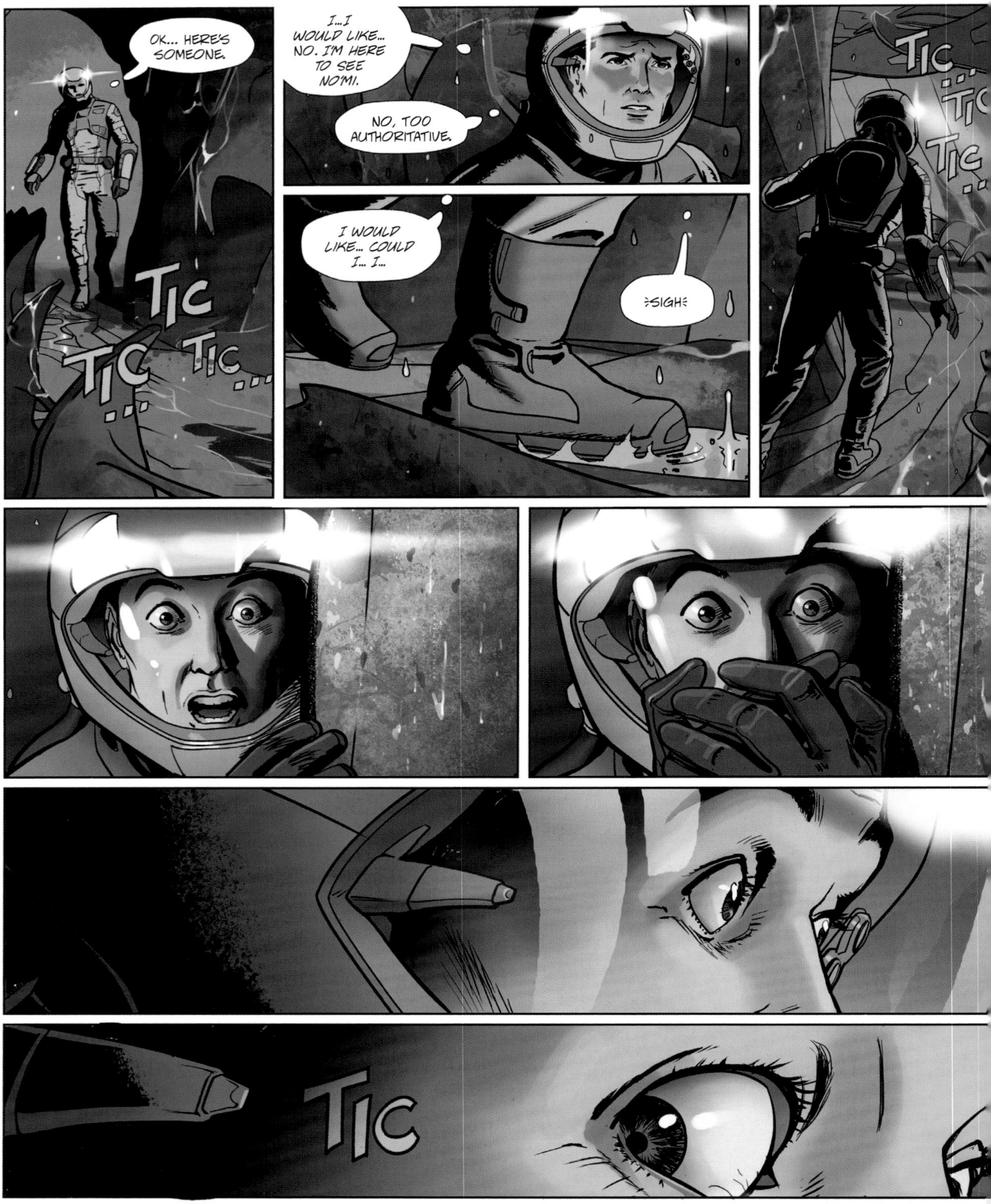
OK... HERE'S SOMEONE.
TIC
TIC TIC...
...
I...I WOULD LIKE... NO. I'M HERE TO SEE NO'MI.
NO, TOO AUTHORITATIVE.
I WOULD LIKE... COULD I... I...
SIGH
TIC... TIC... TIC...
TIC

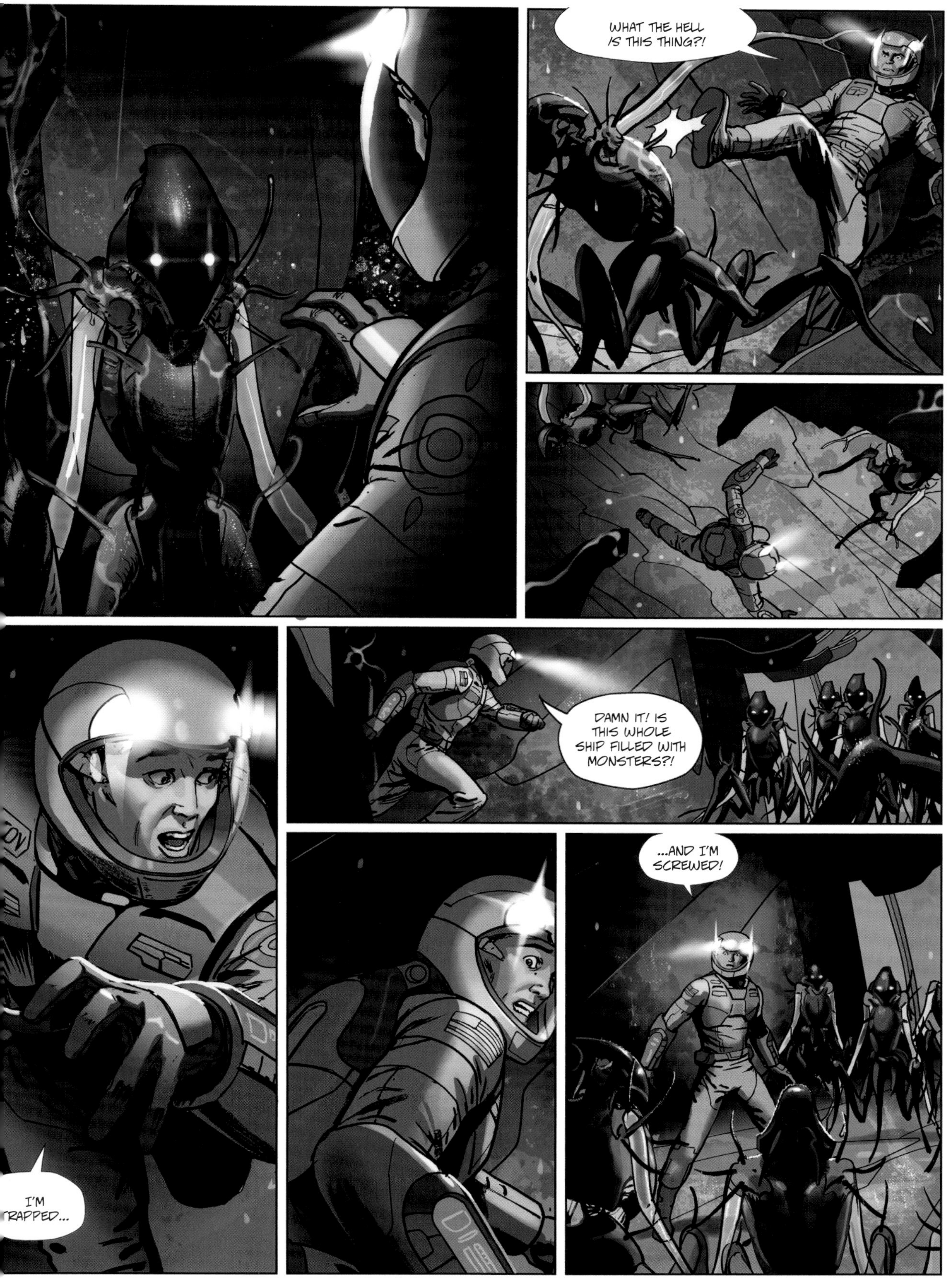

WHAT THE HELL IS THIS THING?!
I'M TRAPPED...
DAMN IT! IS THIS WHOLE SHIP FILLED WITH MONSTERS?!
...AND I'M SCREWED!

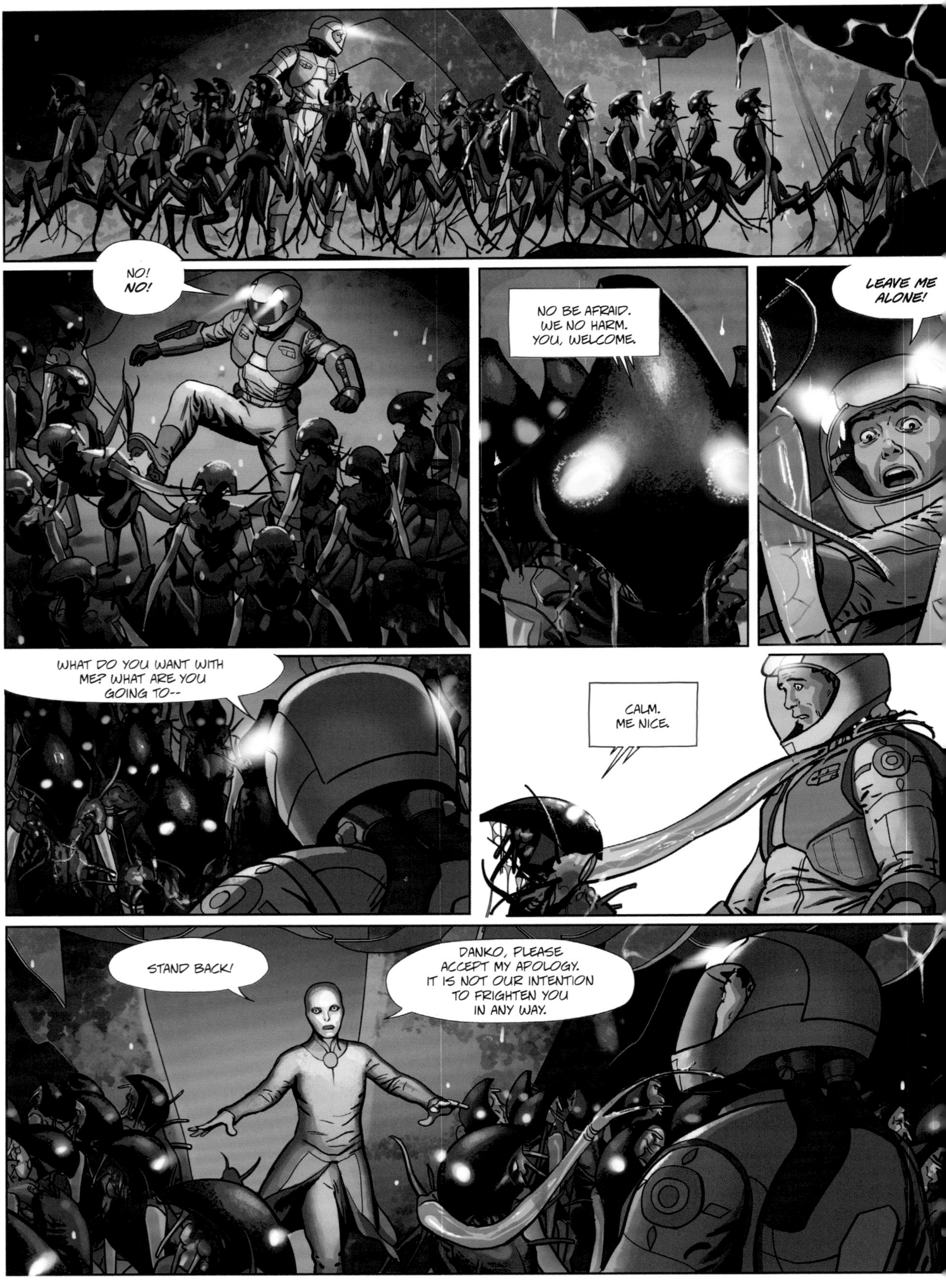
NO!
NO!
NO BE AFRAID. WE NO HARM. YOU, WELCOME.
LEAVE ME ALONE!
WHAT DO YOU WANT WITH ME? WHAT ARE YOU GOING TO--
CALM. ME NICE.
STAND BACK!
DANKO, PLEASE ACCEPT MY APOLOGY. IT IS NOT OUR INTENTION TO FRIGHTEN YOU IN ANY WAY.

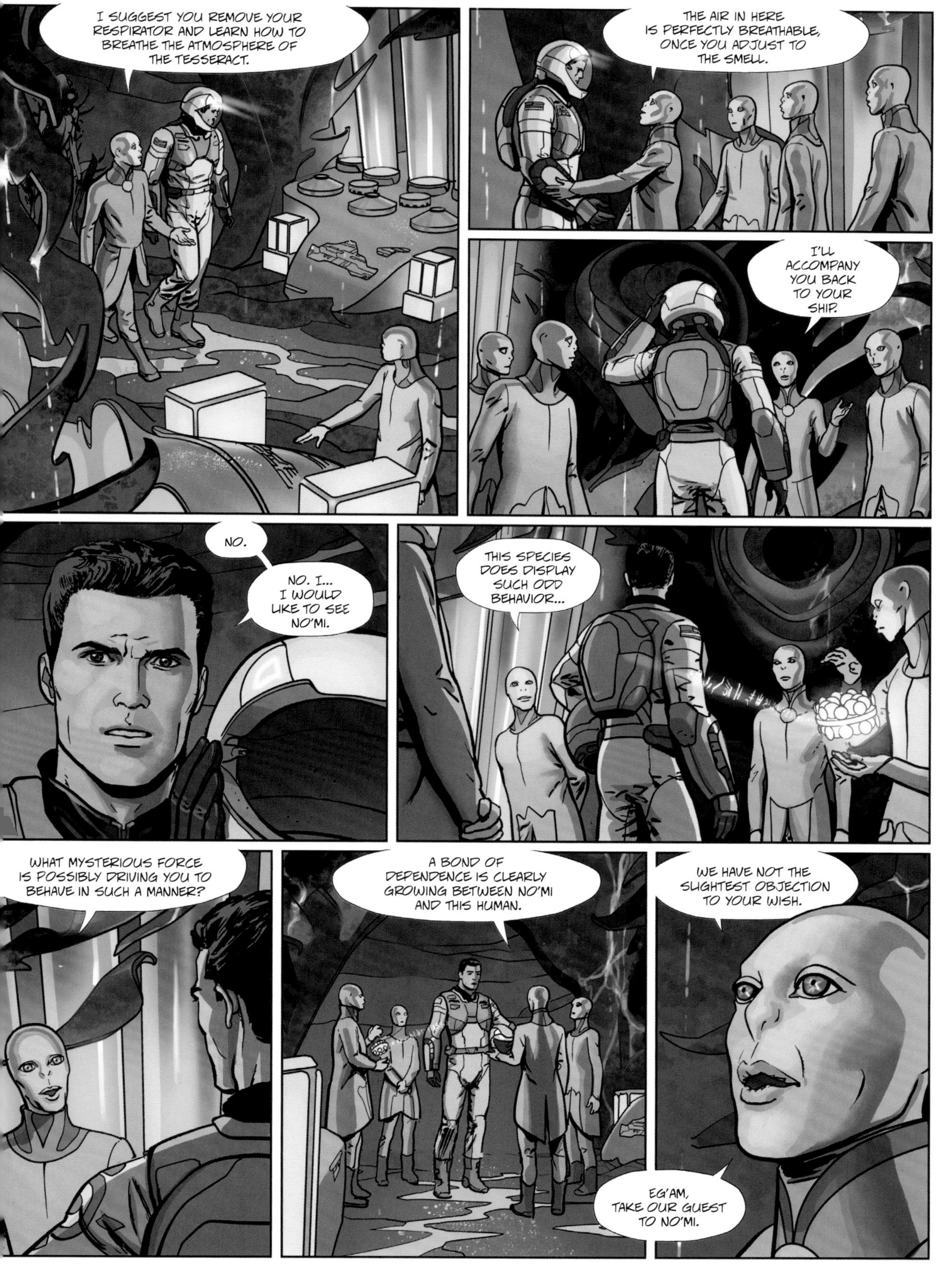
I SUGGEST YOU REMOVE YOUR RESPIRATOR AND LEARN HOW TO BREATHE THE ATMOSPHERE OF THE TESSERACT.
THE AIR IN HERE IS PERFECTLY BREATHABLE, ONCE YOU ADJUST TO THE SMELL.
I'LL ACCOMPANY YOU BACK TO YOUR SHIP.
NO.
NO. I... I WOULD LIKE TO SEE NO'MI.
THIS SPECIES DOES DISPLAY SUCH ODD BEHAVIOR...
WHAT MYSTERIOUS FORCE IS POSSIBLY DRIVING YOU TO BEHAVE IN SUCH A MANNER?
A BOND OF DEPENDENCE IS CLEARLY GROWING BETWEEN NO'MI AND THIS HUMAN.
WE HAVE NOT THE SLIGHTEST OBJECTION TO YOUR WISH.
EG'AM, TAKE OUR GUEST TO NO'MI.

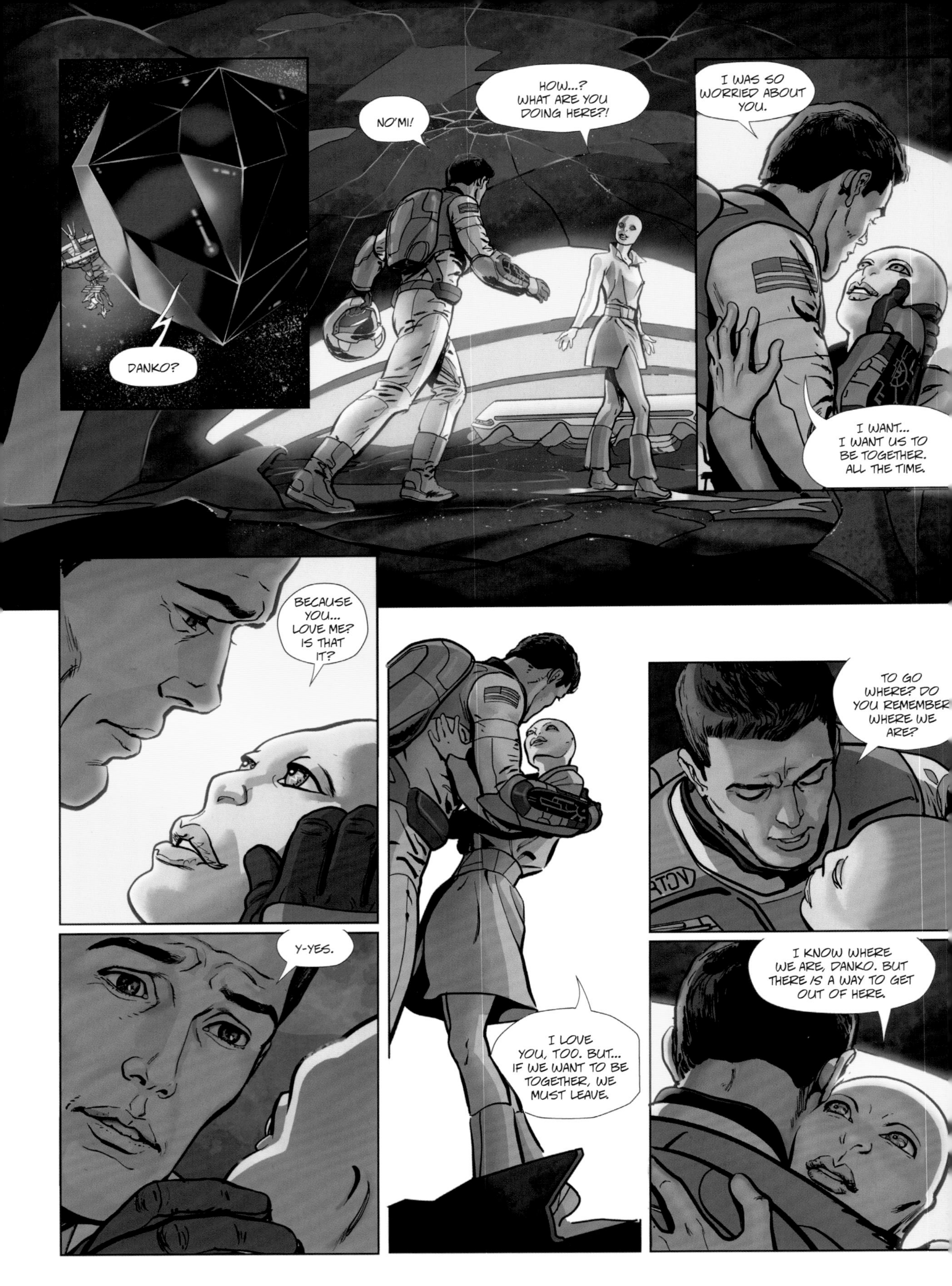
DANKO?
NO'MI!
HOW...? WHAT ARE YOU DOING HERE?!
I WAS SO WORRIED ABOUT YOU.
I WANT... I WANT US TO BE TOGETHER. ALL THE TIME.
BECAUSE YOU... LOVE ME? IS THAT IT?
Y-YES.
I LOVE YOU, TOO. BUT... IF WE WANT TO BE TOGETHER, WE MUST LEAVE.
TO GO WHERE? DO YOU REMEMBER WHERE WE ARE?
I KNOW WHERE WE ARE, DANKO. BUT THERE IS A WAY TO GET OUT OF HERE.

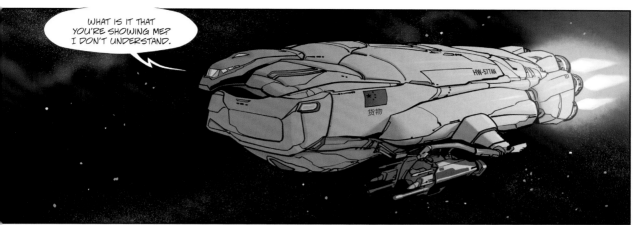

WHAT IS IT THAT YOU'RE SHOWING ME? I DON'T UNDERSTAND.

RIGHT NEXT TO HORIZON, THERE'S A STRANGE STRUCTURE THAT SHOULDN'T...THAT SHOULDN'T BE THERE.

WELL, WHAT IS IT?

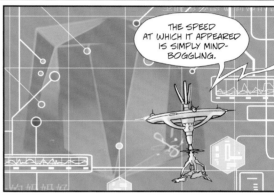

THE SPEED AT WHICH IT APPEARED IS SIMPLY MIND-BOGGLING.

HORIZON SPACE STATION, THIS IS COMMANDER LI JENG SPEAKING, FROM ABOARD THE *TIANKONG* FROM TIANMI...

WE WILL BE PASSING BY IN CLOSE PROXIMITY TO HORIZON...

UNDER THE SPACE ACCORDS OF THE UNITED NATIONS, I REQUEST THAT YOU IDENTIFY THE STRUCTURE CONNECTED TO YOUR BASE.

THIS REQUEST REQUIRES AN IMMEDIATE RESPONSE.

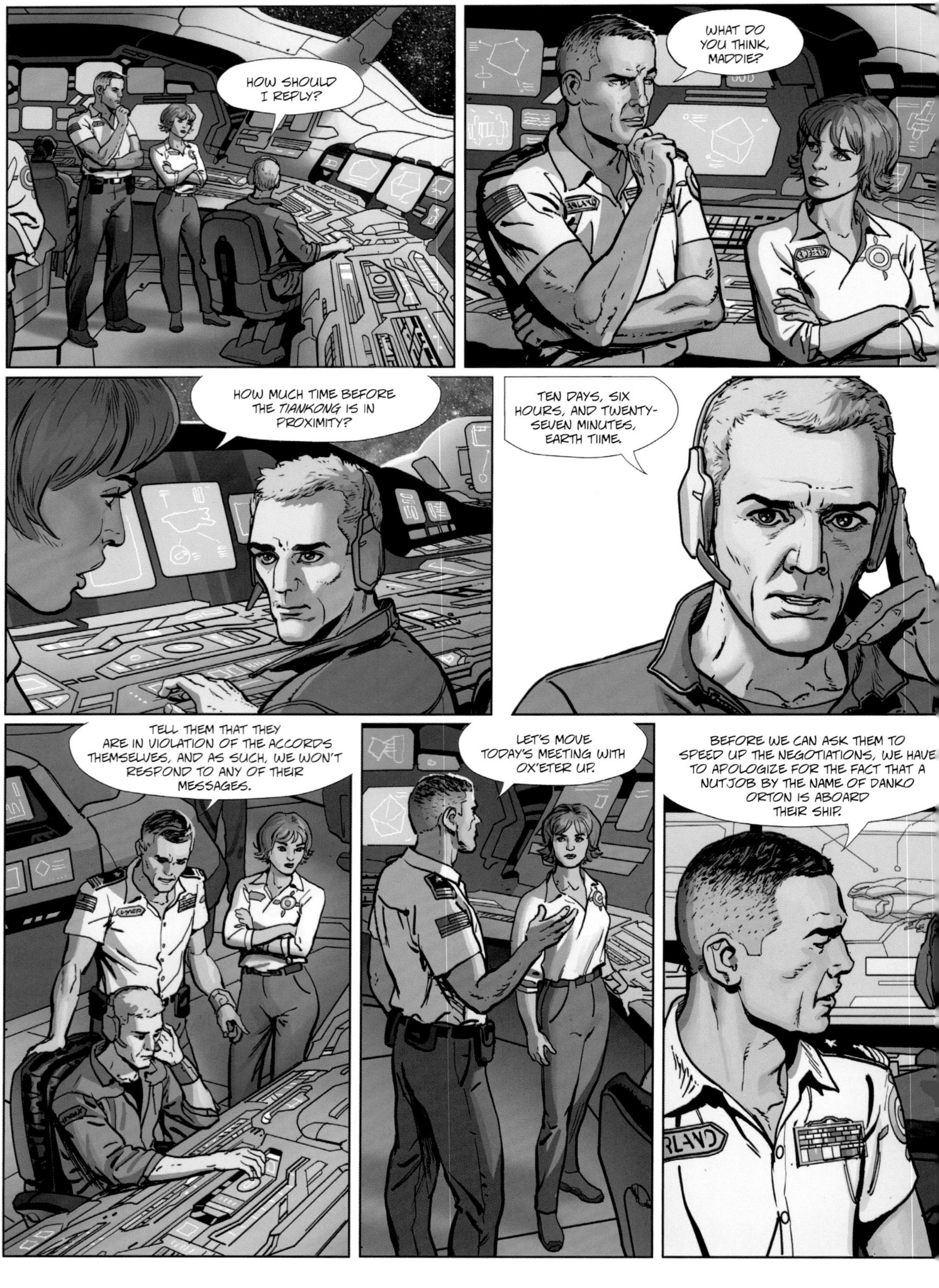
HOW SHOULD I REPLY?
WHAT DO YOU THINK, MADDIE?
HOW MUCH TIME BEFORE THE *TIANKONG* IS IN PROXIMITY?
TEN DAYS, SIX HOURS, AND TWENTY-SEVEN MINUTES, EARTH TIIME.
TELL THEM THAT THEY ARE IN VIOLATION OF THE ACCORDS THEMSELVES, AND AS SUCH, WE WON'T RESPOND TO ANY OF THEIR MESSAGES.
LET'S MOVE TODAY'S MEETING WITH OX'ETER UP.
BEFORE WE CAN ASK THEM TO SPEED UP THE NEGOTIATIONS, WE HAVE TO APOLOGIZE FOR THE FACT THAT A NUTJOB BY THE NAME OF DANKO ORTON IS ABOARD THEIR SHIP.

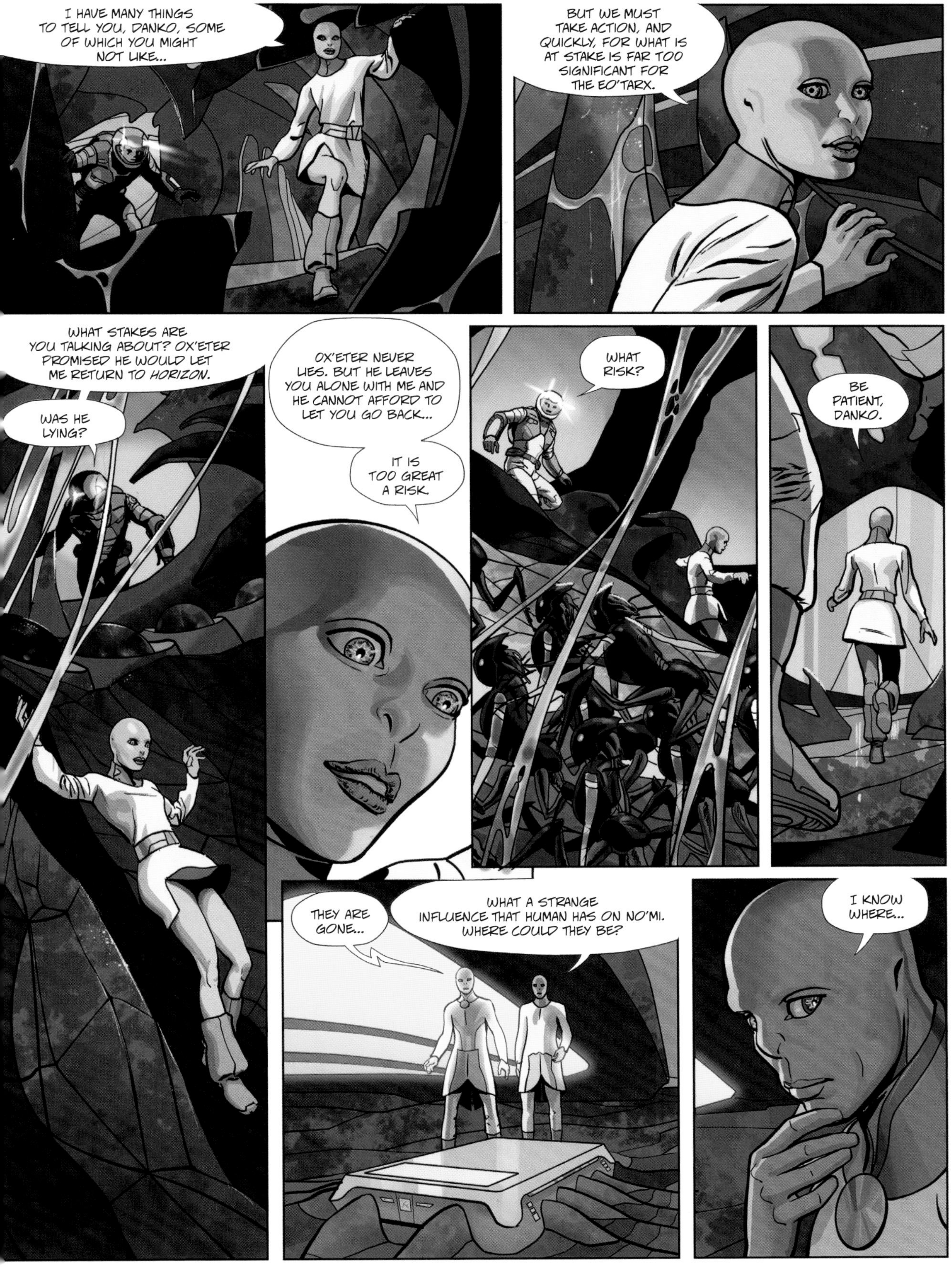
I HAVE MANY THINGS TO TELL YOU, DANKO, SOME OF WHICH YOU MIGHT NOT LIKE...
BUT WE MUST TAKE ACTION, AND QUICKLY, FOR WHAT IS AT STAKE IS FAR TOO SIGNIFICANT FOR THE EO'TARX.
WHAT STAKES ARE YOU TALKING ABOUT? OX'ETER PROMISED HE WOULD LET ME RETURN TO *HORIZON*.
WAS HE LYING?
OX'ETER NEVER LIES. BUT HE LEAVES YOU ALONE WITH ME AND HE CANNOT AFFORD TO LET YOU GO BACK...
IT IS TOO GREAT A RISK.
WHAT RISK?
BE PATIENT, DANKO.
THEY ARE GONE...
WHAT A STRANGE INFLUENCE THAT HUMAN HAS ON NO'MI. WHERE COULD THEY BE?
I KNOW WHERE...

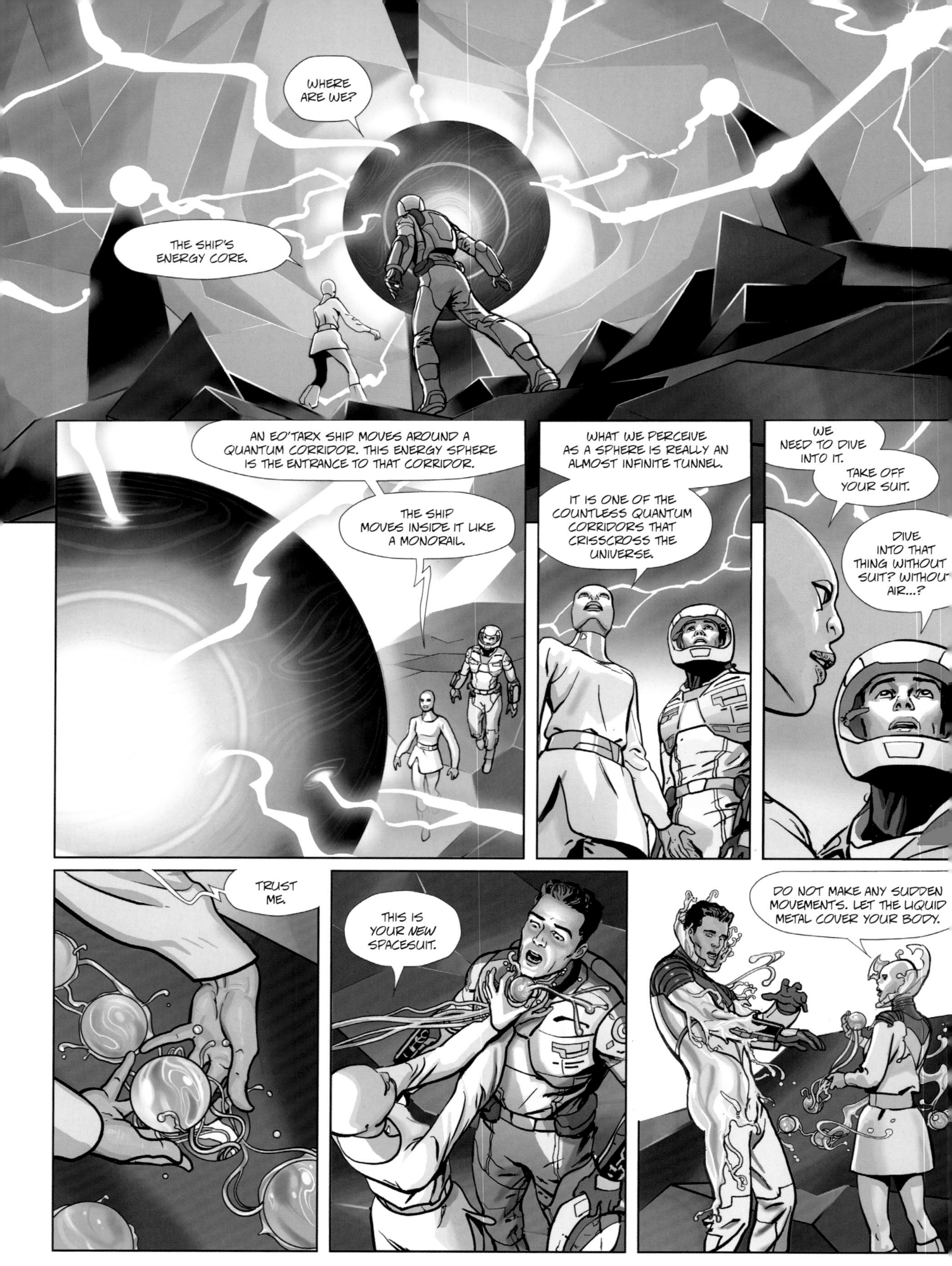
WHERE ARE WE?
THE SHIP'S ENERGY CORE.
AN EO'TARX SHIP MOVES AROUND A QUANTUM CORRIDOR. THIS ENERGY SPHERE IS THE ENTRANCE TO THAT CORRIDOR.
THE SHIP MOVES INSIDE IT LIKE A MONORAIL.
WHAT WE PERCEIVE AS A SPHERE IS REALLY AN ALMOST INFINITE TUNNEL.
IT IS ONE OF THE COUNTLESS QUANTUM CORRIDORS THAT CRISSCROSS THE UNIVERSE.
WE NEED TO DIVE INTO IT.
TAKE OFF YOUR SUIT.
DIVE INTO THAT THING WITHOUT SUIT? WITHOUT AIR...?
TRUST ME.
THIS IS YOUR NEW SPACESUIT.
DO NOT MAKE ANY SUDDEN MOVEMENTS. LET THE LIQUID METAL COVER YOUR BODY.

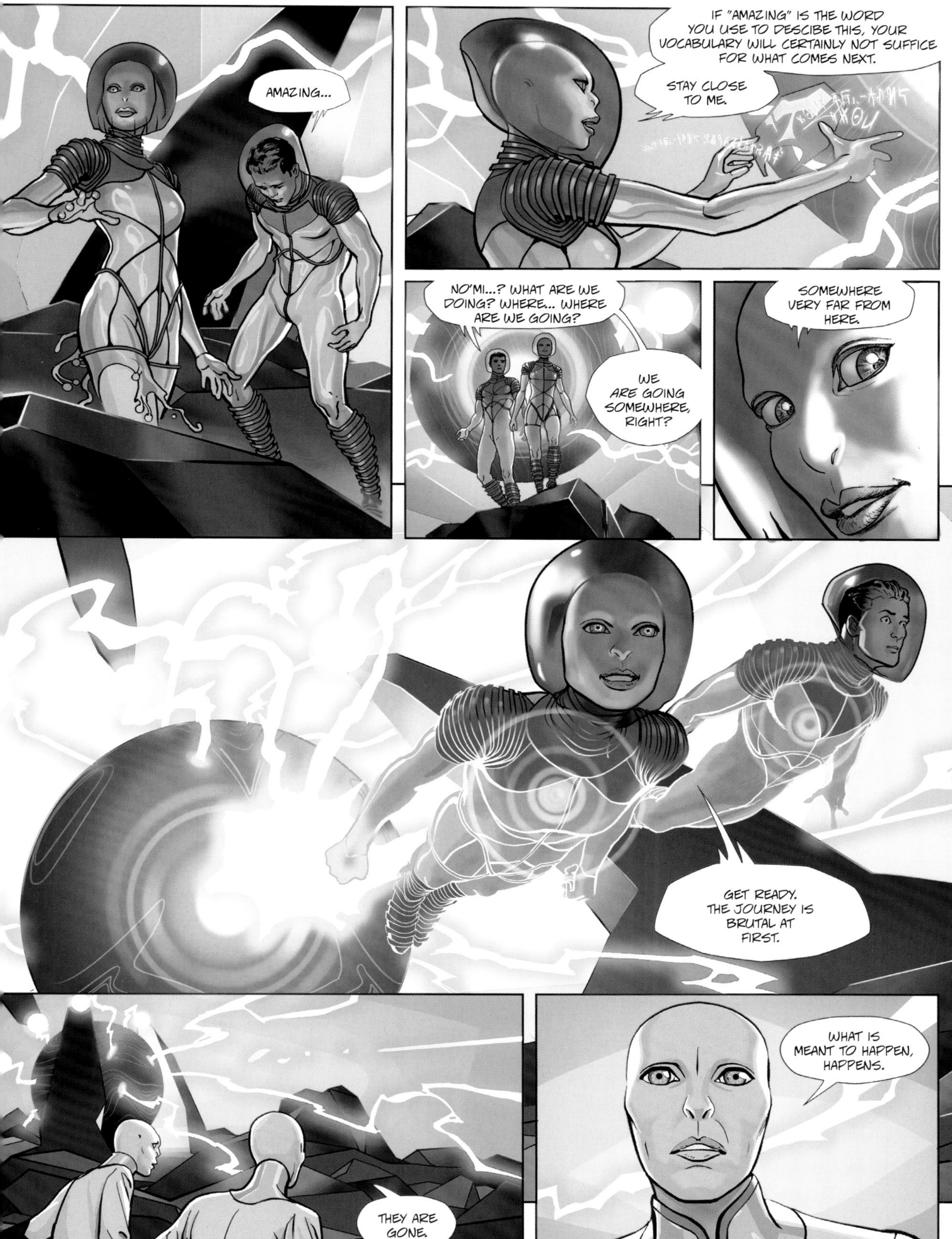
AMAZING...
IF "AMAZING" IS THE WORD YOU USE TO DESCIBE THIS, YOUR VOCABULARY WILL CERTAINLY NOT SUFFICE FOR WHAT COMES NEXT.
STAY CLOSE TO ME.
NO'MI...? WHAT ARE WE DOING? WHERE... WHERE ARE WE GOING?
WE ARE GOING SOMEWHERE, RIGHT?
SOMEWHERE VERY FAR FROM HERE.
GET READY. THE JOURNEY IS BRUTAL AT FIRST.
THEY ARE GONE.
WHAT IS MEANT TO HAPPEN, HAPPENS.

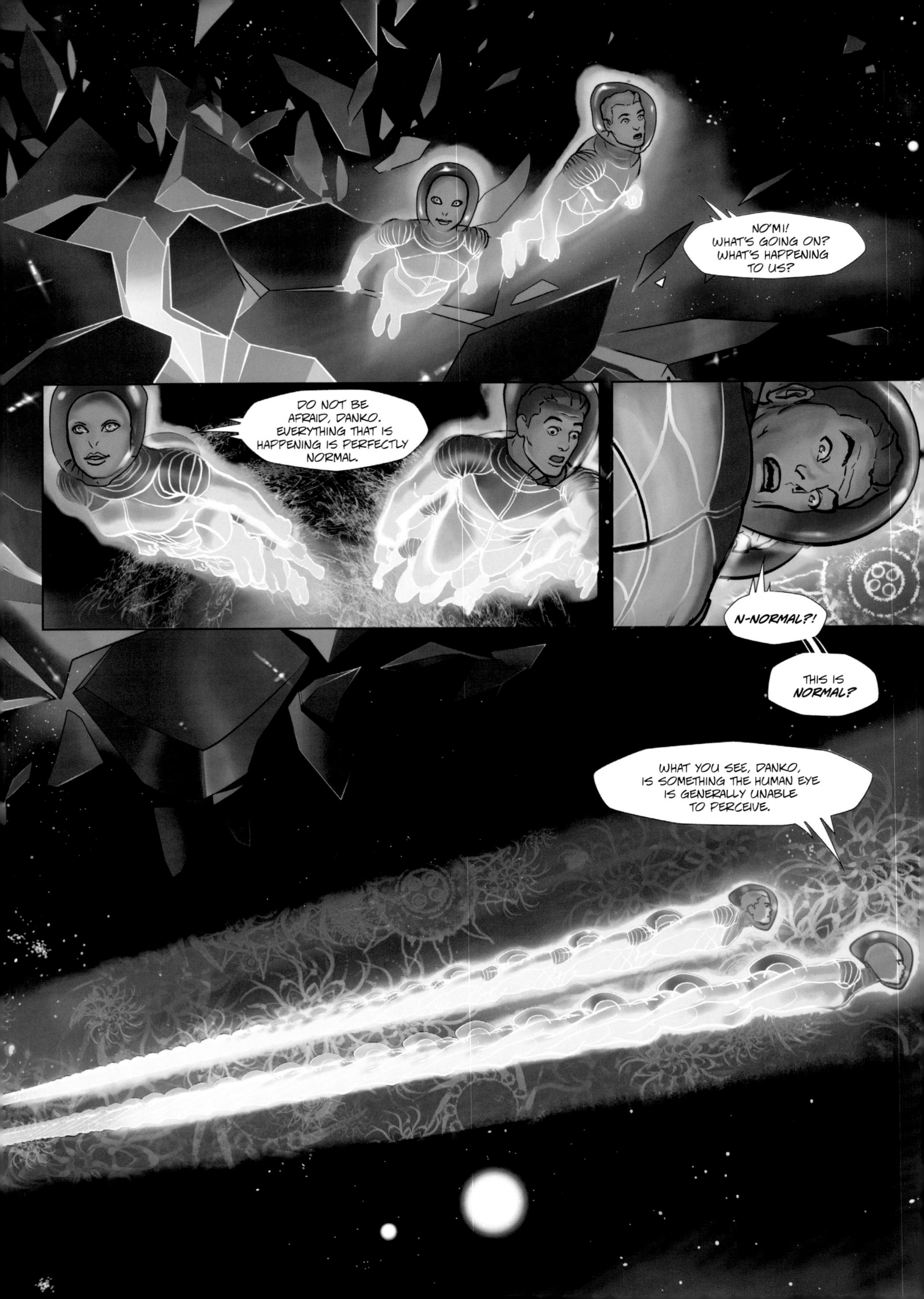
NO'MI! WHAT'S GOING ON? WHAT'S HAPPENING TO US?
DO NOT BE AFRAID, DANKO. EVERYTHING THAT IS HAPPENING IS PERFECTLY NORMAL.
N-NORMAL?!
THIS IS NORMAL?
WHAT YOU SEE, DANKO, IS SOMETHING THE HUMAN EYE IS GENERALLY UNABLE TO PERCEIVE.

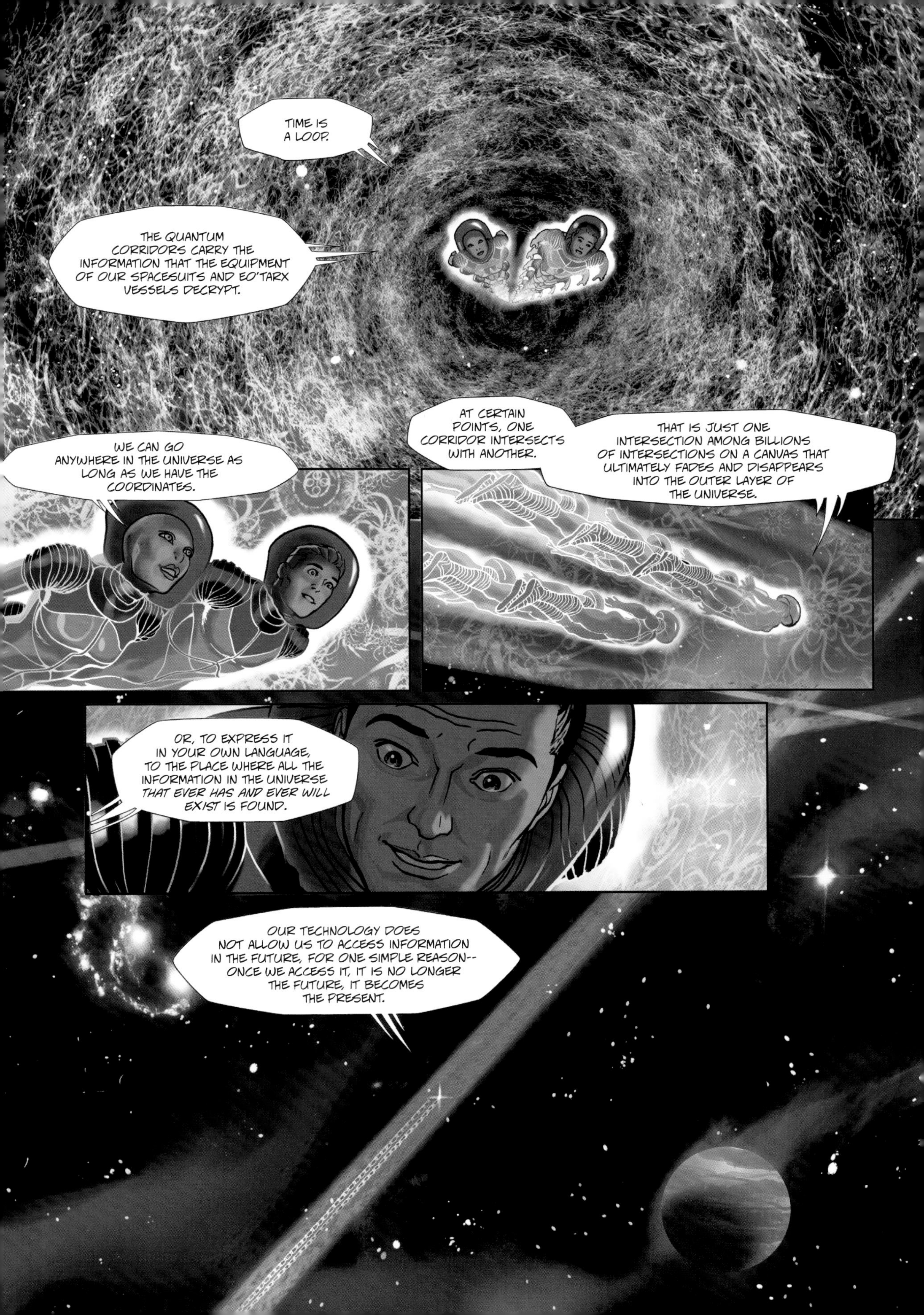
TIME IS A LOOP.
THE QUANTUM CORRIDORS CARRY THE INFORMATION THAT THE EQUIPMENT OF OUR SPACESUITS AND EO'TARX VESSELS DECRYPT.
WE CAN GO ANYWHERE IN THE UNIVERSE AS LONG AS WE HAVE THE COORDINATES.
AT CERTAIN POINTS, ONE CORRIDOR INTERSECTS WITH ANOTHER.
THAT IS JUST ONE INTERSECTION AMONG BILLIONS OF INTERSECTIONS ON A CANVAS THAT ULTIMATELY FADES AND DISAPPEARS INTO THE OUTER LAYER OF THE UNIVERSE.
OR, TO EXPRESS IT IN YOUR OWN LANGUAGE, TO THE PLACE WHERE ALL THE INFORMATION IN THE UNIVERSE THAT EVER HAS AND EVER WILL EXIST IS FOUND.
OUR TECHNOLOGY DOES NOT ALLOW US TO ACCESS INFORMATION IN THE FUTURE, FOR ONE SIMPLE REASON-- ONCE WE ACCESS IT, IT IS NO LONGER THE FUTURE, IT BECOMES THE PRESENT.

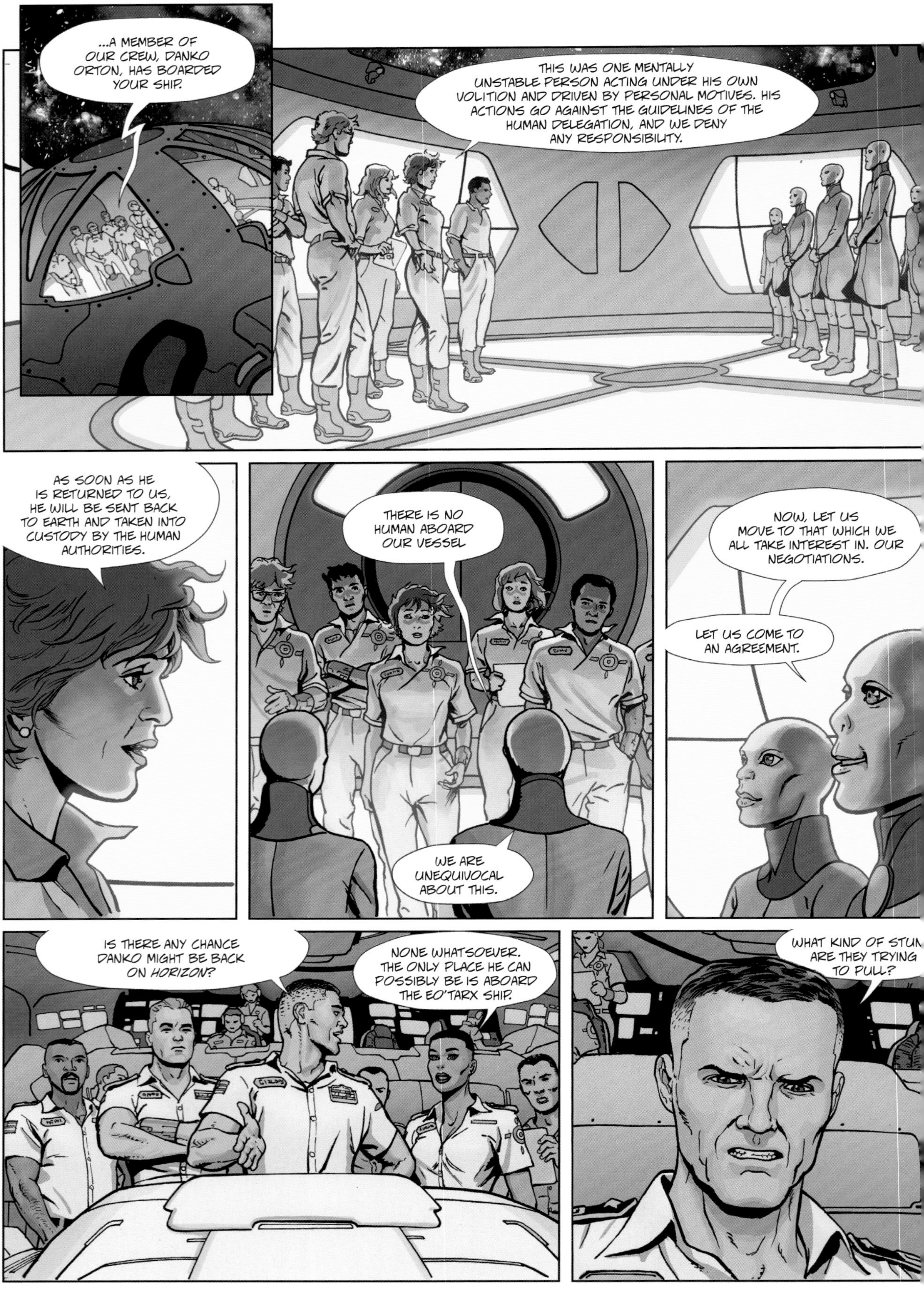
...A MEMBER OF OUR CREW, DANKO ORTON, HAS BOARDED YOUR SHIP.
THIS WAS ONE MENTALLY UNSTABLE PERSON ACTING UNDER HIS OWN VOLITION AND DRIVEN BY PERSONAL MOTIVES. HIS ACTIONS GO AGAINST THE GUIDELINES OF THE HUMAN DELEGATION, AND WE DENY ANY RESPONSIBILITY.
AS SOON AS HE IS RETURNED TO US, HE WILL BE SENT BACK TO EARTH AND TAKEN INTO CUSTODY BY THE HUMAN AUTHORITIES.
THERE IS NO HUMAN ABOARD OUR VESSEL
WE ARE UNEQUIVOCAL ABOUT THIS.
NOW, LET US MOVE TO THAT WHICH WE ALL TAKE INTEREST IN. OUR NEGOTIATIONS.
LET US COME TO AN AGREEMENT.
IS THERE ANY CHANCE DANKO MIGHT BE BACK ON *HORIZON*?
NONE WHATSOEVER. THE ONLY PLACE HE CAN POSSIBLY BE IS ABOARD THE EO'TARX SHIP.
WHAT KIND OF STUN ARE THEY TRYING TO PULL?

THIS JUST GOES TO SHOW THAT WHAT NO'MI TOLD DANKO ABOUT HOW HONEST THE EO'TARX ARE AND ABOUT HOW THEY'RE INCAPABLE OF LYING...

...WAS NOTHING BUT *A BIG FAT LIE.*

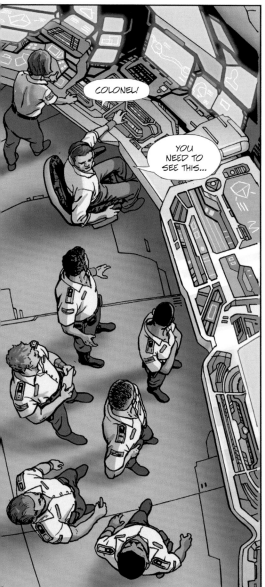

COLONEL!

YOU NEED TO SEE THIS...

I WANT TO CONTINUE THIS MEETING ALONE WITH YOU, ELLIS.

WHY DON'T WE ASK THEM TO TURN OFF THE CAMERAS?

WHAT THE...? WHAT THE HELL DOES THIS MEAN? IS THIS *ROUND TWO?*

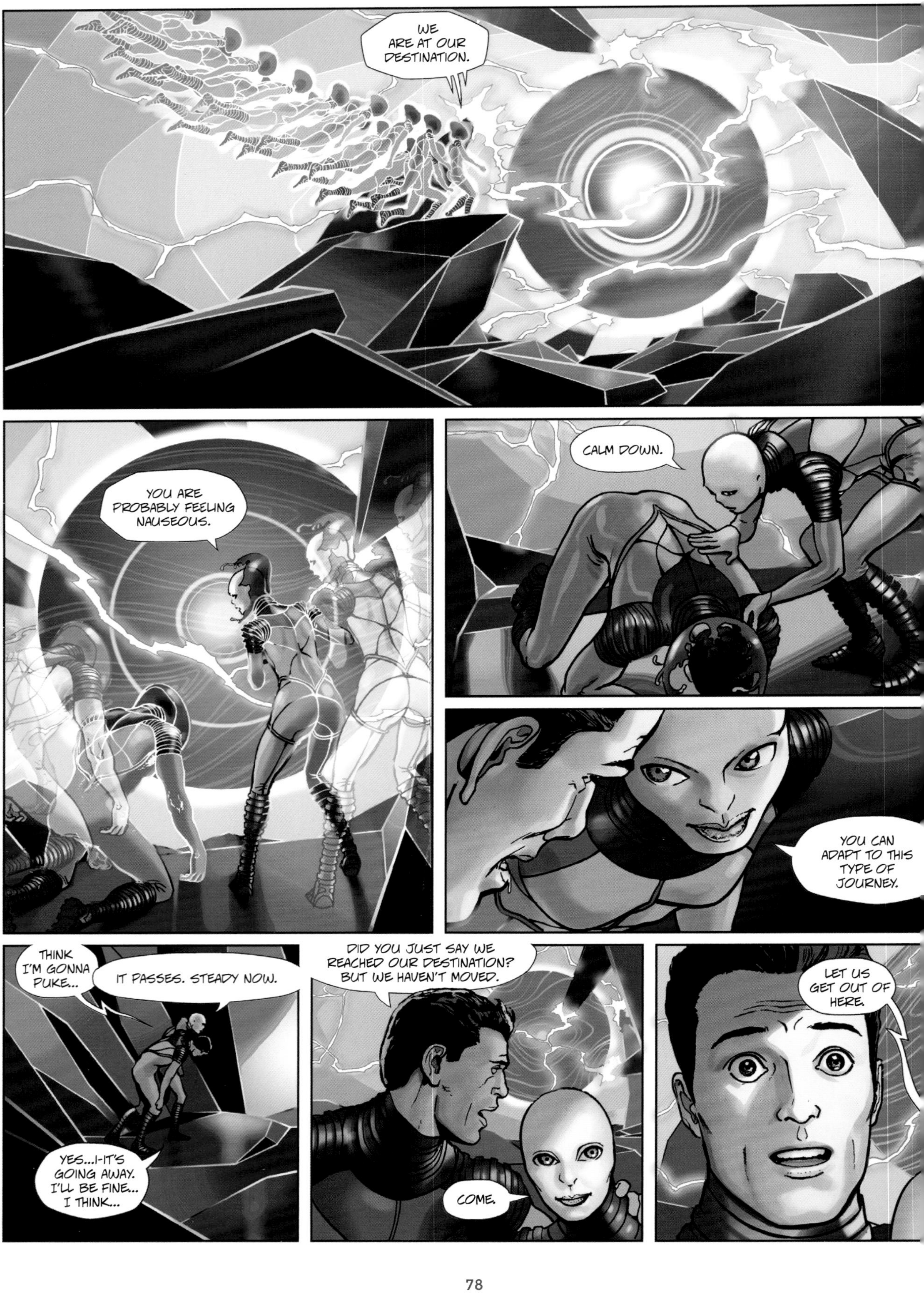

WE ARE AT OUR DESTINATION.
YOU ARE PROBABLY FEELING NAUSEOUS.
CALM DOWN.
YOU CAN ADAPT TO THIS TYPE OF JOURNEY.
THINK I'M GONNA PUKE...
IT PASSES. STEADY NOW.
YES...I-IT'S GOING AWAY. I'LL BE FINE... I THINK...
DID YOU JUST SAY WE REACHED OUR DESTINATION? BUT WE HAVEN'T MOVED.
COME.
LET US GET OUT OF HERE.

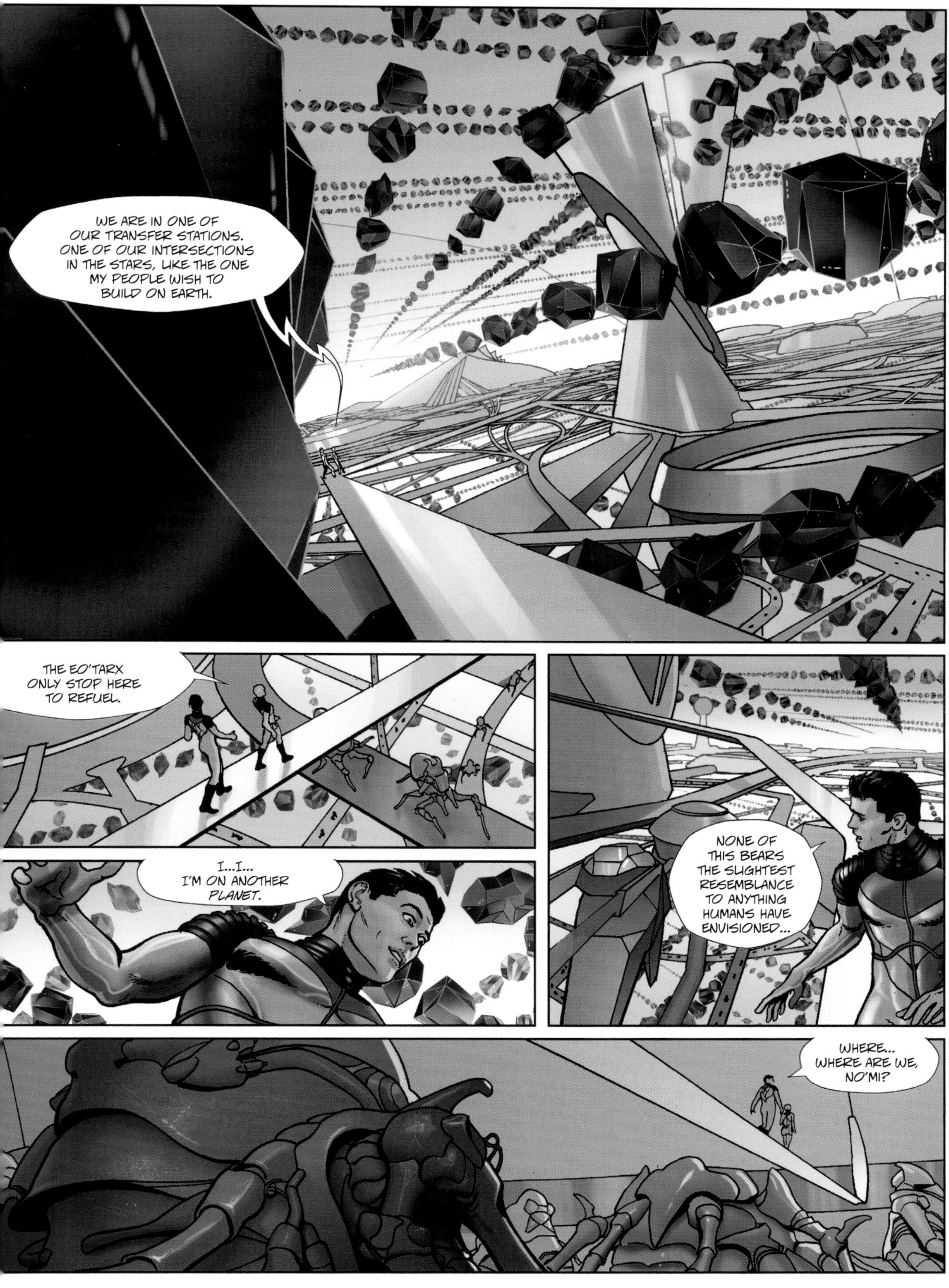
WE ARE IN ONE OF OUR TRANSFER STATIONS. ONE OF OUR INTERSECTIONS IN THE STARS, LIKE THE ONE MY PEOPLE WISH TO BUILD ON EARTH.
THE EO'TARX ONLY STOP HERE TO REFUEL.
I...I... I'M ON ANOTHER PLANET.
NONE OF THIS BEARS THE SLIGHTEST RESEMBLANCE TO ANYTHING HUMANS HAVE ENVISIONED...
WHERE... WHERE ARE WE, NO'MI?

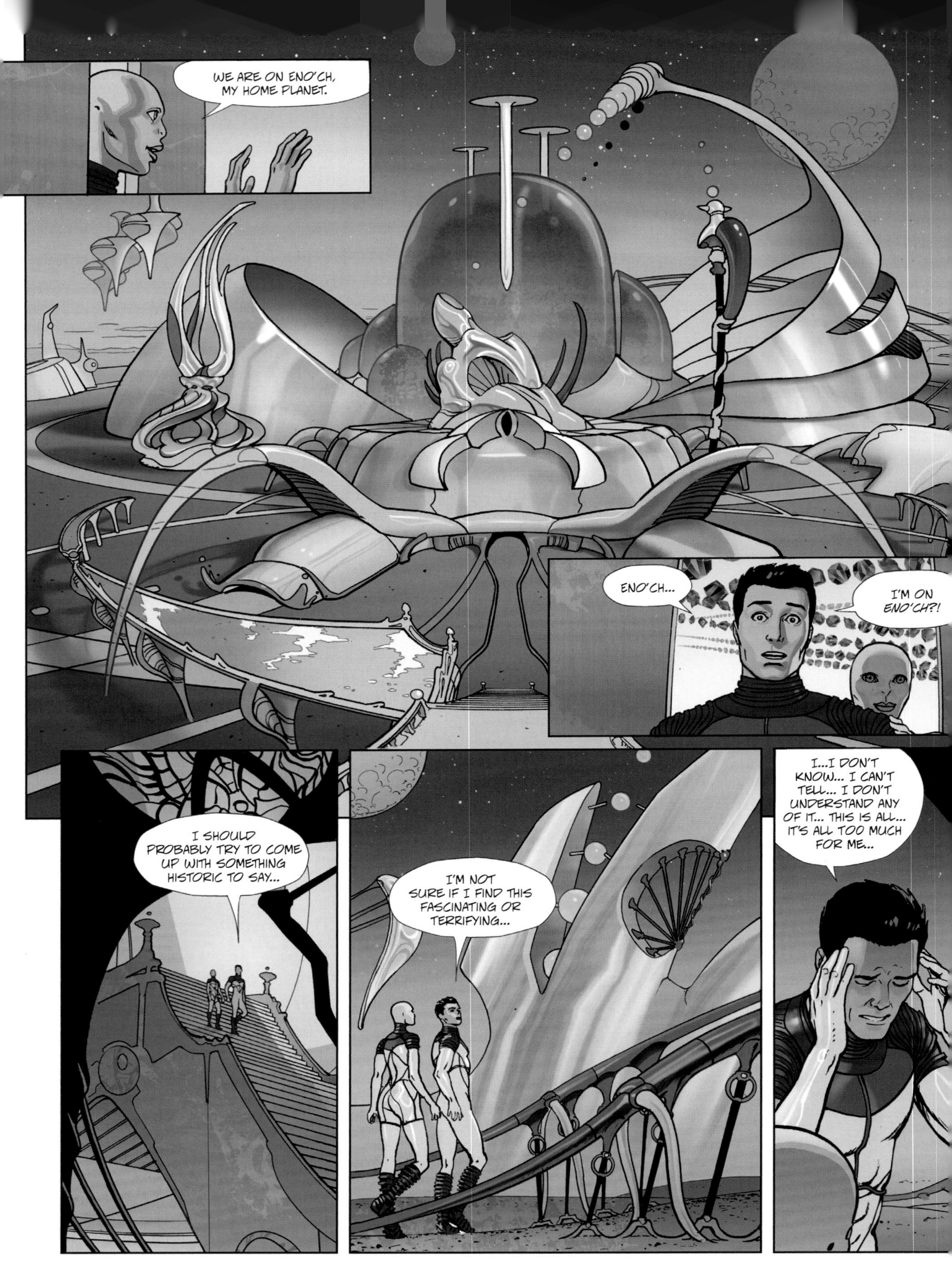
WE ARE ON ENO'CH, MY HOME PLANET.
ENO'CH...
I'M ON ENO'CH?!
I SHOULD PROBABLY TRY TO COME UP WITH SOMETHING HISTORIC TO SAY...
I'M NOT SURE IF I FIND THIS FASCINATING OR TERRIFYING...
I...I DON'T KNOW... I CAN'T TELL... I DON'T UNDERSTAND ANY OF IT... THIS IS ALL... IT'S ALL TOO MUCH FOR ME...

DO NOT BE AFRAID.
I DON'T THINK I'M AFRAID. WHAT I'M FEELING IS UNLIKE ANYTHING I'VE EVER FELT BEFORE...
I'D BE HARD PRESSED TO TELL THE DIFFERENCE BETWEEN A HOUSE AND A VEHICLE...
AND YET THERE SEEMS TO BE A HARMONIOUS LOGIC TO ALL THE COMPLEXITY.
HEY, WHY IS EVERYTHING SO QUIET? NOTHING IS MOVING, IT'S LIKE EVERYTHING HAS BEEN ABANDONED.
THE EO'TARX ARE NOMADS, DUE TO OUR DISCOVERY OF THE QUANTUM CORRIDORS.
ONLY A HUNDRED OR SO OF US LIVE ON ENO'CH, IT IS A PLACE WHERE YOU AND I CAN BE FREE AND HAPPY.
BRUF
WHAT THE HELL IS THAT THING?!

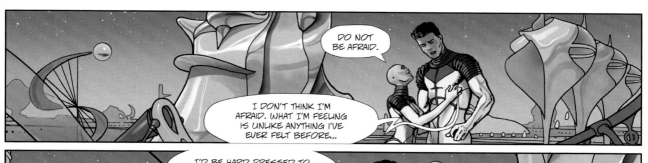

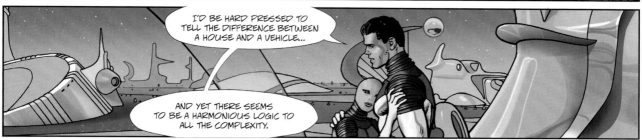

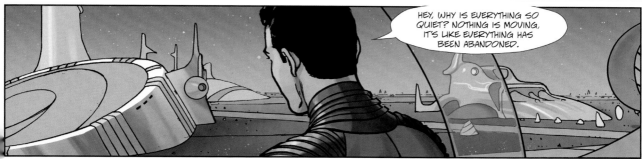

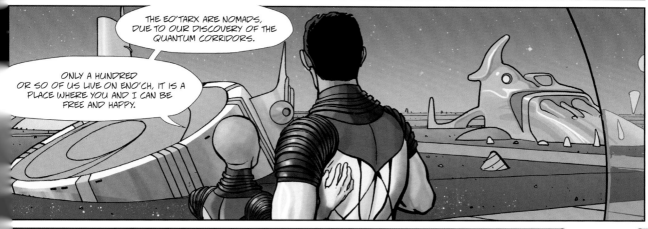

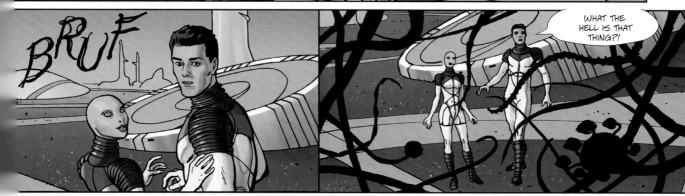

FEAR NOT, DANKO.

THIS IS VO'GT, THE SOLE GUARDIAN OF THIS INTERSECTION OF THE STARS.

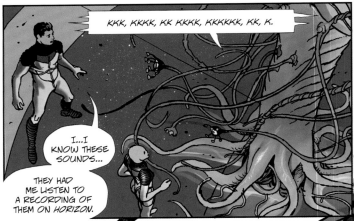

KKK, KKKK, KK KKKK, KKKKKK, KK, K.

I...I KNOW THESE SOUNDS...

THEY HAD ME LISTEN TO A RECORDING OF THEM ON *HORIZON*.

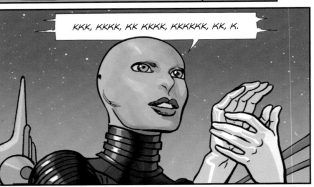

KKK, KKKK, KK KKKK, KKKKKK, KK, K.

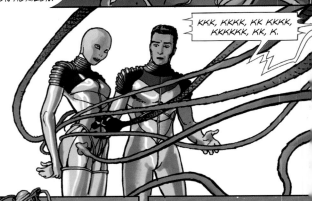

KKK, KKKK, KK KKKK, KKKKKK, KK, K.

HE HAS OTHER THINGS TO SEE TO.

WHY DID IT TOUCH YOU LIKE THAT? WHAT DID IT SAY TO YOU?

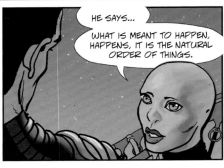

HE SAYS...

WHAT IS MEANT TO HAPPEN, HAPPENS, IT IS THE NATURAL ORDER OF THINGS.

ARE YOU... PREGNANT?

NO'MI?

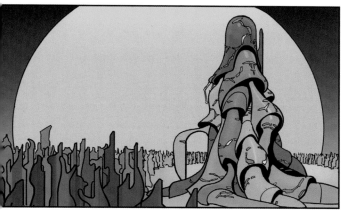

WHY DIDN'T YOU TELL ME?

IT IS COMPLEX... VERY COMPLEX.

I CANNOT SAY I TRULY KNOW MYSELF...

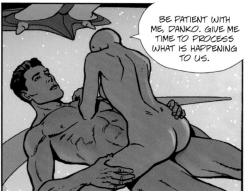

BE PATIENT WITH ME, DANKO. GIVE ME TIME TO PROCESS WHAT IS HAPPENING TO US.

I HAVE SO MUCH TO TELL YOU.

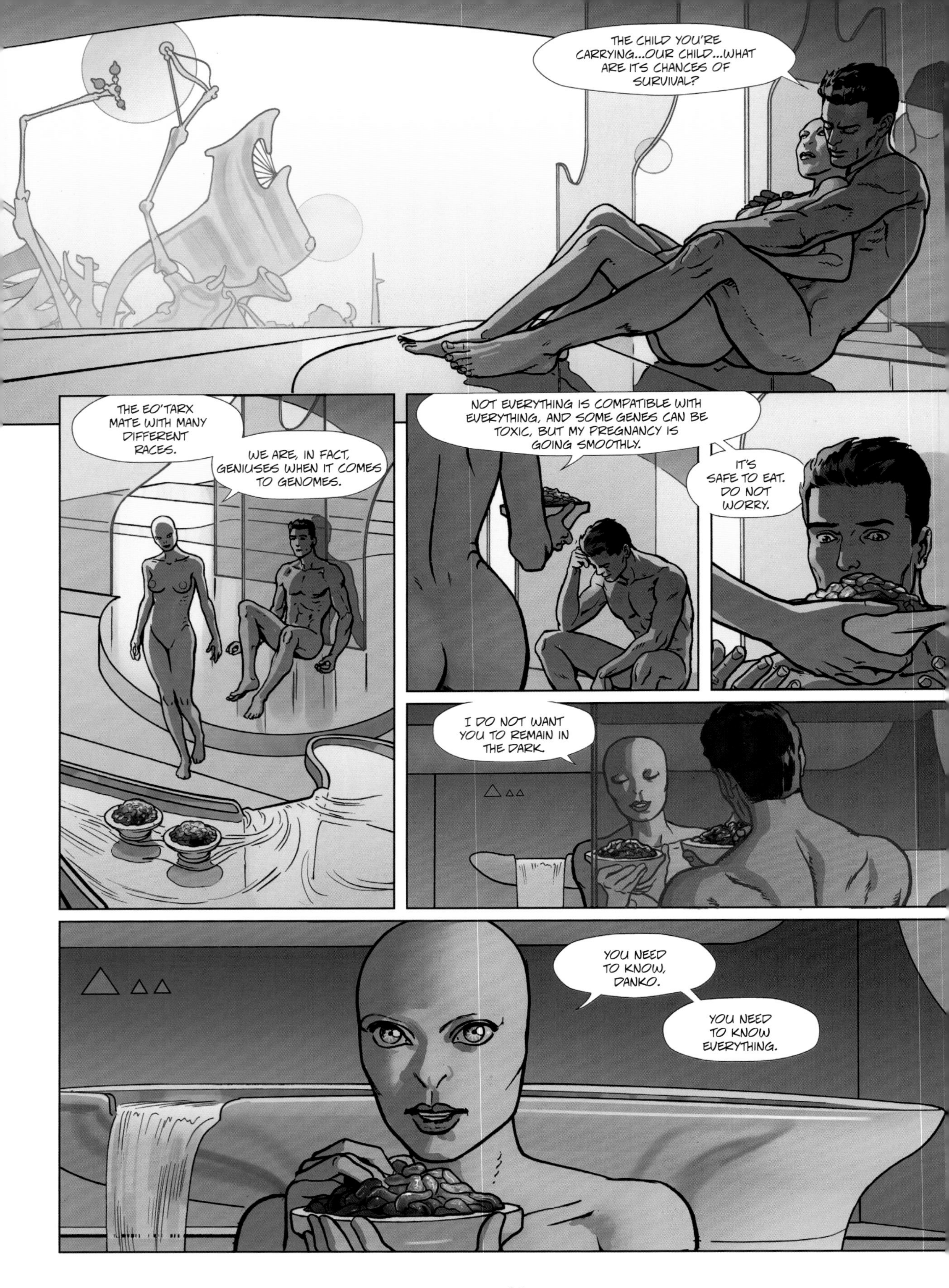

THE CHILD YOU'RE CARRYING...OUR CHILD...WHAT ARE ITS CHANCES OF SURVIVAL?
THE EO'TARX MATE WITH MANY DIFFERENT RACES.
WE ARE, IN FACT, GENIUSES WHEN IT COMES TO GENOMES.
NOT EVERYTHING IS COMPATIBLE WITH EVERYTHING, AND SOME GENES CAN BE TOXIC, BUT MY PREGNANCY IS GOING SMOOTHLY.
IT'S SAFE TO EAT. DO NOT WORRY.
I DO NOT WANT YOU TO REMAIN IN THE DARK.
YOU NEED TO KNOW, DANKO.
YOU NEED TO KNOW EVERYTHING.

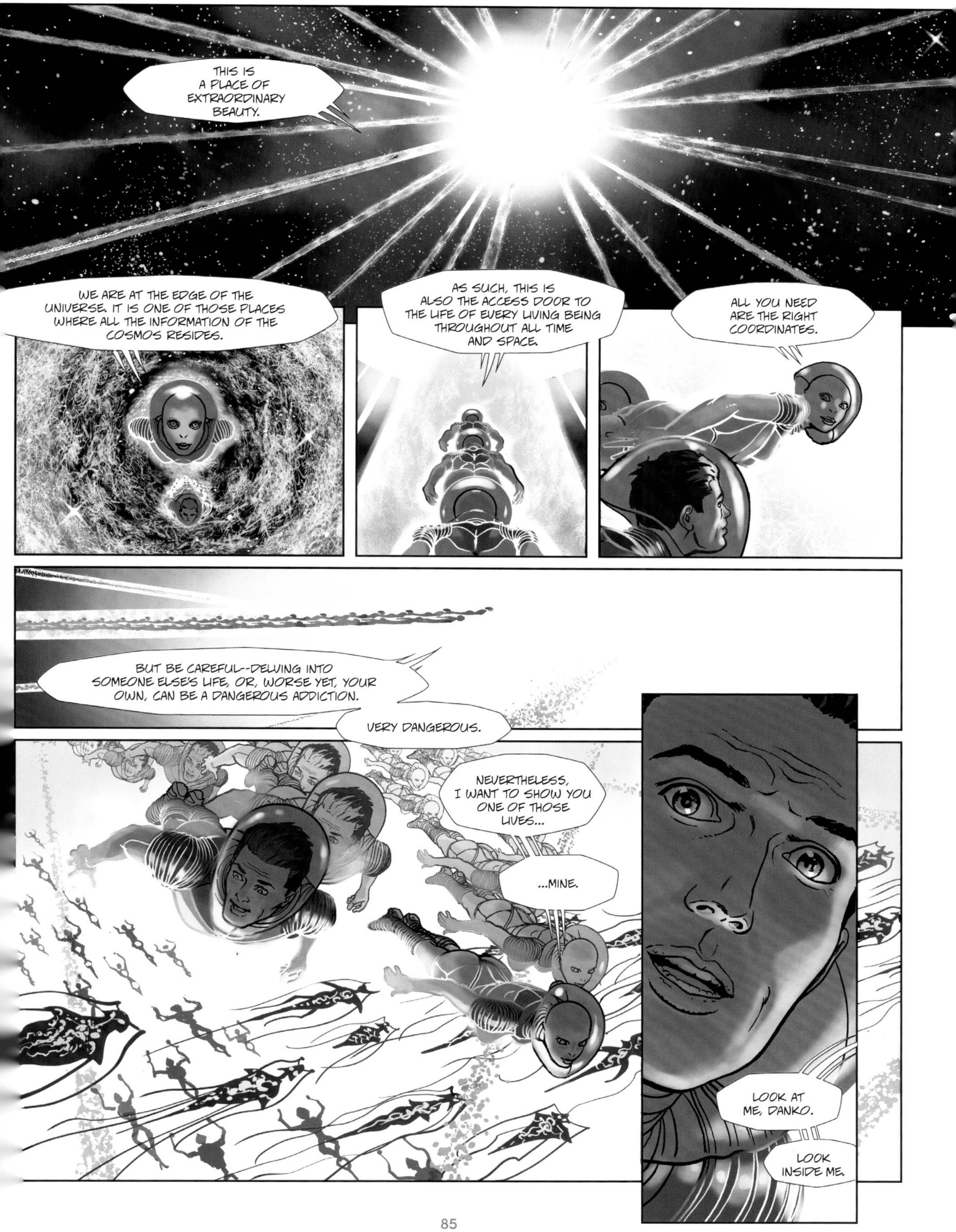
THIS IS A PLACE OF EXTRAORDINARY BEAUTY.
WE ARE AT THE EDGE OF THE UNIVERSE. IT IS ONE OF THOSE PLACES WHERE ALL THE INFORMATION OF THE COSMOS RESIDES.
AS SUCH, THIS IS ALSO THE ACCESS DOOR TO THE LIFE OF EVERY LIVING BEING THROUGHOUT ALL TIME AND SPACE.
ALL YOU NEED ARE THE RIGHT COORDINATES.
BUT BE CAREFUL--DELVING INTO SOMEONE ELSE'S LIFE, OR, WORSE YET, YOUR OWN, CAN BE A DANGEROUS ADDICTION.
VERY DANGEROUS.
NEVERTHELESS, I WANT TO SHOW YOU ONE OF THOSE LIVES...
...MINE.
LOOK AT ME, DANKO.
LOOK INSIDE ME.

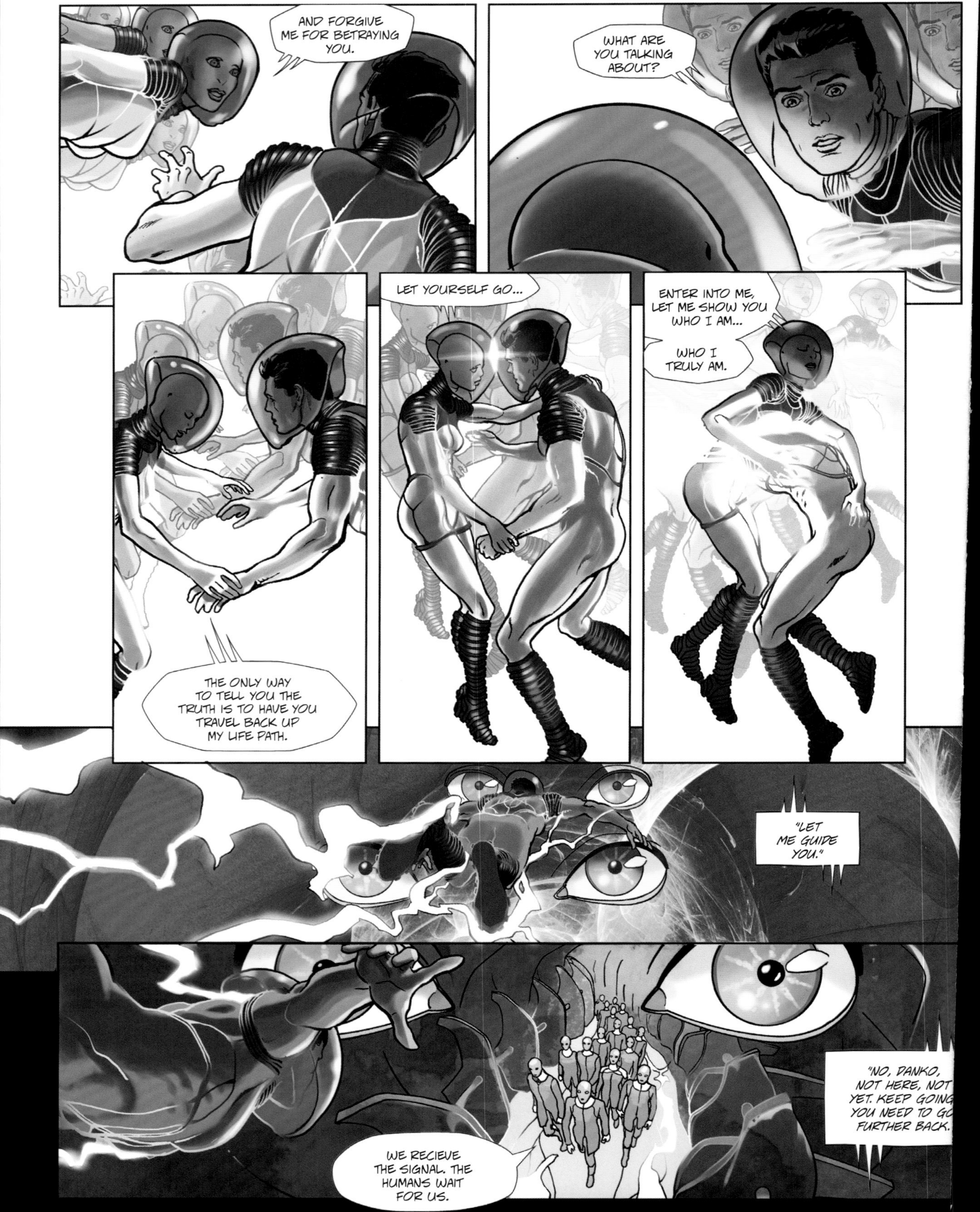
AND FORGIVE ME FOR BETRAYING YOU.
WHAT ARE YOU TALKING ABOUT?
THE ONLY WAY TO TELL YOU THE TRUTH IS TO HAVE YOU TRAVEL BACK UP MY LIFE PATH.
LET YOURSELF GO...
ENTER INTO ME, LET ME SHOW YOU WHO I AM...
WHO I TRULY AM.
"LET ME GUIDE YOU."
"NO, DANKO, NOT HERE, NOT YET. KEEP GOING YOU NEED TO GO FURTHER BACK.
WE RECIEVE THE SIGNAL. THE HUMANS WAIT FOR US.

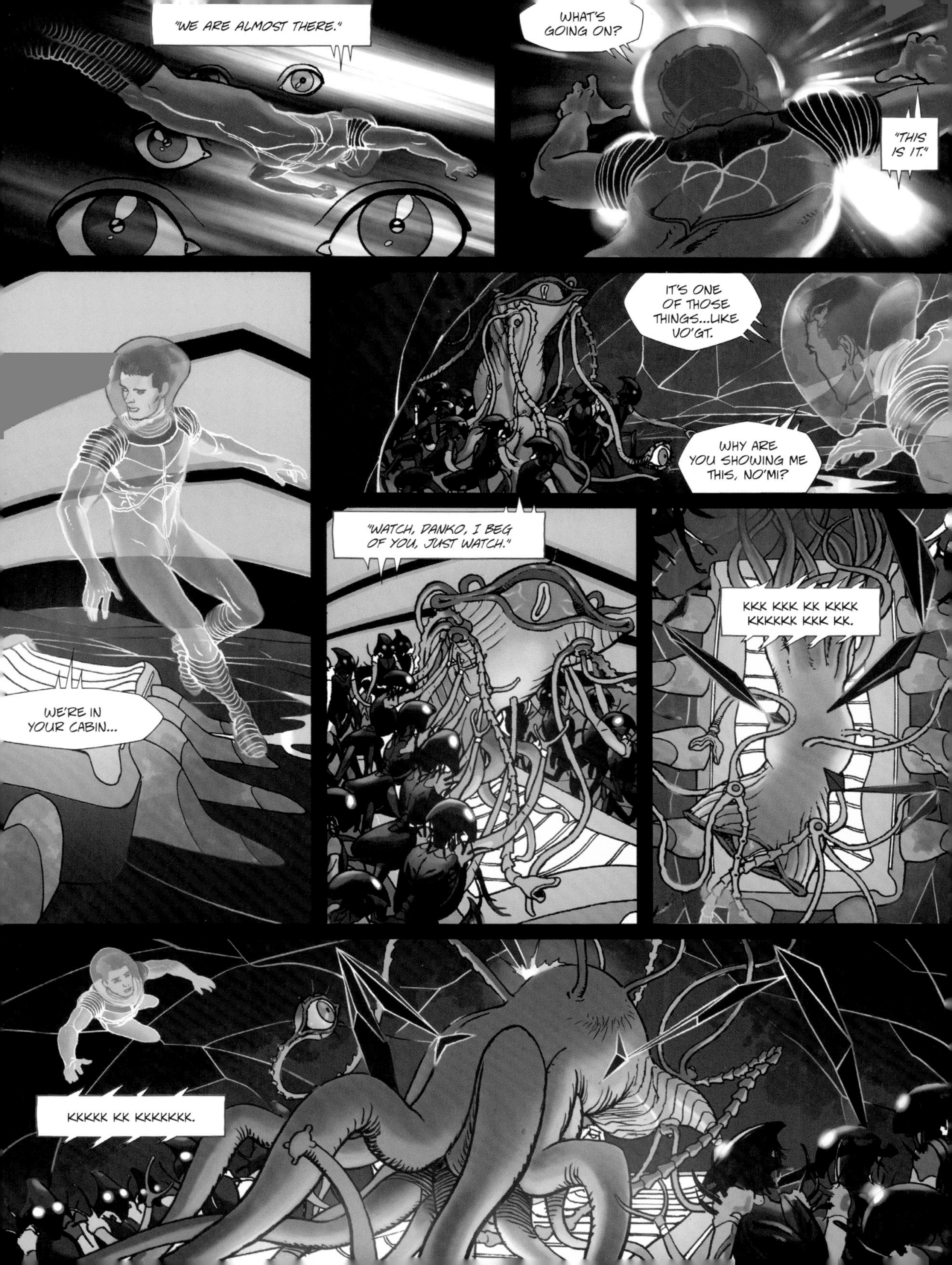
"WE ARE ALMOST THERE."
WHAT'S GOING ON?
"THIS IS IT."
WE'RE IN YOUR CABIN...
IT'S ONE OF THOSE THINGS...LIKE VO'GT.
WHY ARE YOU SHOWING ME THIS, NO'MI?
"WATCH, DANKO, I BEG OF YOU, JUST WATCH."
KKK KKK KK KKKK KKKKKK KKK KK.
KKKKK KK KKKKKKK.

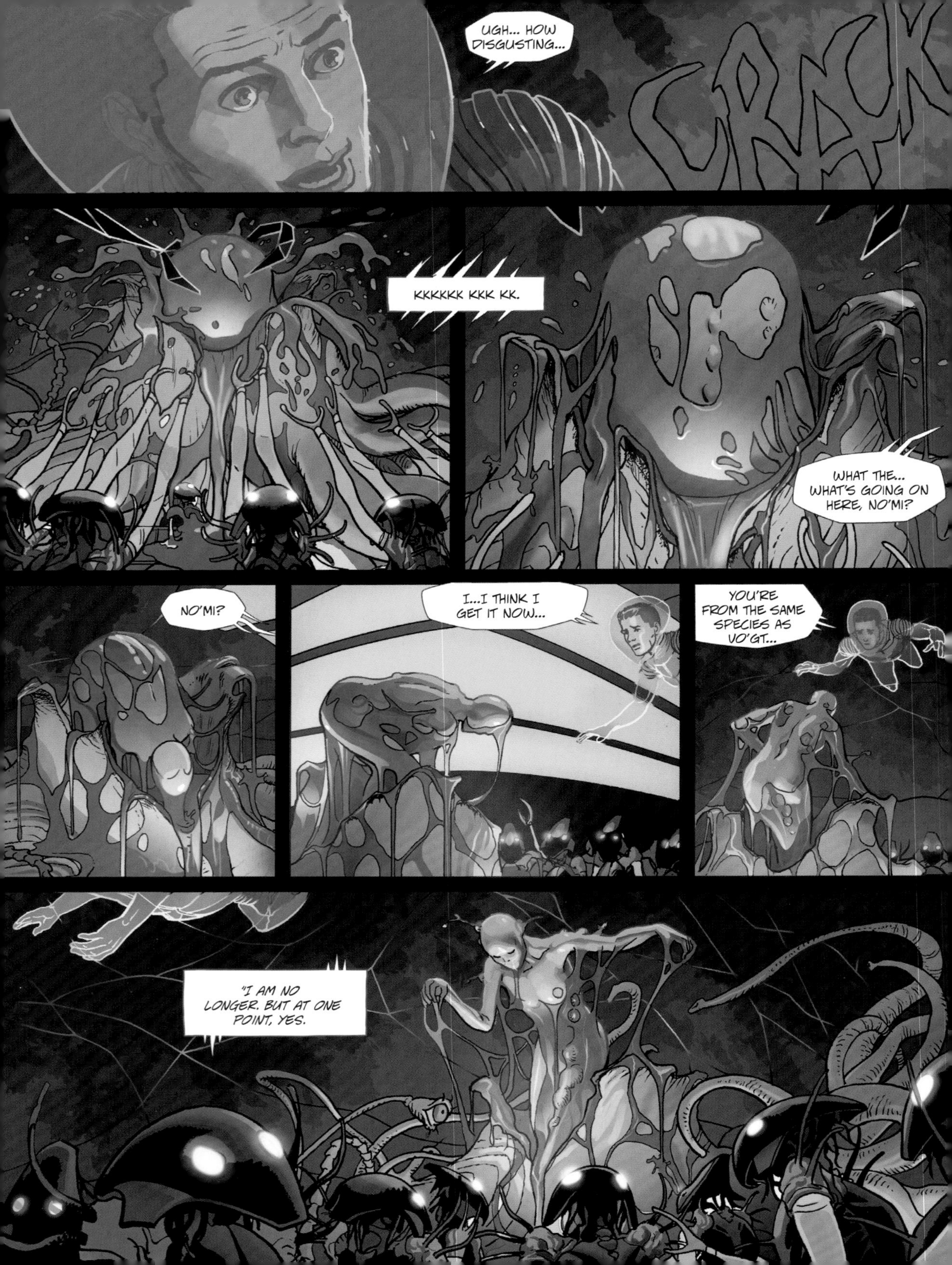
UGH... HOW DISGUSTING...
CRACK
KKKKKK KKK KK.
WHAT THE... WHAT'S GOING ON HERE, NO'MI?
NO'MI?
I...I THINK I GET IT NOW...
YOU'RE FROM THE SAME SPECIES AS VO'GT...
"I AM NO LONGER. BUT AT ONE POINT, YES.

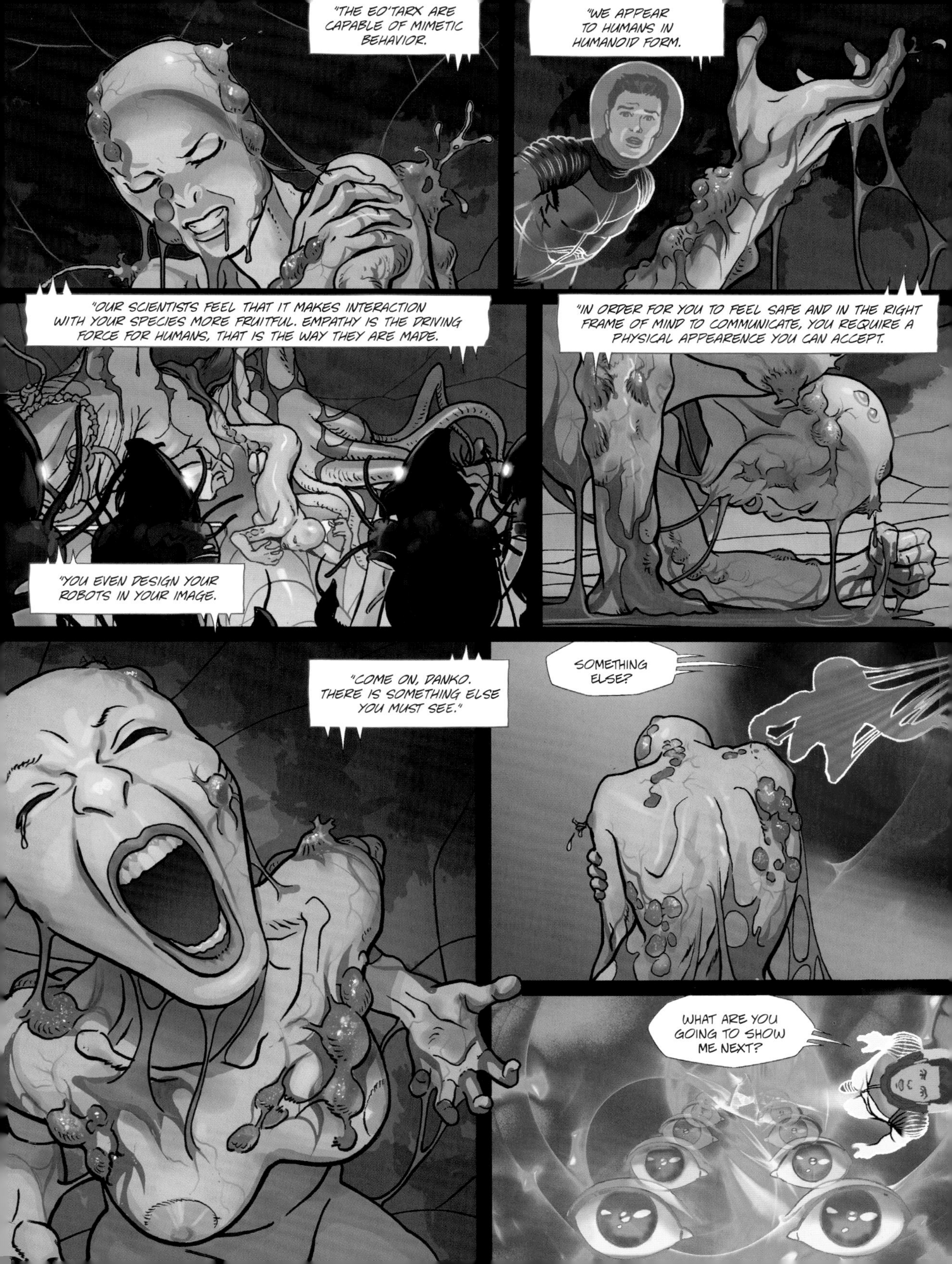
"THE EO'TARX ARE CAPABLE OF MIMETIC BEHAVIOR.
"WE APPEAR TO HUMANS IN HUMANOID FORM.
"OUR SCIENTISTS FEEL THAT IT MAKES INTERACTION WITH YOUR SPECIES MORE FRUITFUL. EMPATHY IS THE DRIVING FORCE FOR HUMANS, THAT IS THE WAY THEY ARE MADE.
"YOU EVEN DESIGN YOUR ROBOTS IN YOUR IMAGE.
"IN ORDER FOR YOU TO FEEL SAFE AND IN THE RIGHT FRAME OF MIND TO COMMUNICATE, YOU REQUIRE A PHYSICAL APPEARENCE YOU CAN ACCEPT.
"COME ON, DANKO. THERE IS SOMETHING ELSE YOU MUST SEE."
SOMETHING ELSE?
WHAT ARE YOU GOING TO SHOW ME NEXT?

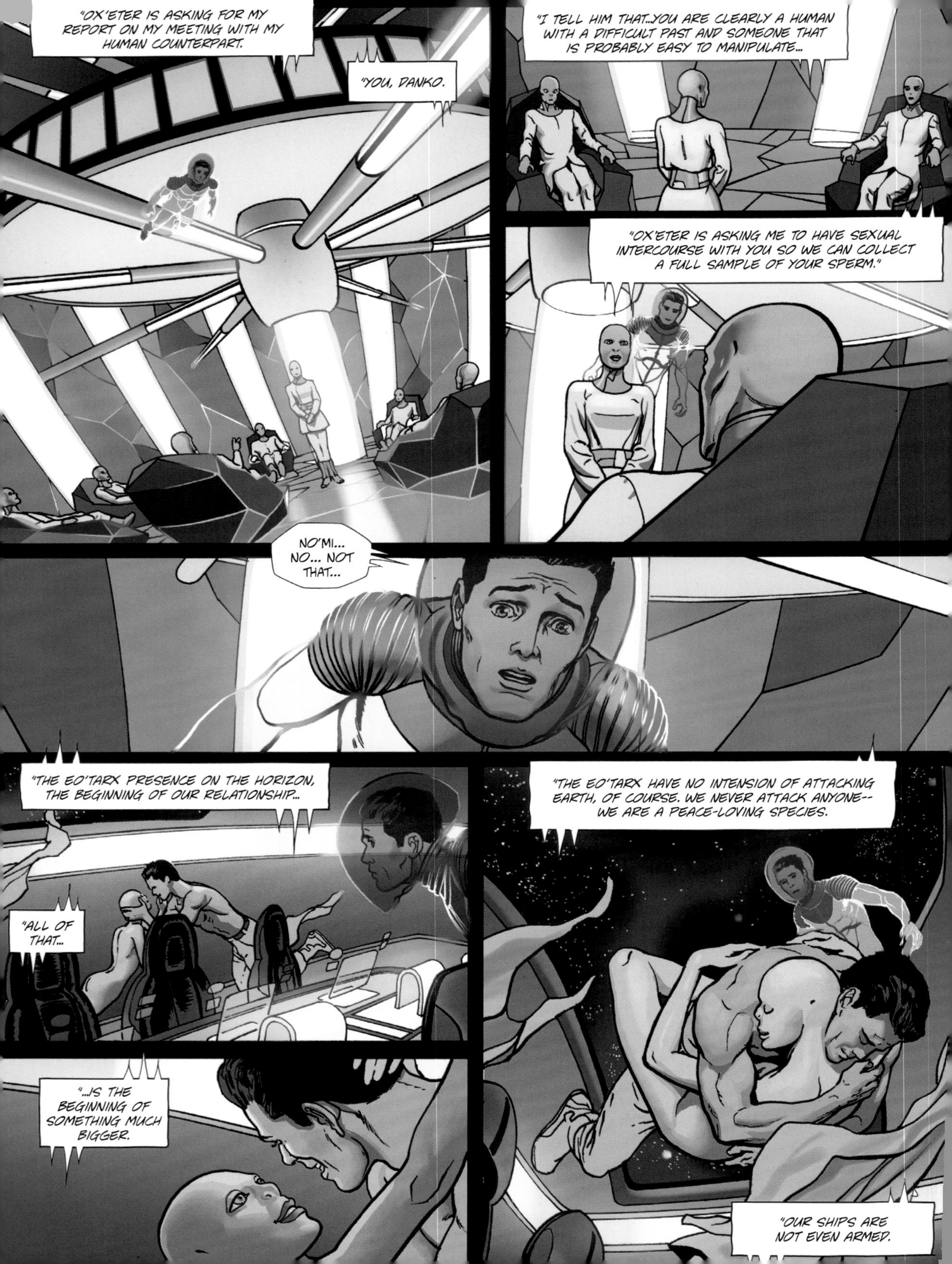
"OX'ETER IS ASKING FOR MY REPORT ON MY MEETING WITH MY HUMAN COUNTERPART.
"YOU, DANKO.
"I TELL HIM THAT...YOU ARE CLEARLY A HUMAN WITH A DIFFICULT PAST AND SOMEONE THAT IS PROBABLY EASY TO MANIPULATE...
"OX'ETER IS ASKING ME TO HAVE SEXUAL INTERCOURSE WITH YOU SO WE CAN COLLECT A FULL SAMPLE OF YOUR SPERM."
NO'MI... NO... NOT THAT...
"THE EO'TARX PRESENCE ON THE HORIZON, THE BEGINNING OF OUR RELATIONSHIP...
"ALL OF THAT...
"...IS THE BEGINNING OF SOMETHING MUCH BIGGER.
"THE EO'TARX HAVE NO INTENSION OF ATTACKING EARTH, OF COURSE. WE NEVER ATTACK ANYONE-- WE ARE A PEACE-LOVING SPECIES.
"OUR SHIPS ARE NOT EVEN ARMED.

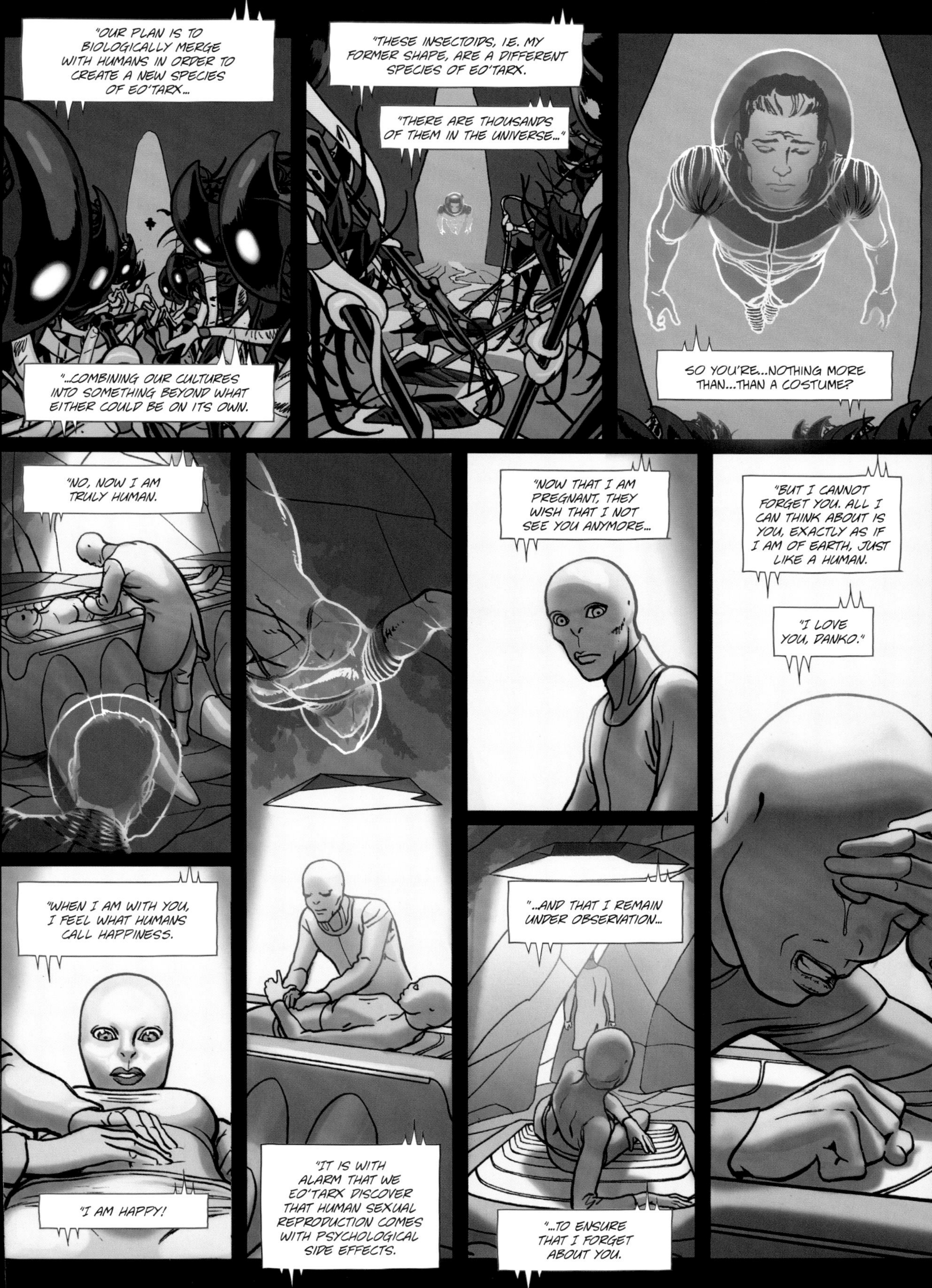
"OUR PLAN IS TO BIOLOGICALLY MERGE WITH HUMANS IN ORDER TO CREATE A NEW SPECIES OF EO'TARX...
"...COMBINING OUR CULTURES INTO SOMETHING BEYOND WHAT EITHER COULD BE ON ITS OWN.
"THESE INSECTOIDS, I.E. MY FORMER SHAPE, ARE A DIFFERENT SPECIES OF EO'TARX.
"THERE ARE THOUSANDS OF THEM IN THE UNIVERSE..."
SO YOU'RE...NOTHING MORE THAN...THAN A COSTUME?
"NO, NOW I AM TRULY HUMAN.
"NOW THAT I AM PREGNANT, THEY WISH THAT I NOT SEE YOU ANYMORE...
"BUT I CANNOT FORGET YOU. ALL I CAN THINK ABOUT IS YOU, EXACTLY AS IF I AM OF EARTH, JUST LIKE A HUMAN.
"I LOVE YOU, DANKO."
"WHEN I AM WITH YOU, I FEEL WHAT HUMANS CALL HAPPINESS.
"I AM HAPPY!
"IT IS WITH ALARM THAT WE EO'TARX DISCOVER THAT HUMAN SEXUAL REPRODUCTION COMES WITH PSYCHOLOGICAL SIDE EFFECTS.
"...AND THAT I REMAIN UNDER OBSERVATION...
"...TO ENSURE THAT I FORGET ABOUT YOU.

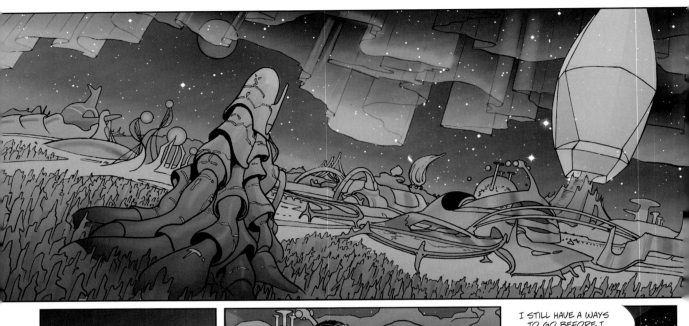

I STILL HAVE A WAYS TO GO BEFORE I CAN ACCEPT WHAT YOU CONFESSED TO ME, TRUE.

YOU CANNOT ACCEPT THIS, CAN YOU?

BUT THAT'S NOT WHY I CAN'T SLEEP...

AND SINCE YOU CAN'T SLEEP EITHER...

...I HAVE A FAVOR TO ASK YOU.

I WANT YOU TO HELP ME ANSWER A QUESTION THAT'S BEEN HAUNTING ME...

DO YOU KNOW HOW TO FIND THE COORDINATES TO EVY'S LIFE PATH?

YOU NEED CLOSURE. I WILL HELP YOU.

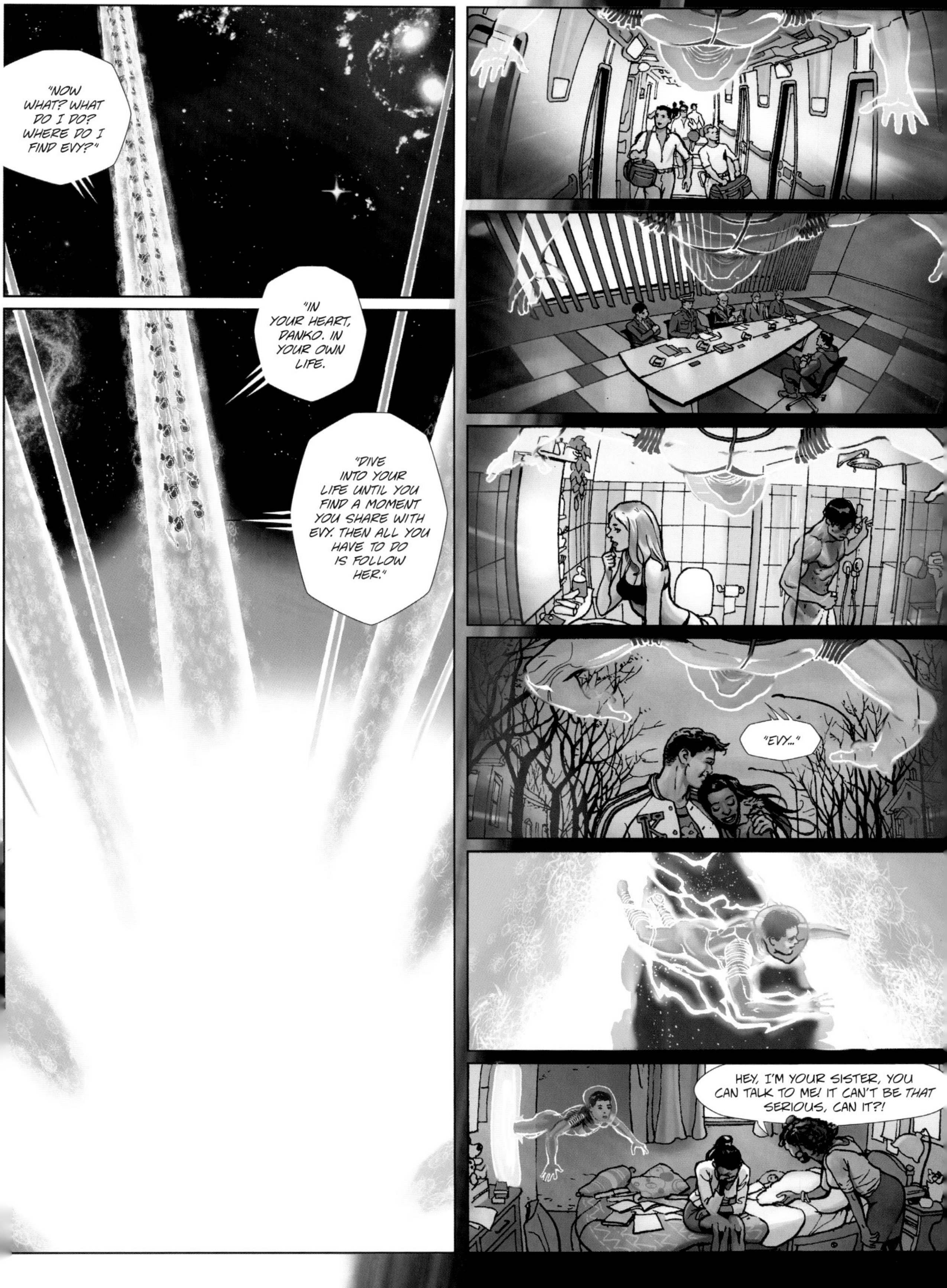
"NOW WHAT? WHAT DO I DO? WHERE DO I FIND EVY?"
"IN YOUR HEART, DANKO. IN YOUR OWN LIFE.
"DIVE INTO YOUR LIFE UNTIL YOU FIND A MOMENT YOU SHARE WITH EVY. THEN ALL YOU HAVE TO DO IS FOLLOW HER."
"EVY..."
HEY, I'M YOUR SISTER, YOU CAN TALK TO ME! IT CAN'T BE THAT SERIOUS, CAN IT?!

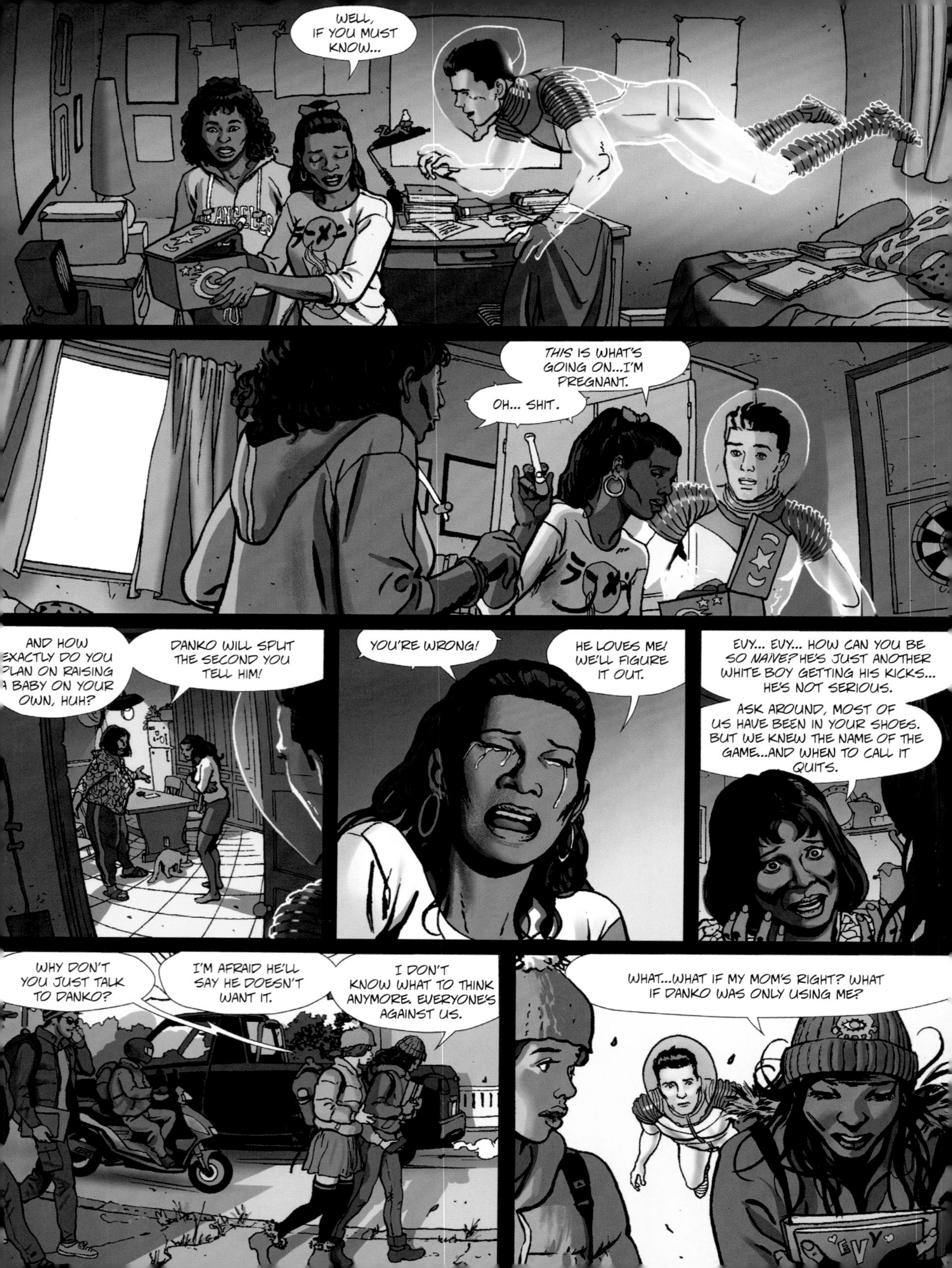

WELL, IF YOU MUST KNOW...
THIS IS WHAT'S GOING ON...I'M PREGNANT.
OH... SHIT.
AND HOW EXACTLY DO YOU PLAN ON RAISING A BABY ON YOUR OWN, HUH?
DANKO WILL SPLIT THE SECOND YOU TELL HIM!
YOU'RE WRONG!
HE LOVES ME! WE'LL FIGURE IT OUT.
EVY... EVY... HOW CAN YOU BE SO NAIVE? HE'S JUST ANOTHER WHITE BOY GETTING HIS KICKS... HE'S NOT SERIOUS.
ASK AROUND, MOST OF US HAVE BEEN IN YOUR SHOES. BUT WE KNEW THE NAME OF THE GAME...AND WHEN TO CALL IT QUITS.
WHY DON'T YOU JUST TALK TO DANKO?
I'M AFRAID HE'LL SAY HE DOESN'T WANT IT.
I DON'T KNOW WHAT TO THINK ANYMORE. EVERYONE'S AGAINST US.
WHAT...WHAT IF MY MOM'S RIGHT? WHAT IF DANKO WAS ONLY USING ME?

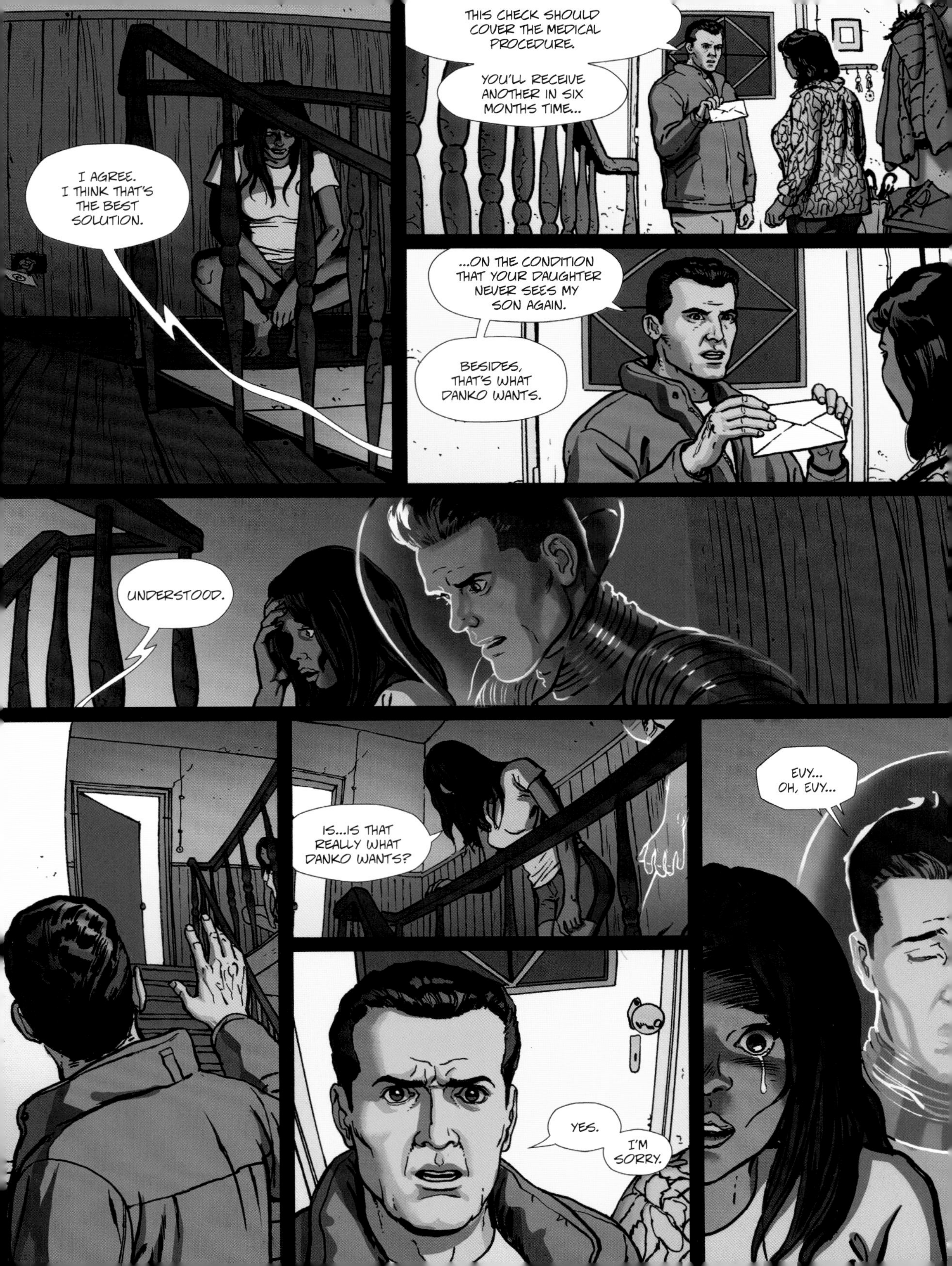
I AGREE. I THINK THAT'S THE BEST SOLUTION.
THIS CHECK SHOULD COVER THE MEDICAL PROCEDURE.
YOU'LL RECEIVE ANOTHER IN SIX MONTHS TIME...
...ON THE CONDITION THAT YOUR DAUGHTER NEVER SEES MY SON AGAIN.
BESIDES, THAT'S WHAT DANKO WANTS.
UNDERSTOOD.
IS...IS THAT REALLY WHAT DANKO WANTS?
EUY... OH, EUY...
YES.
I'M SORRY.

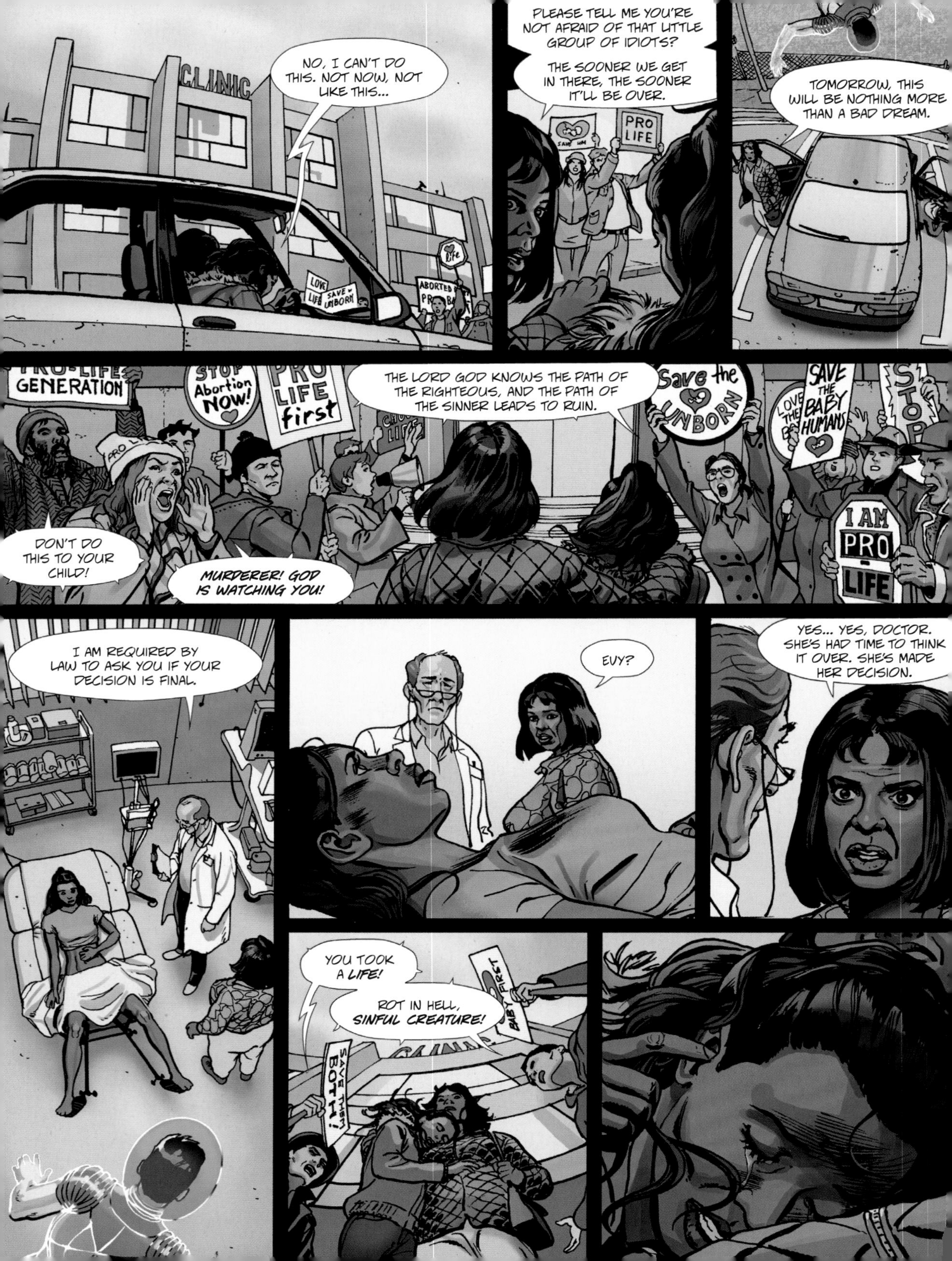

CLINIC
NO, I CAN'T DO THIS. NOT NOW, NOT LIKE THIS...
LOVE LIFE
SAVE the UNBORN
ABORTED
PLEASE TELL ME YOU'RE NOT AFRAID OF THAT LITTLE GROUP OF IDIOTS?
THE SOONER WE GET IN THERE, THE SOONER IT'LL BE OVER.
PRO LIFE
TOMORROW, THIS WILL BE NOTHING MORE THAN A BAD DREAM.
PRO-LIFE GENERATION
STOP Abortion NOW!
PRO LIFE first
THE LORD GOD KNOWS THE PATH OF THE RIGHTEOUS, AND THE PATH OF THE SINNER LEADS TO RUIN.
Save the UNBORN
SAVE THE BABY HUMANS
STOP
I AM PRO LIFE
DON'T DO THIS TO YOUR CHILD!
MURDERER! GOD IS WATCHING YOU!
I AM REQUIRED BY LAW TO ASK YOU IF YOUR DECISION IS FINAL.
EVY?
YES... YES, DOCTOR. SHE'S HAD TIME TO THINK IT OVER. SHE'S MADE HER DECISION.
YOU TOOK A LIFE!
ROT IN HELL, SINFUL CREATURE!
BABY FIRST
SAVE THEM BOTH!

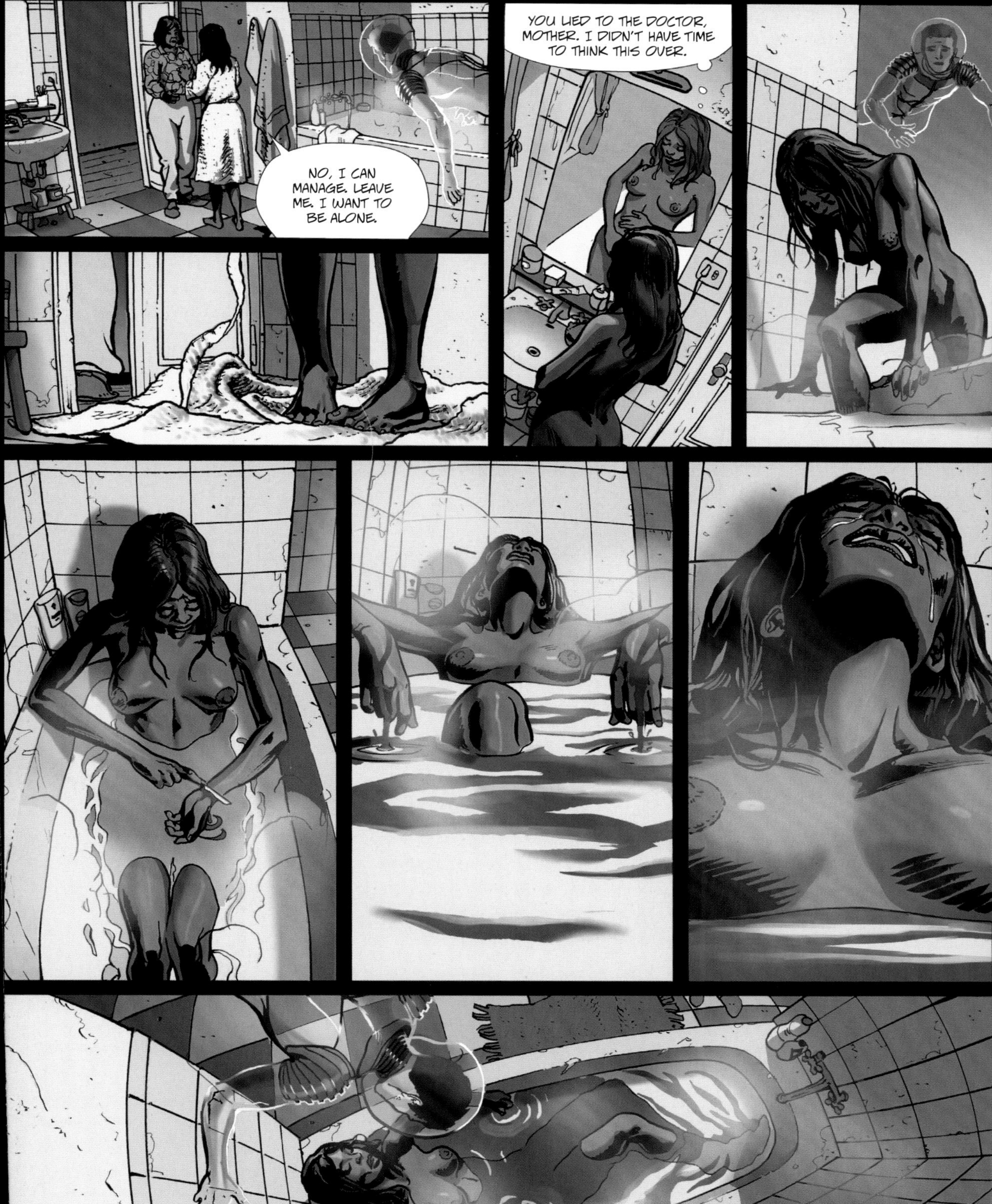
NO, I CAN MANAGE. LEAVE ME. I WANT TO BE ALONE.
YOU LIED TO THE DOCTOR, MOTHER. I DIDN'T HAVE TIME TO THINK THIS OVER.
"EVY..."

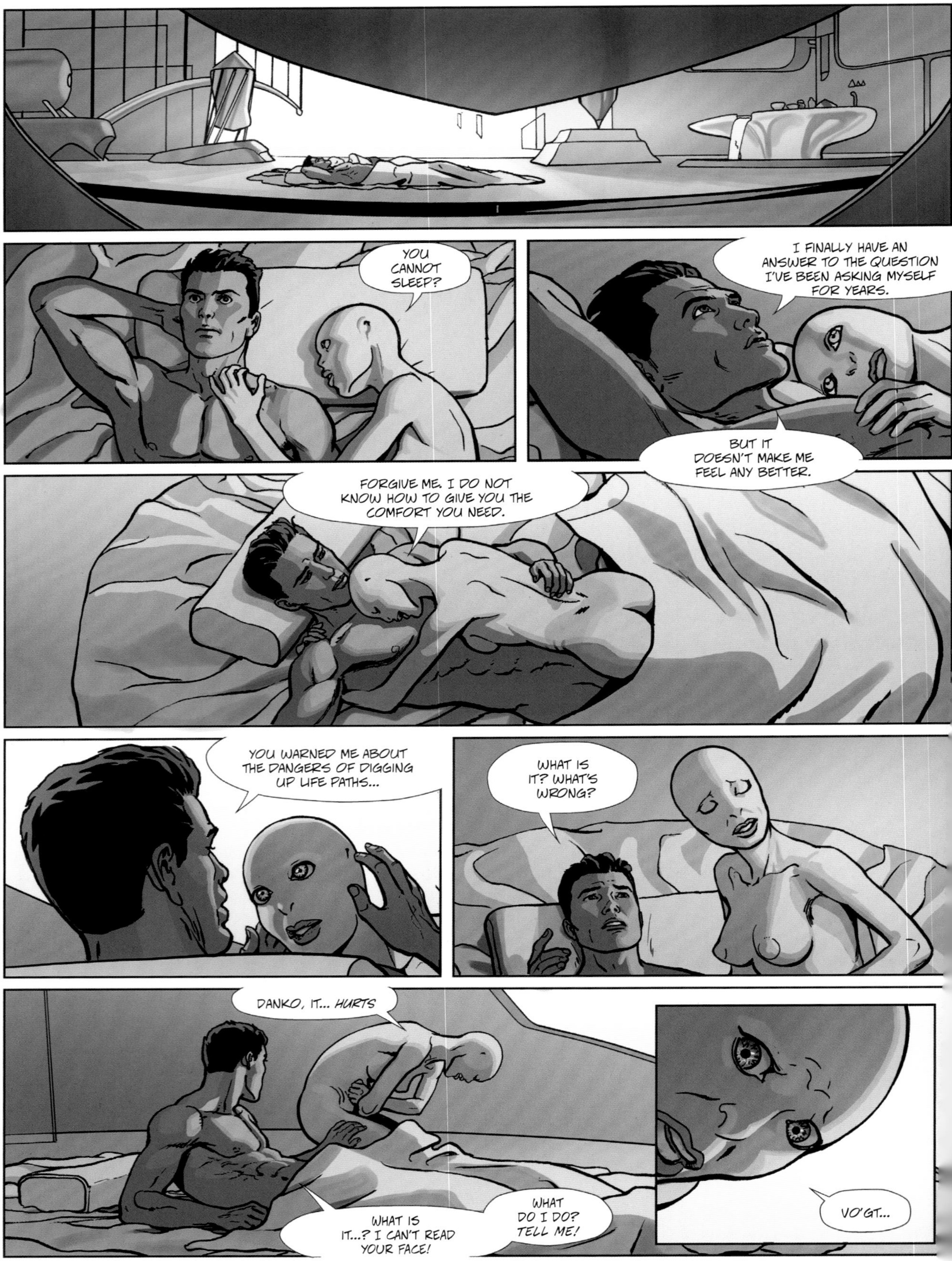
YOU CANNOT SLEEP?
I FINALLY HAVE AN ANSWER TO THE QUESTION I'VE BEEN ASKING MYSELF FOR YEARS.
BUT IT DOESN'T MAKE ME FEEL ANY BETTER.
FORGIVE ME. I DO NOT KNOW HOW TO GIVE YOU THE COMFORT YOU NEED.
YOU WARNED ME ABOUT THE DANGERS OF DIGGING UP LIFE PATHS...
WHAT IS IT? WHAT'S WRONG?
DANKO, IT... *HURTS*
WHAT IS IT...? I CAN'T READ YOUR FACE!
WHAT DO I DO? *TELL ME!*
VO'GT...

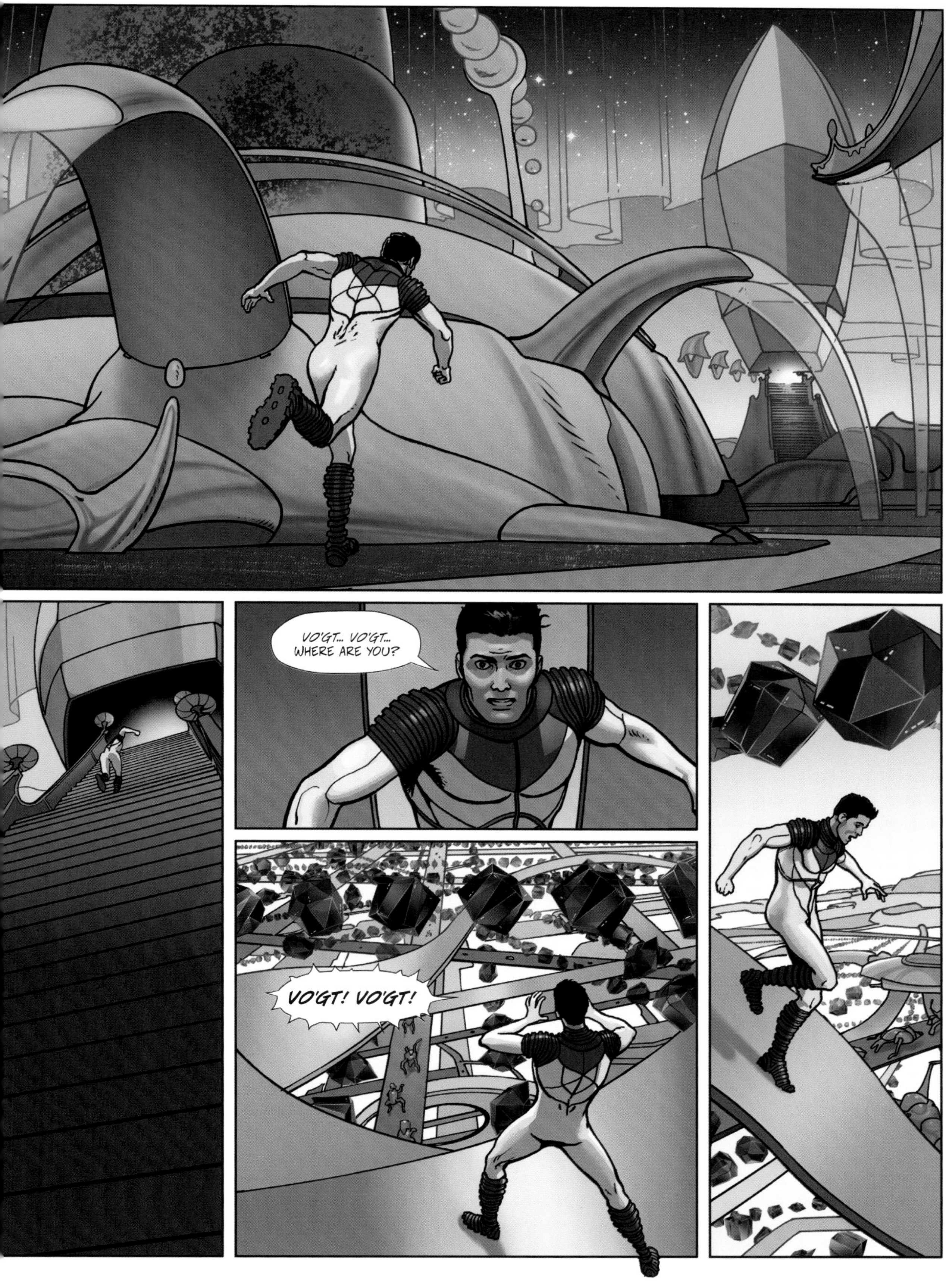
VO'GT... VO'GT...
WHERE ARE YOU?
VO'GT! VO'GT!

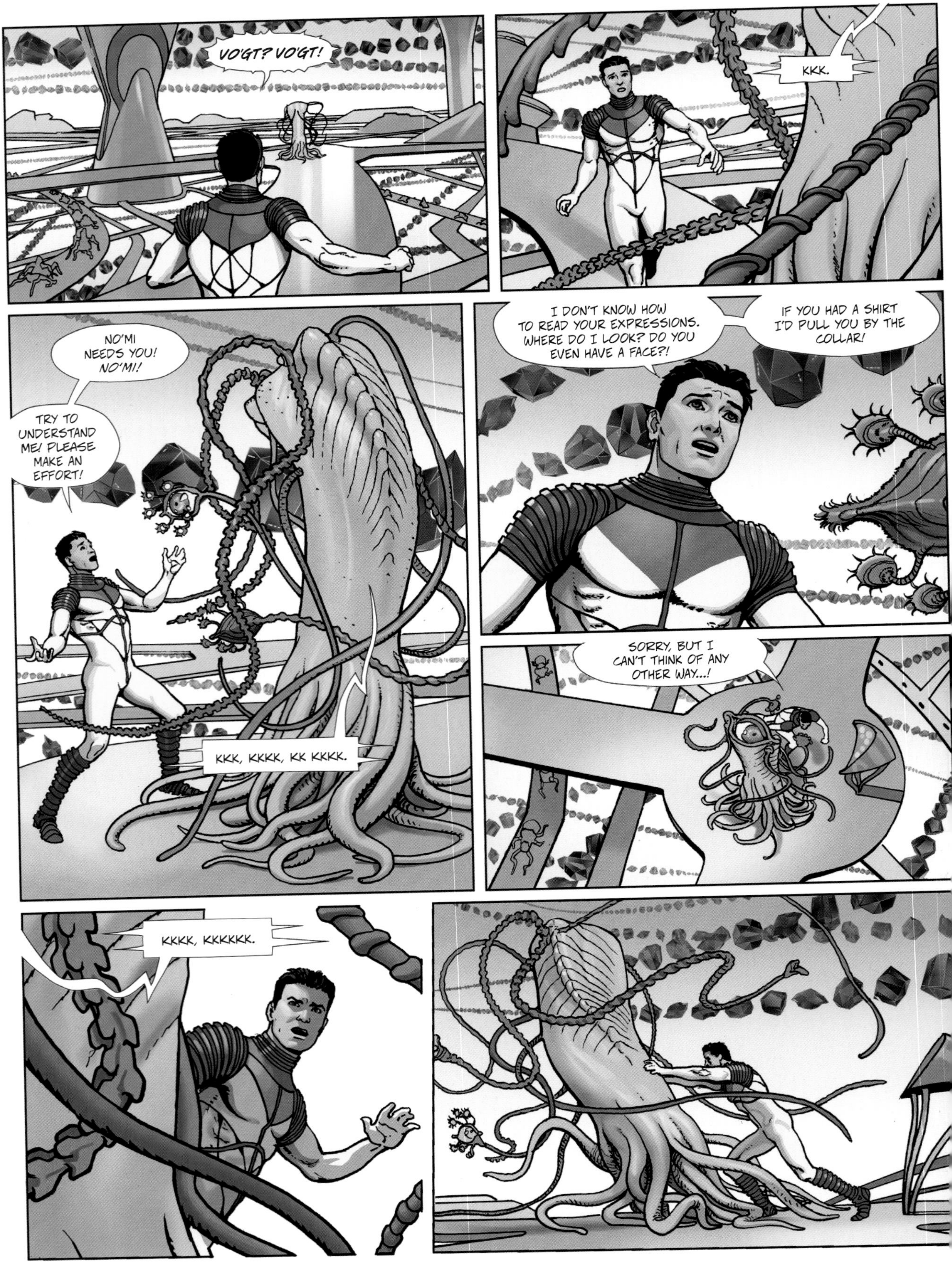
VO'GT? VO'GT!
KKK.
NO'MI NEEDS YOU! NO'MI!
TRY TO UNDERSTAND ME! PLEASE MAKE AN EFFORT!
KKK, KKKK, KK KKKK.
I DON'T KNOW HOW TO READ YOUR EXPRESSIONS. WHERE DO I LOOK? DO YOU EVEN HAVE A FACE?!
IF YOU HAD A SHIRT I'D PULL YOU BY THE COLLAR!
SORRY, BUT I CAN'T THINK OF ANY OTHER WAY...!
KKKK, KKKKKK.

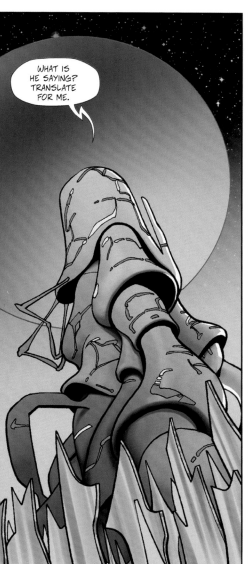

WHAT IS HE SAYING? TRANSLATE FOR ME.

HE IS NOT SAYING ANYTHING. BE PATIENT.

WHAT IS HE SHOWING US?

WHAT IS INSIDE MY BODY.

THE CHILD... IS TOO BIG FOR ME TO SURIVIVE GIVING BIRTH.

WH... WHAT?!

VO'GT IS UNABLE TO PERFORM THE REQUIRED MEDICAL INTERVENTION. HE IS LOOKING AT A MUTATION HE IS NOT FAMILIAR WITH.

AND MOST OF ALL...

HE DOES NOT SEE THE POINT, BECAUSE AS YOU KNOW, WHAT IS MEANT TO HAPPEN, HAPPENS.

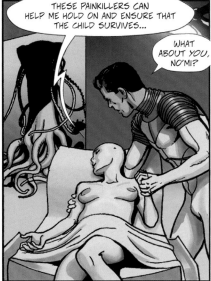

THESE PAINKILLERS CAN HELP ME HOLD ON AND ENSURE THAT THE CHILD SURVIVES...

WHAT ABOUT YOU, NO'MI?

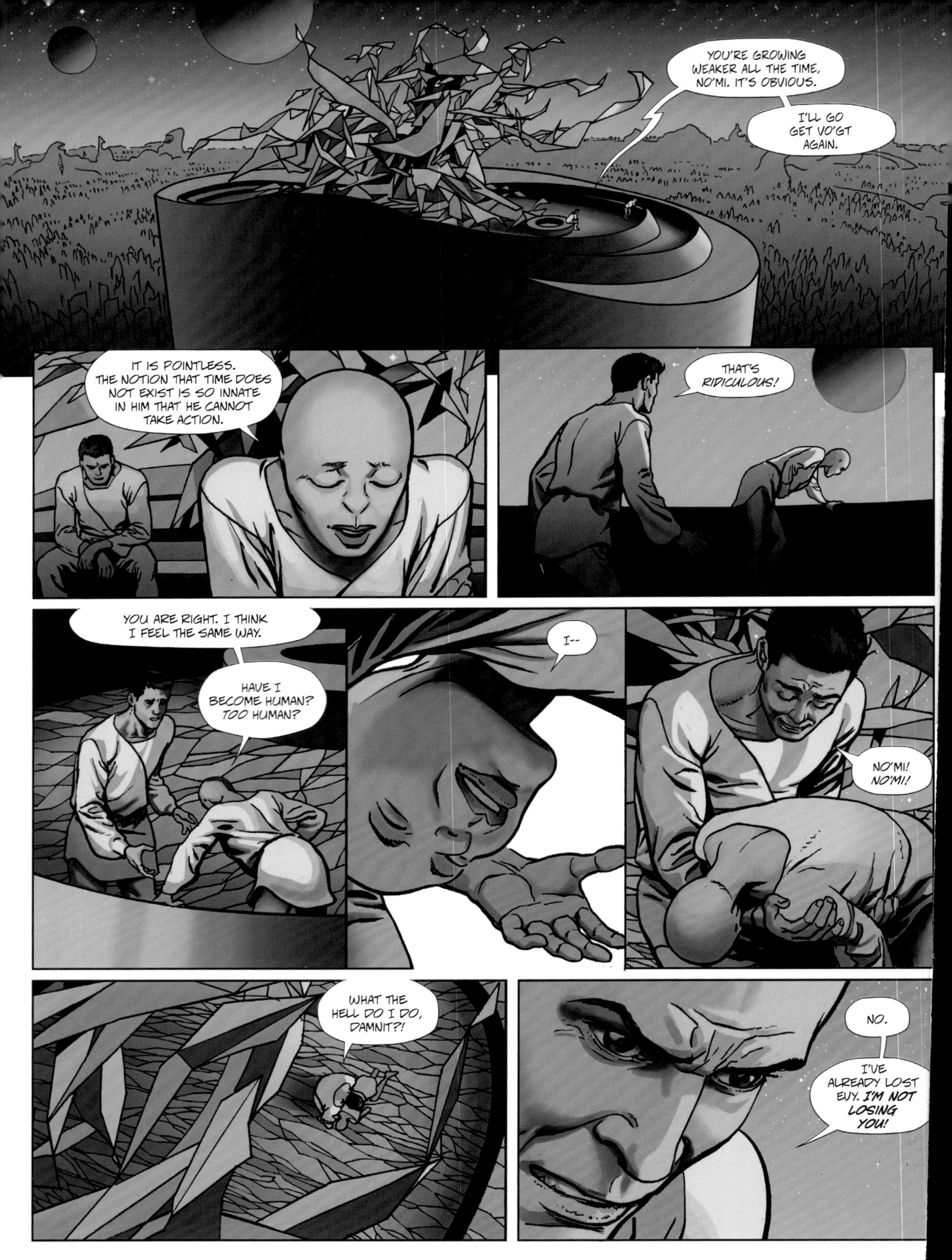

YOU'RE GROWING WEAKER ALL THE TIME, NO'MI. IT'S OBVIOUS.
I'LL GO GET VO'GT AGAIN.
IT IS POINTLESS. THE NOTION THAT TIME DOES NOT EXIST IS SO INNATE IN HIM THAT HE CANNOT TAKE ACTION.
THAT'S *RIDICULOUS!*
YOU ARE RIGHT. I THINK I FEEL THE SAME WAY.
HAVE I BECOME HUMAN? *TOO* HUMAN?
I--
NO'MI! *NO'MI!*
WHAT THE HELL DO I DO, DAMNIT?!
NO.
I'VE ALREADY LOST EVY. ***I'M NOT LOSING YOU!***

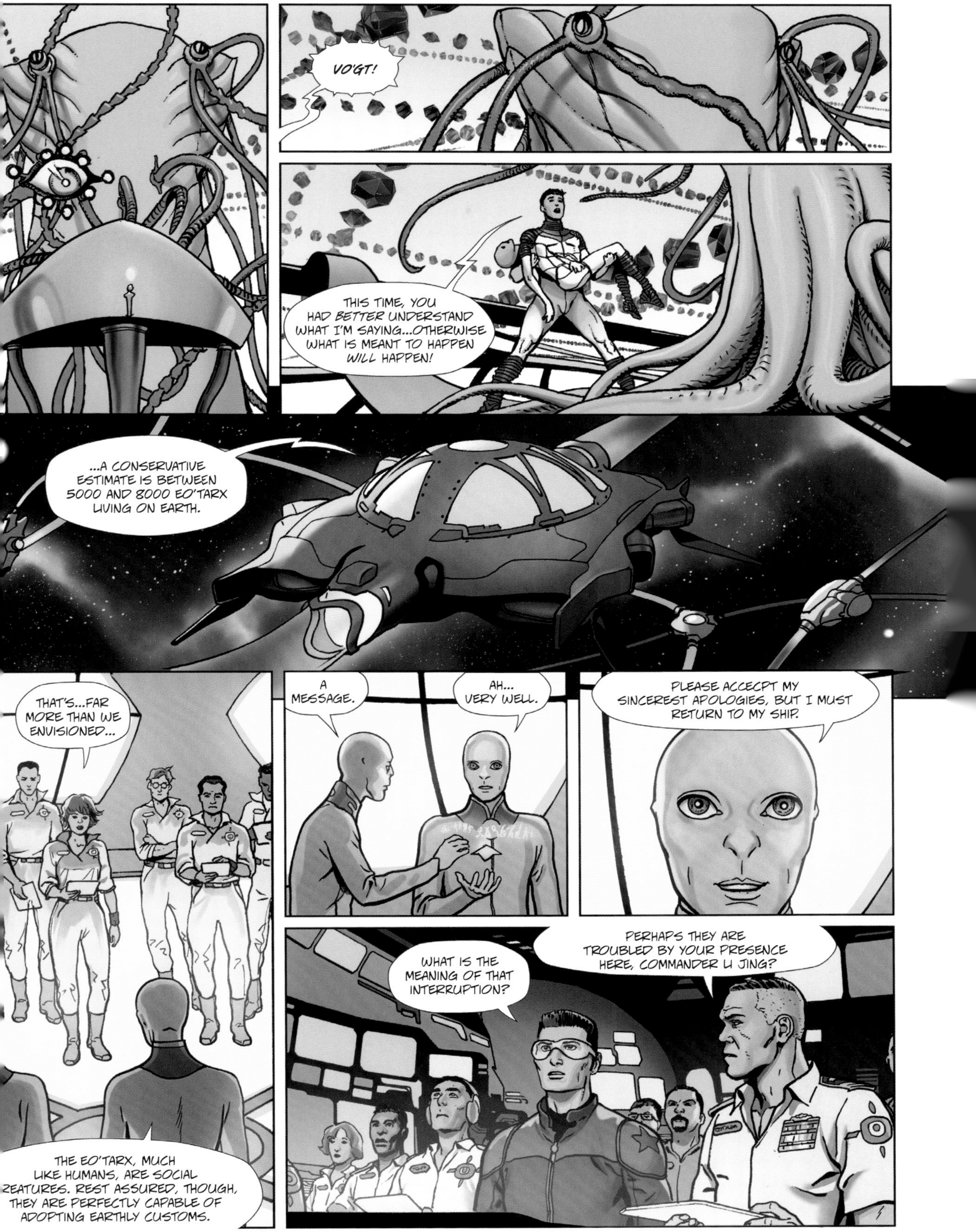
VO'GT!
THIS TIME, YOU HAD *BETTER* UNDERSTAND WHAT I'M SAYING...OTHERWISE WHAT IS MEANT TO HAPPEN *WILL* HAPPEN!
...A CONSERVATIVE ESTIMATE IS BETWEEN 5000 AND 8000 EO'TARX LIVING ON EARTH.
THAT'S...FAR MORE THAN WE ENVISIONED...
THE EO'TARX, MUCH LIKE HUMANS, ARE SOCIAL CREATURES. REST ASSURED, THOUGH, THEY ARE PERFECTLY CAPABLE OF ADOPTING EARTHLY CUSTOMS.
A MESSAGE.
AH... VERY WELL.
PLEASE ACCECPT MY SINCEREST APOLOGIES, BUT I MUST RETURN TO MY SHIP.
WHAT IS THE MEANING OF THAT INTERRUPTION?
PERHAPS THEY ARE TROUBLED BY YOUR PRESENCE HERE, COMMANDER LI JING?

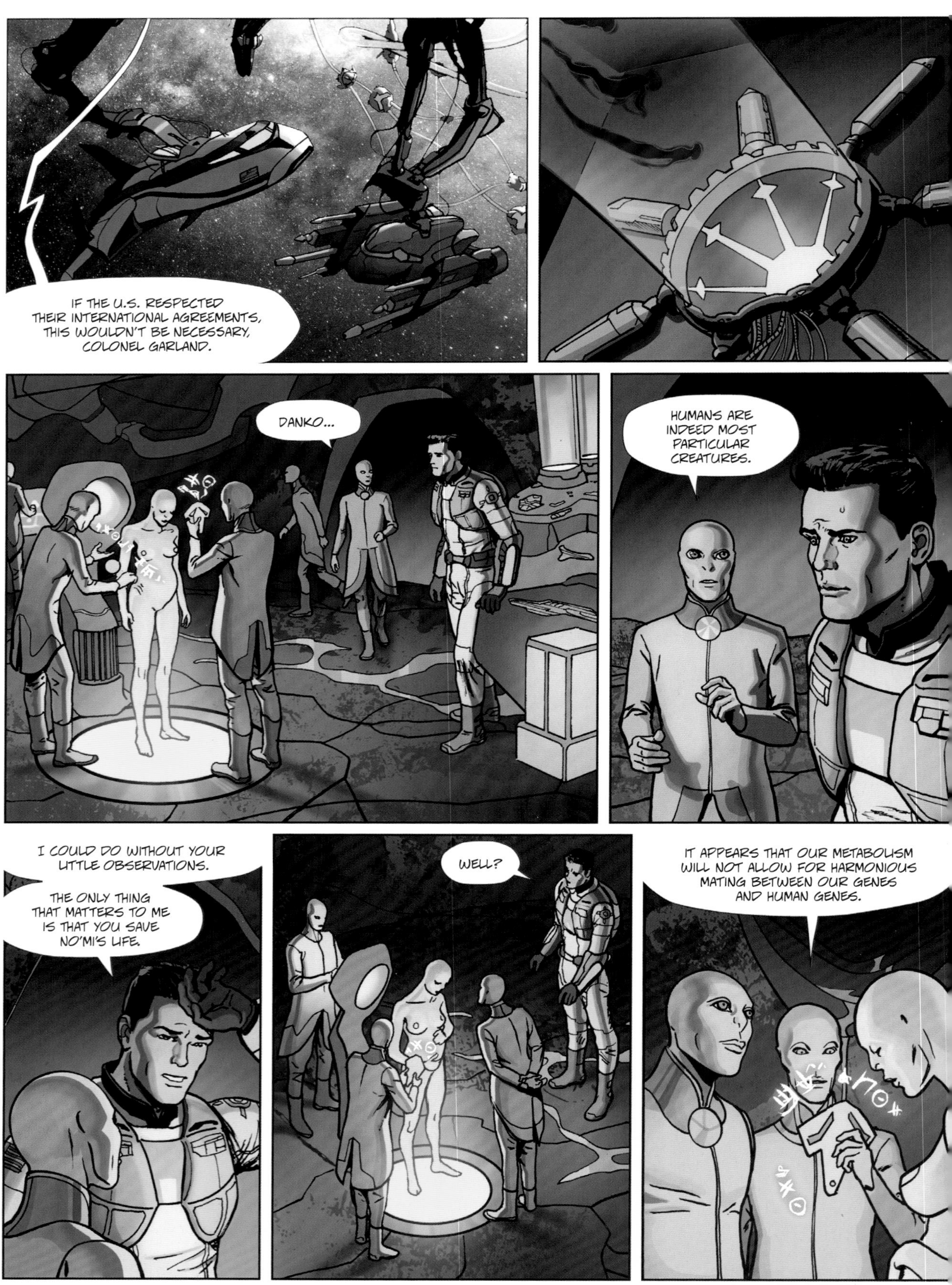
IF THE U.S. RESPECTED THEIR INTERNATIONAL AGREEMENTS, THIS WOULDN'T BE NECESSARY, COLONEL GARLAND.
DANKO...
HUMANS ARE INDEED MOST PARTICULAR CREATURES.
I COULD DO WITHOUT YOUR LITTLE OBSERVATIONS.
THE ONLY THING THAT MATTERS TO ME IS THAT YOU SAVE NO'MI'S LIFE.
WELL?
IT APPEARS THAT OUR METABOLISM WILL NOT ALLOW FOR HARMONIOUS MATING BETWEEN OUR GENES AND HUMAN GENES.

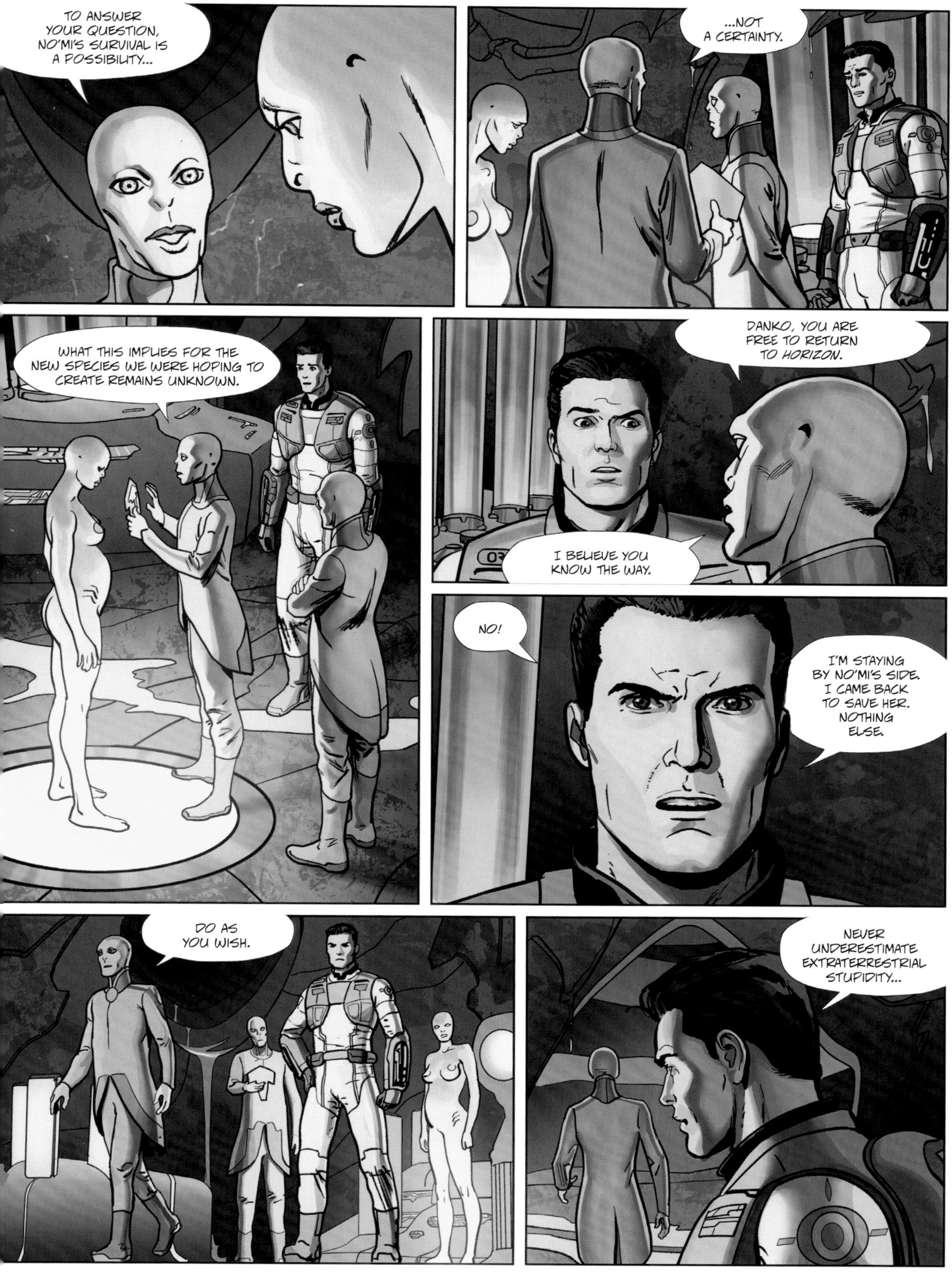

TO ANSWER YOUR QUESTION, NO'MI'S SURVIVAL IS A POSSIBILITY...
...NOT A CERTAINTY.
WHAT THIS IMPLIES FOR THE NEW SPECIES WE WERE HOPING TO CREATE REMAINS UNKNOWN.
DANKO, YOU ARE FREE TO RETURN TO *HORIZON*.
I BELIEVE YOU KNOW THE WAY.
NO!
I'M STAYING BY NO'MI'S SIDE. I CAME BACK TO SAVE HER. NOTHING ELSE.
DO AS YOU WISH.
NEVER UNDERESTIMATE EXTRATERRESTRIAL STUPIDITY...

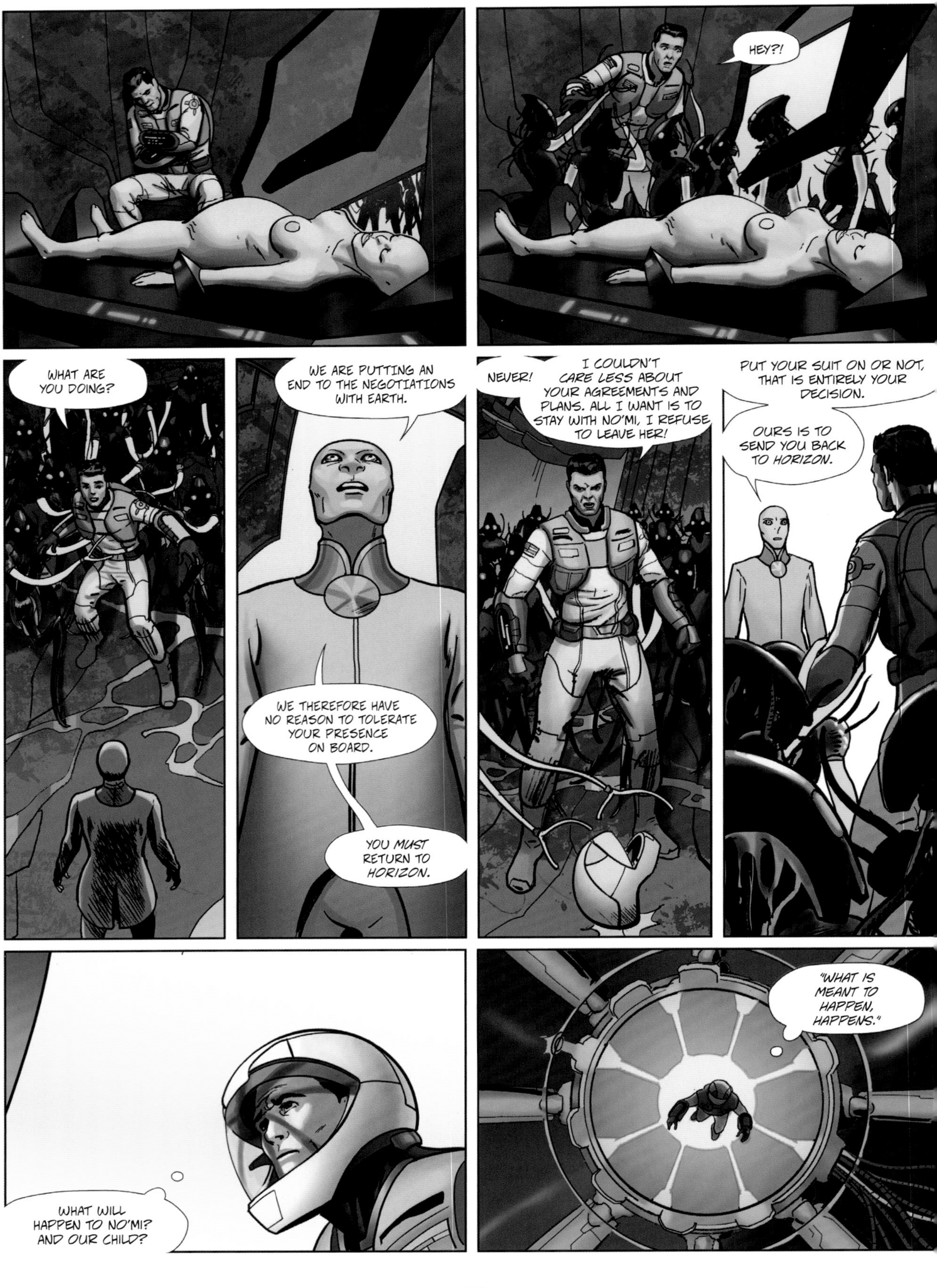
HEY?!
WHAT ARE YOU DOING?
WE ARE PUTTING AN END TO THE NEGOTIATIONS WITH EARTH.
WE THEREFORE HAVE NO REASON TO TOLERATE YOUR PRESENCE ON BOARD.
YOU MUST RETURN TO HORIZON.
NEVER!
I COULDN'T CARE LESS ABOUT YOUR AGREEMENTS AND PLANS. ALL I WANT IS TO STAY WITH NO'MI, I REFUSE TO LEAVE HER!
PUT YOUR SUIT ON OR NOT, THAT IS ENTIRELY YOUR DECISION.
OURS IS TO SEND YOU BACK TO HORIZON.
WHAT WILL HAPPEN TO NO'MI? AND OUR CHILD?
"WHAT IS MEANT TO HAPPEN, HAPPENS."

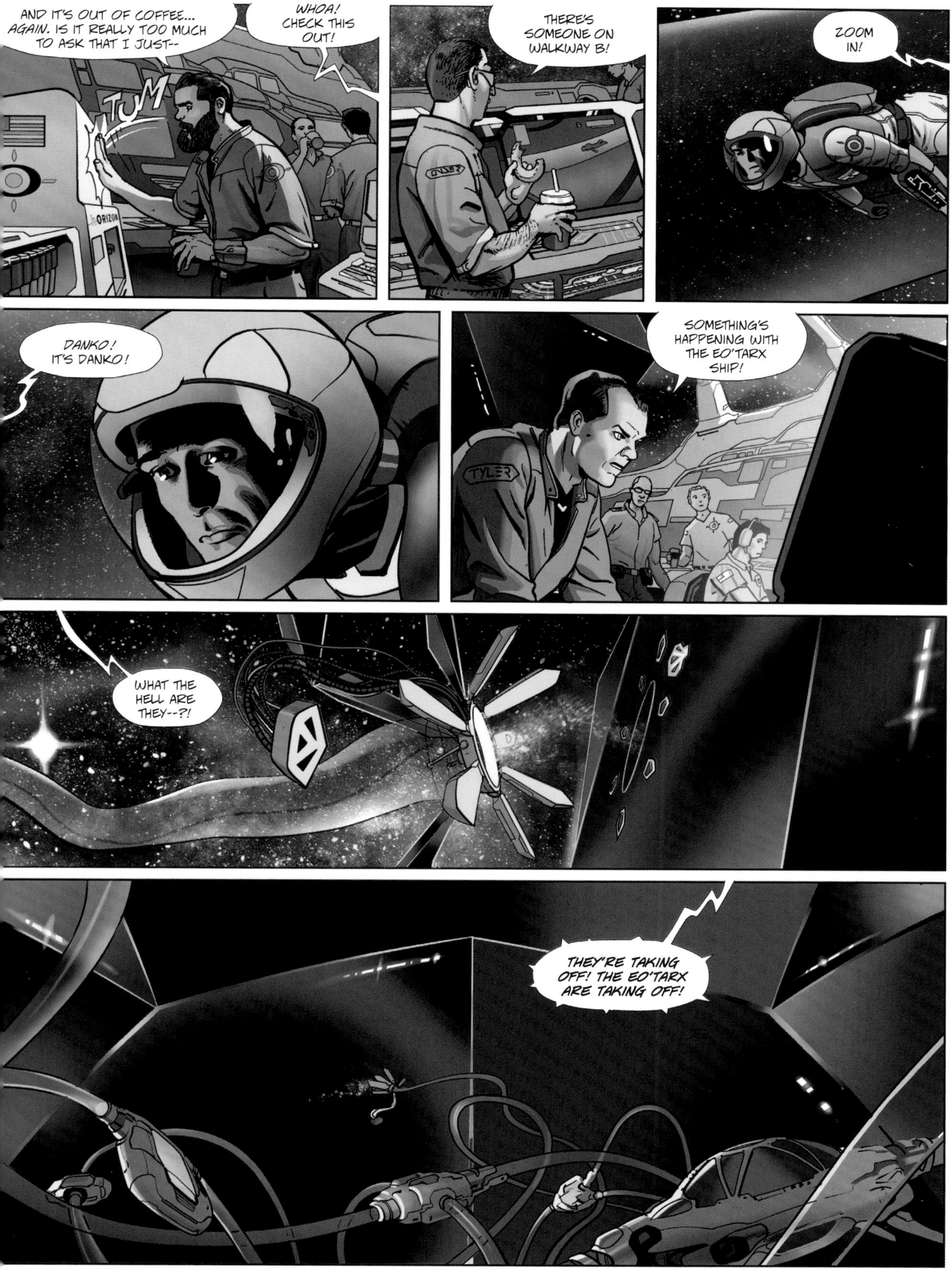
AND IT'S OUT OF COFFEE... AGAIN. IS IT REALLY TOO MUCH TO ASK THAT I JUST--
TUM
WHOA! CHECK THIS OUT!
THERE'S SOMEONE ON WALKWAY B!
ZOOM IN!
DANKO! IT'S DANKO!
SOMETHING'S HAPPENING WITH THE EO'TARX SHIP!
WHAT THE HELL ARE THEY--?!
THEY'RE TAKING OFF! THE EO'TARX ARE TAKING OFF!

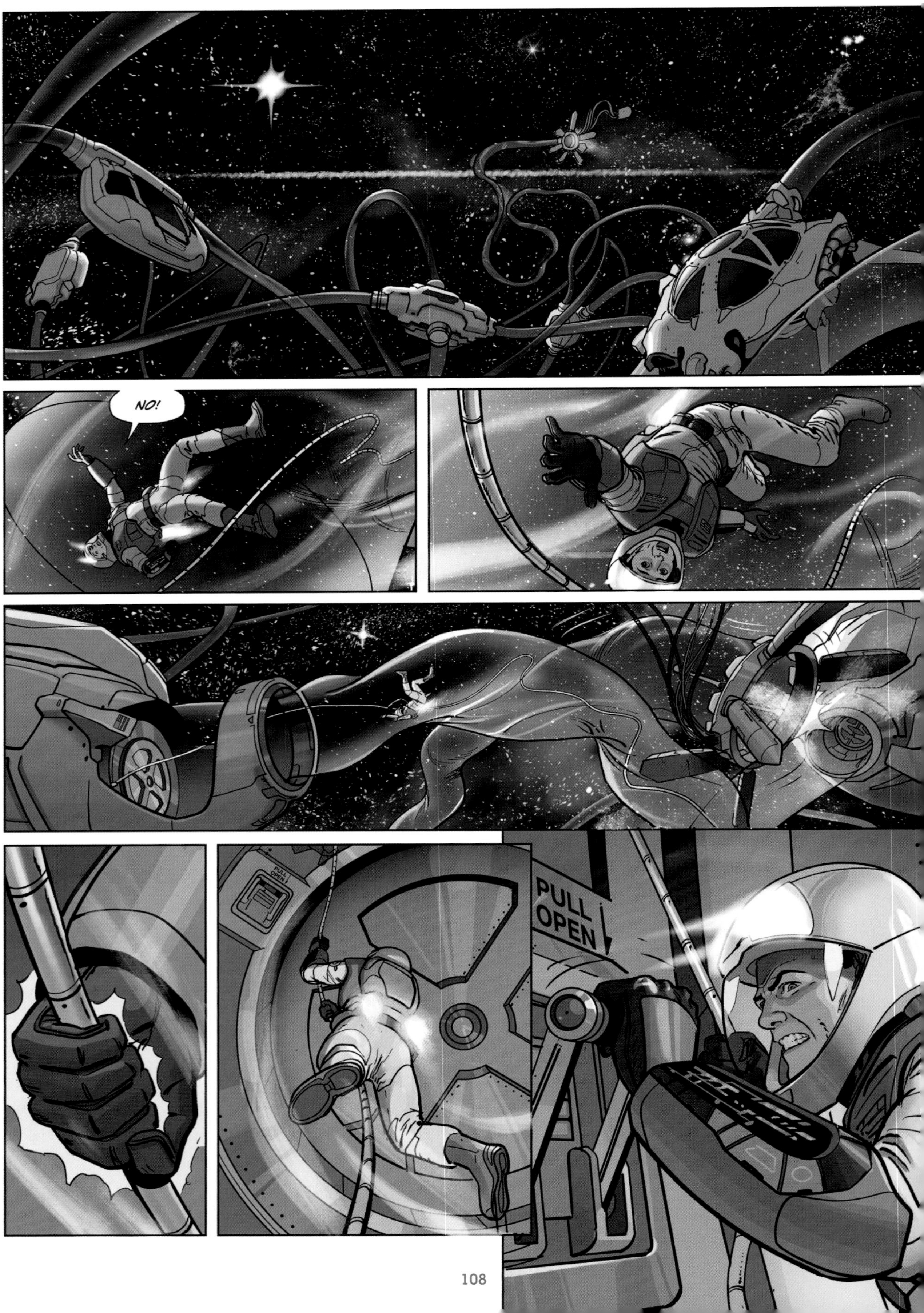
NO!
PULL OPEN
PULL OPEN

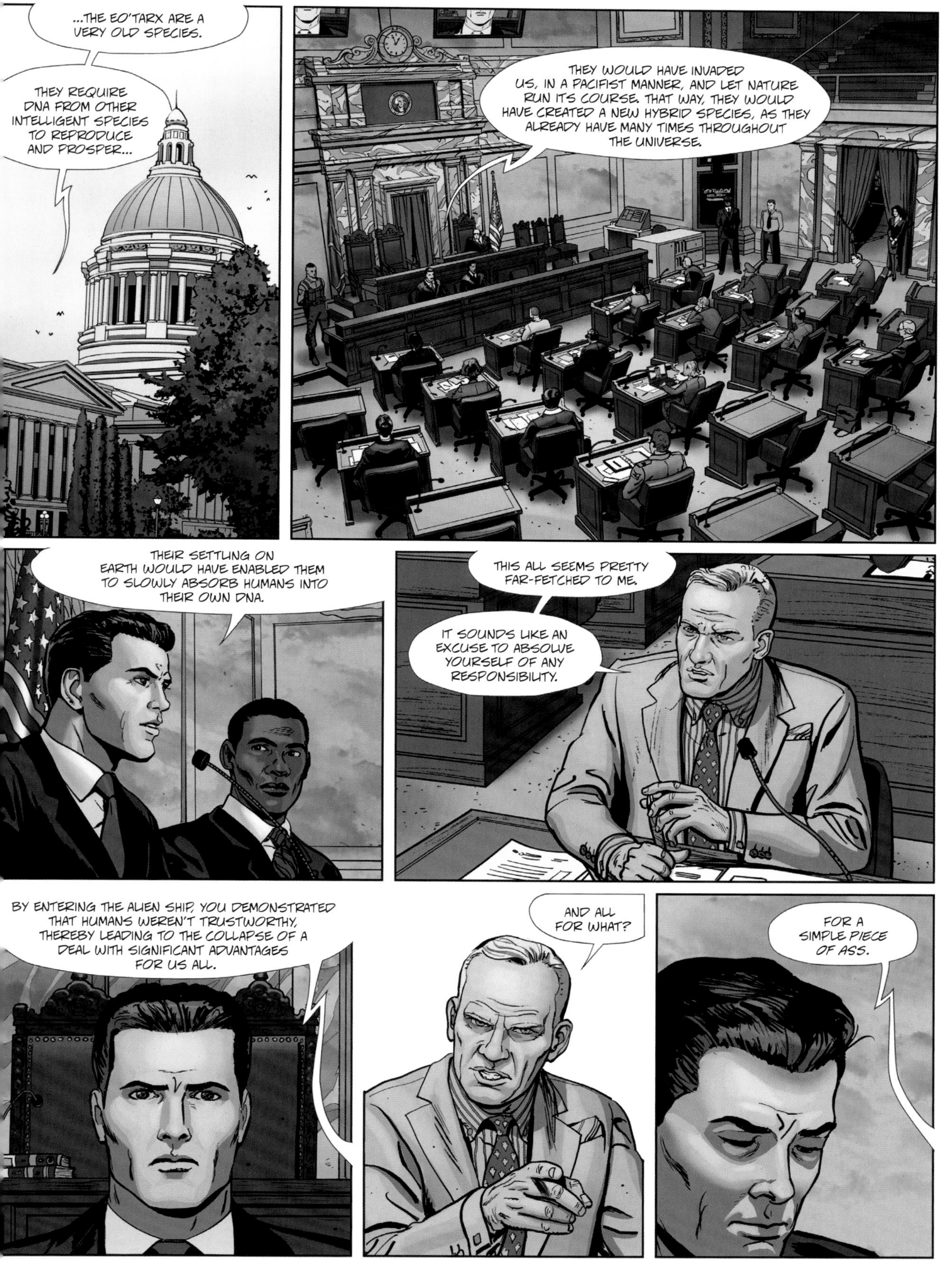
...THE EO'TARX ARE A VERY OLD SPECIES.
THEY REQUIRE DNA FROM OTHER INTELLIGENT SPECIES TO REPRODUCE AND PROSPER...
THEY WOULD HAVE INVADED US, IN A PACIFIST MANNER, AND LET NATURE RUN ITS COURSE. THAT WAY, THEY WOULD HAVE CREATED A NEW HYBRID SPECIES, AS THEY ALREADY HAVE MANY TIMES THROUGHOUT THE UNIVERSE.
THEIR SETTLING ON EARTH WOULD HAVE ENABLED THEM TO SLOWLY ABSORB HUMANS INTO THEIR OWN DNA.
THIS ALL SEEMS PRETTY FAR-FETCHED TO ME.
IT SOUNDS LIKE AN EXCUSE TO ABSOLVE YOURSELF OF ANY RESPONSIBILITY.
BY ENTERING THE ALIEN SHIP, YOU DEMONSTRATED THAT HUMANS WEREN'T TRUSTWORTHY, THEREBY LEADING TO THE COLLAPSE OF A DEAL WITH SIGNIFICANT ADVANTAGES FOR US ALL.
AND ALL FOR WHAT?
FOR A SIMPLE PIECE OF ASS.

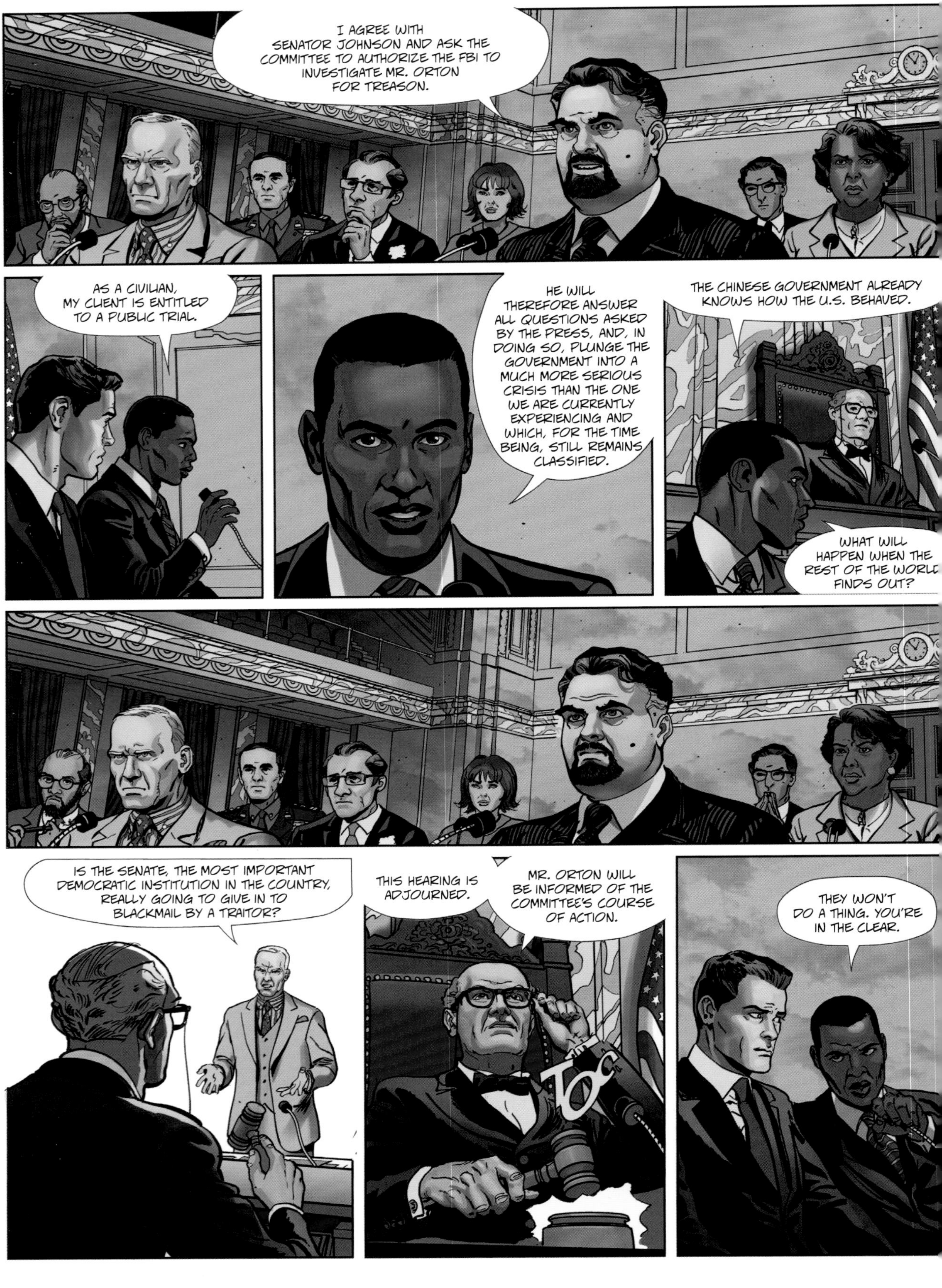
I AGREE WITH SENATOR JOHNSON AND ASK THE COMMITTEE TO AUTHORIZE THE FBI TO INVESTIGATE MR. ORTON FOR TREASON.
AS A CIVILIAN, MY CLIENT IS ENTITLED TO A PUBLIC TRIAL.
HE WILL THEREFORE ANSWER ALL QUESTIONS ASKED BY THE PRESS, AND, IN DOING SO, PLUNGE THE GOVERNMENT INTO A MUCH MORE SERIOUS CRISIS THAN THE ONE WE ARE CURRENTLY EXPERIENCING AND WHICH, FOR THE TIME BEING, STILL REMAINS CLASSIFIED.
THE CHINESE GOVERNMENT ALREADY KNOWS HOW THE U.S. BEHAVED.
WHAT WILL HAPPEN WHEN THE REST OF THE WORLD FINDS OUT?
IS THE SENATE, THE MOST IMPORTANT DEMOCRATIC INSTITUTION IN THE COUNTRY, REALLY GOING TO GIVE IN TO BLACKMAIL BY A TRAITOR?
THIS HEARING IS ADJOURNED.
MR. ORTON WILL BE INFORMED OF THE COMMITTEE'S COURSE OF ACTION.
TOC
THEY WON'T DO A THING. YOU'RE IN THE CLEAR.

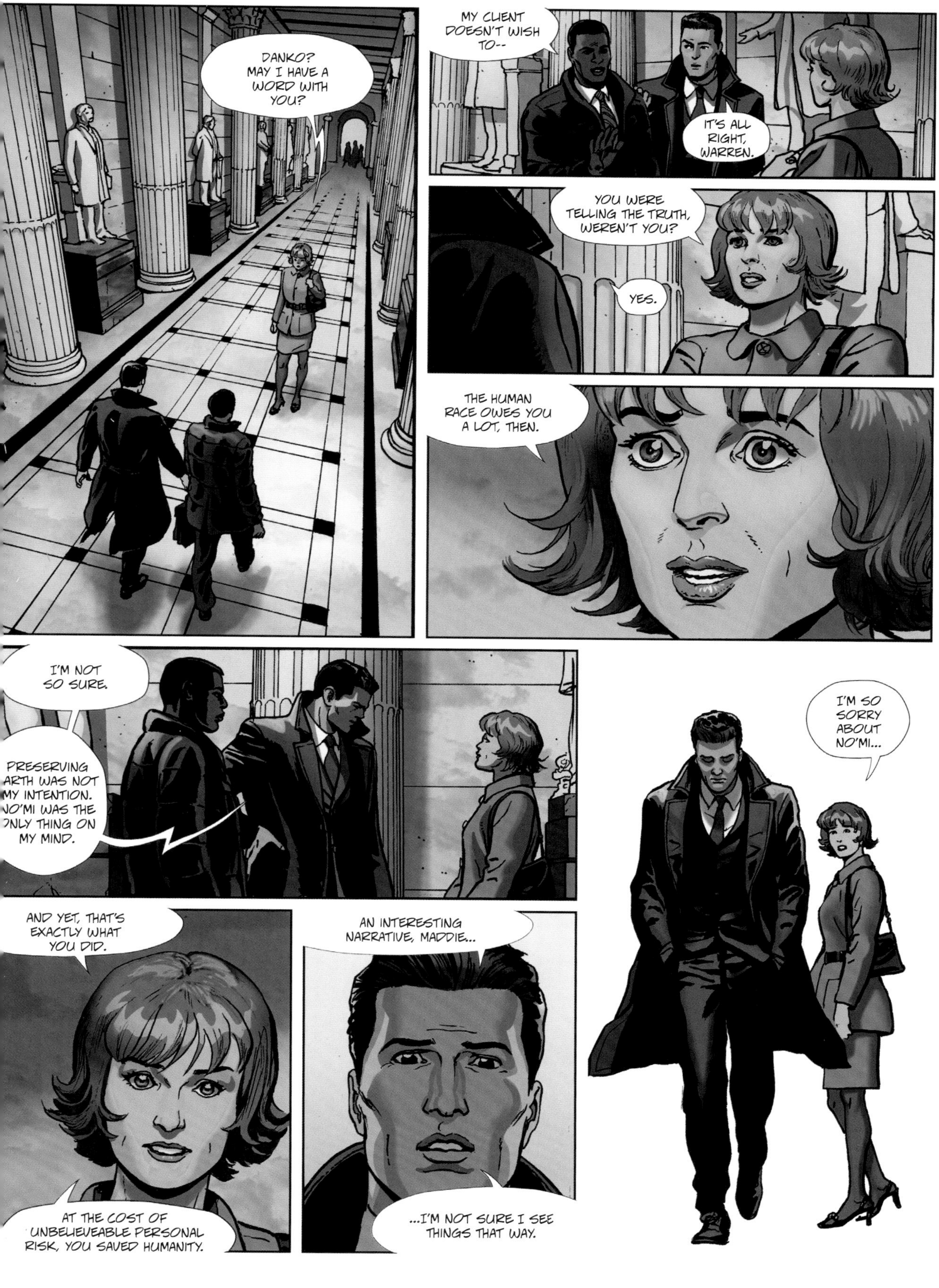
DANKO? MAY I HAVE A WORD WITH YOU?
MY CLIENT DOESN'T WISH TO--
IT'S ALL RIGHT, WARREN.
YOU WERE TELLING THE TRUTH, WEREN'T YOU?
YES.
THE HUMAN RACE OWES YOU A LOT, THEN.
I'M NOT SO SURE.
PRESERVING ARTH WAS NOT MY INTENTION. O'MI WAS THE NLY THING ON MY MIND.
AND YET, THAT'S EXACTLY WHAT YOU DID.
AT THE COST OF UNBELIEVEABLE PERSONAL RISK, YOU SAVED HUMANITY.
AN INTERESTING NARRATIVE, MADDIE...
...I'M NOT SURE I SEE THINGS THAT WAY.
I'M SO SORRY ABOUT NO'MI...

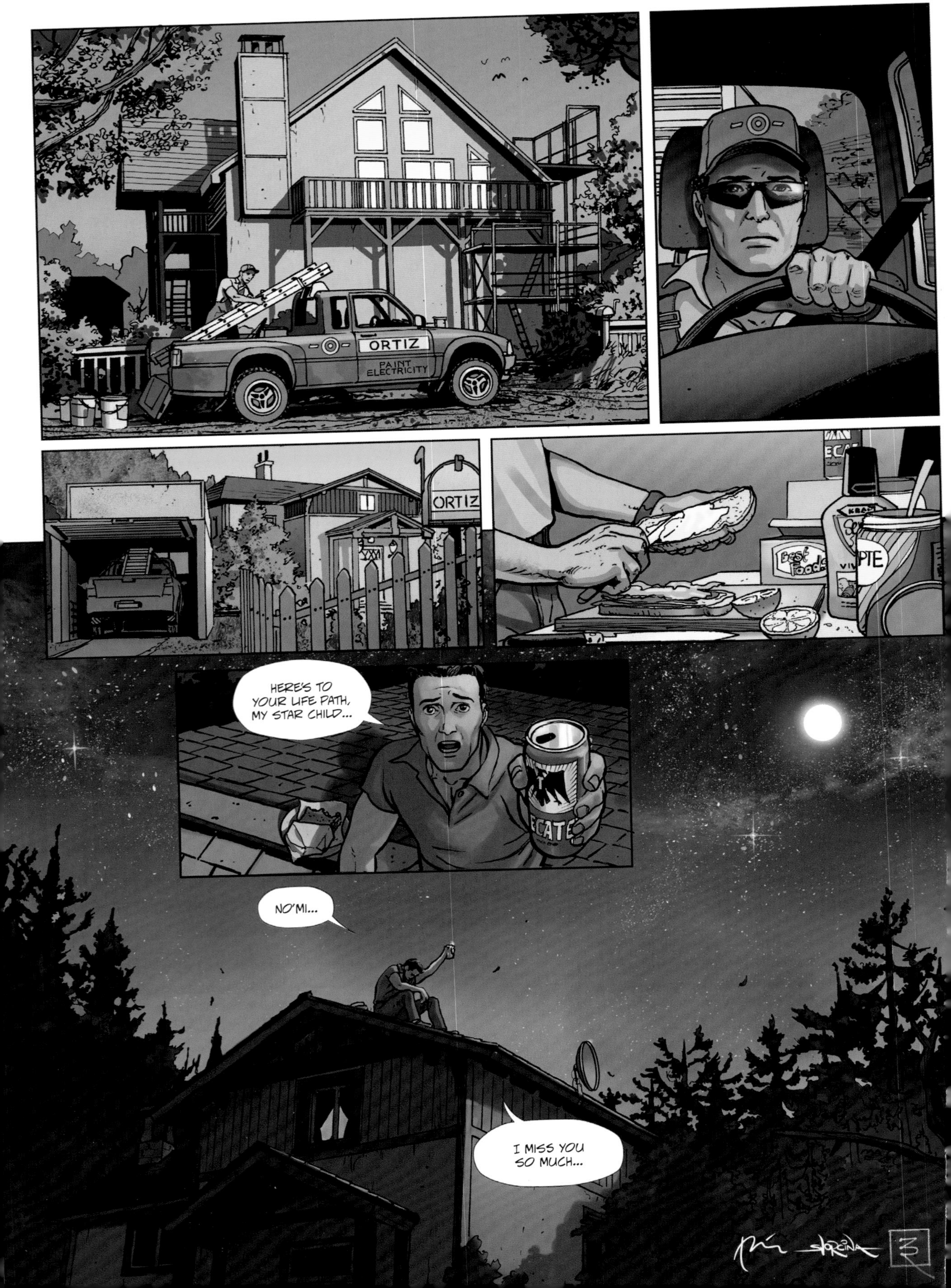
ORTIZ
PAINT ELECTRICITY
ORTIZ
HERE'S TO YOUR LIFE PATH, MY STAR CHILD...
NO'MI...
I MISS YOU SO MUCH...